MW01133293

A GAME OF CAT AND MOUSE

BY

SUZANNE FLOYD

2-6-17

Chet,
Thank you.
Suzanne Floyd

Cover art by Bella Media Management

Contact me at: www.SuzanneFloyd.com

I dedicate this book to my husband Paul and our daughters, Camala and Shannon, and family. Thanks for your support and encouragement.

PROLOGUE

The school bus stopped in the middle of the block, and several young boys clamored down the steps ahead of Jennifer Miller. Manners weren't something practiced much in the shabby homes on her street, and something she didn't expect anyway. Keeping her gaze trained on the ground in front of her, Jennifer reluctantly took several steps towards her house. Since Eddie came home, home was the last place she wanted to be.

"Hey, Jen, what're all the cops doin' at your place? Looks like the whole friggin' force is there." Rafael Gonzales knew better than to use any stronger words. Jennifer had given him a black eye once for swearing at her. She was one girl who could and would take care of herself.

When his words finally penetrated her troubled thoughts Jennifer looked up to see yellow police tape strung along the sidewalk. Several policemen kept the gawking neighbors at bay. Jennifer's heart seemed to jump into her throat. Only something terrible would bring this many police all at once. Only one thing.

Without realizing she was running Jennifer reached the police tape, only to be stopped by one of the policemen guarding the yard. "Whoa there, little girl, you can't come in here. Just step back."

"I live here. Where are my folks? What happened to them?" Jennifer fought to get past.

Before the policeman could reply, Eddie came out of the house, concern showing on his handsome face. "That's my sister, let her through!" he demanded, starting towards

Jennifer. "Oh, Sis, I'm so sorry." Instinctively, Jennifer backed away, but stopped after taking several steps. Showing fear only made matters worse; a lesson she'd learned long ago.

"This your sister?" A gruff, middle-aged man followed Eddie out of the house. "How long you been out here?"

Eddie pushed Jennifer behind him, staying between her and the man. "She just got home from school. I haven't even told her yet." To anyone watching it might seem like a protective gesture, but Jennifer knew better. It was all part of the show.

"Told me what? What happened to Mom and Dad? Where are they?" Eddie still wouldn't let her go around him. Doing her best to ignore Eddie, Jennifer looked around at the other man. "Where are my parents?" she demanded, trying to sound grown up and keep the quiver out of her voice. Another lesson she'd learned long ago was that the police weren't always on your side, and they didn't always care about the people they were supposed to protect.

"Let's go inside, Little Girl. I'd like to talk to you."

"Her name's Jennifer and she's NOT going in there!" Eddie shouted, almost fooling Jennifer into believing that he really did care about her. "You can talk to her right out here."

"You're not calling the shots here, kid. Now let's go." He took another step toward them, and Jennifer could feel the tension and anger burning through Eddie.

"That's enough, Sergeant Hardy! I'll handle it from here." A woman several years younger than the man came out of the house. Anger seemed to boil just below the surface in the sergeant, but Jennifer didn't understand it or care. She only wanted to know what had happened to her parents, to have her worst fears confirmed. Being left to guess was worse than the truth.

Suzanne Floyd

After what seemed like an eternity, Sergeant Hardy clomped back into the house. "I'm sorry about that, Jennifer." The woman turned to her with a sad smile. "I'm Lieutenant Vargas. Let's go over here so we can talk." She nodded toward the large shade tree in a neighbor's yard. Eddie started to follow, but Lieutenant Vargas stopped him, keeping one hand on Jennifer's shoulder. "She's going to be all right, Eddie. Just let me talk to her alone." Her smile now seemed overly charming.

Eddie puffed up under the smile, offering a suggestive one of his own. "All right, Lieutenant. I just didn't want that guy near my little sister." He sent an angry glare towards the house where the sergeant had disappeared.

"I understand, Eddie. I won't let anything happen to her." Turning back to Jennifer, Lieutenant Vargas led her farther away from the house, and Eddie.

Jennifer shrunk from the woman's touch. If Eddie fooled her that easily, the woman couldn't be very smart. "Where are my parents? What happened to them?"

Suspicion momentarily flashed in Lieutenant Vargas' dark eyes. "What makes you think something happened to them?"

"You're here, aren't you?" Jennifer countered, not intimidated by the older woman. "All of you." Her angry gaze took in the activity going on in her front yard. "It wouldn't take this many cops to handle a burglary. Especially not in this neighborhood. Normally you don't even bother to show up."

"You're right, Jennifer, something bad did happen," the lieutenant sighed wearily. "Someone broke into your house today while you and Eddie were in school. Your parents must have surprised the burglars and..." She paused. This was the hardest part of her job.

"They're dead, aren't they," Jennifer whispered, hoping the lieutenant would deny it yet knowing she wouldn't.

"Yes, Jennifer. I'm so sorry. The house has been

7

ransacked. Whoever did this was probably looking for money to buy drugs. Do you know if your parents kept money in the house?" What money, Jennifer thought bitterly. Her folks were dirt poor or they wouldn't be living in this neighborhood. She didn't put her thoughts into words though, just giving her head a small shake. "Eddie found them when he came home from class," the lieutenant continued softly. "Again, I'm sorry."

Jennifer was no longer listening. Eddie hadn't found them; he'd killed them. There might not be any evidence; any DNA or fingerprints from Eddie would be expected since he lived here. The police would overlook anything that could point to him, but she knew this was Eddie's doing.

Eddie had spent the last four years in a mental hospital. She didn't even want to think about the things he'd done to land himself there. When he turned 18, the doctors had declared him 'cured' and ready to face society, no longer a threat to himself or anyone else. That only goes to show how much the doctors know, Jennifer thought disparagingly. Eddie had been a threat to their parents and her for as long as Jennifer could remember.

But his record was locked away and couldn't be used against him. It wouldn't even do any good to tell the lieutenant about it because he had been a minor at the time. Everyone was just supposed to pretend it had never happened.

"We have officers going around the neighborhood now," Lieutenant Vargas broke in on her troubled thoughts. "Maybe someone saw something. But even if they didn't, we will find the people responsible for this. There's no such thing as the perfect crime."

Jennifer's disbelieving look momentarily threw Lieutenant Vargas. How did a 14-year-old get that cynical? "What is it you don't believe, Jennifer? We are going to find out who did this. People hooked on drugs aren't smart enough to make sure they don't leave evidence behind. Especially when they're hopped up on dope or looking for their next score." She tried to reassure the young girl, but could see it wasn't working.

"What if it wasn't a druggie?" Jennifer asked defiantly.

"What do you mean? Do you know something I should know about?" Lieutenant Vargas eyed her suspiciously.

Jennifer shook her head. "Just asking, playing devil's advocate."

This surprised Lieutenant Vargas even more. Why would a 14-year-old know that term? "We will find whoever did this." But the look Jennifer threw her way almost staggered the lieutenant, a look of doubt and almost hatred.

Drug deals could be made on any street corner within a mile of her house; prostitutes plied their trade in broad daylight. And she was supposed to believe that the cops cared enough about her parents to look for their killer? I don't think so, Jennifer told herself. Besides, they didn't have to look very far. Eddie is right in front of them, and they still can't or won't look at him.

"Jennifer, we will find the ones responsible," Lieutenant Vargas reassured her again. "Now I have to get back in there. Child Protective Services will be here to get you in a little while. Until then, please stay out here and away from the house."

"No! CPS isn't taking her away!" Without the lieutenant realizing it, Eddie had managed to get close enough to eavesdrop on their conversation. "She's my sister, and I'll take care of her."

A shudder of fear and revulsion shook Jennifer. Her life wouldn't be worth living if she had to stay with him.

"Eddie, you're only 18. You just started college. You can't take care of yourself and Jennifer." Thinking that was the end of the discussion, Lieutenant Vargas hurried off.

Jennifer knew Eddie wouldn't let it drop though. When he wanted something done his way, he always managed to get it, one way or another.

Eddie watched as Lieutenant Vargas hurried back to the house. "No way in hell I'm going to let CPS take her," he muttered to himself. "No way!"

Jennifer's heart sank in her chest. Even if he had to kidnap her, she felt certain Eddie would get what he wanted, from her and from the system that was supposed to protect her. She knew "the system wasn't worth a plug nickel" as her father was fond of saying. For years Eddie had molested her, mistreated their parents, tortured small animals, and vandalized neighbors' houses. No one had paid the least bit of attention. It was only when he had attacked an elderly lady that the system had stepped in and put Eddie away.

Those four years Eddie was gone were the safest Jennifer had felt in her life. It would start all over again, only on a grander scale, if Eddie got custody of her.

During her short life Jennifer had dealt with a number of CPS workers. All were dour, middle-aged, gray haired women really not interested in helping the children in their charge. Most were just marking time until retirement. When a pretty young woman drove up in a CPS van, Jennifer was more than a little surprised.

Apparently so was Eddie, pleasantly so. Turning on the charm, he crossed the shabby yard, opening the door for her in a gallant manner. "Are you the social worker here to take my little sister away from me?" His tone was harmless, but a razor's edge underscored the words.

"I'm Brenda Jones, yes." She held out her hand for him to shake. "But I'm not here to separate you and your sister. In cases where an older sibling is just eighteen, it's best for all parties if the younger ones go into foster care, at least for the time being."

Anger flared in Eddie's light eyes, but the young woman was looking at Jennifer now. "Hi, honey. Have you been able to get any of your things out of the house?" Although Brenda Jones looked only a few years older than Jennifer, and they were almost the same size, she was treating Jennifer like a very young child.

"She hasn't been allowed in the house yet," Eddie answered for her. "I'm the one who found our folks, and I don't want my sister seeing what's left of them." His words were graphic enough to cause both Jennifer and Brenda Jones to pale.

"Of course," Brenda quickly agreed. "I understand. Someone can send her clothes later. I just need to talk to someone inside and then we can go." She headed toward the house with Eddie right beside her, arguing his case.

Trying to put on a cheerful face when she returned a few minutes later, Brenda Jones looked far paler than she had just moments ago. Jennifer didn't know if that meant the woman had seen how her parents died, or if Eddie had made some veiled threats.

Still treating Jennifer like a small child, she reached out to take her hand. "Let's go, Sweetie. You'll see Eddie tomorrow. We'll manage to work out something to keep the two of you together."

With a sinking heart, Jennifer ignored the proffered hand and headed for the car. Eddie had worked his charm again, and would get his own way. Besides, in Arizona, CPS didn't have a stellar reputation for protecting children from the people who wanted to harm them. As they saw it, it was their job to keep families together no matter the cost to the children. That meant it was up to her to protect herself.

"Sis, wait." Materializing almost magically, Eddie was beside her before she could get into the van. Gathering her in a warm embrace, he whispered softly. "We will be together. No one is going to keep us apart." He stepped back, smiling with satisfaction. The image he'd left in the social worker's mind was of a loving brother, and the fear he'd inflicted on his younger sister would keep her in line.

Eddie stayed where he was until the van was out of sight, then went looking for Lieutenant Vargas.

~~~

A week later, frustration and anger nearly overwhelmed Eddie. Brenda Jones was proving to be a harder nut to crack than he expected. "Why are you doing this? It's cruel. We've already lost our parents; we only have each other now. Why won't you let me have...take care of Jennifer?" he amended quickly.

Brenda sighed wearily, "Eddie, we've gone over this time and time again. It's what is best for both of you. I'm not doing this to hurt you or Jennifer.

"Does this have anything to do with my past?" He managed to put on a look that was both embarrassed and ashamed.

Brenda lovingly stroked his face. "Eddie, you know better than that. You've explained how that happened. You were a victim as much as that woman was. You were just a kid listening to the wrong people. You should have told the police about them, and you wouldn't have been blamed. You didn't have to take the punishment all by yourself. But the department has a policy that young children should be put in foster care, and not become a burden on older siblings when they are so young themselves. I've explained all that and I happen to agree." She continued to stroke his face, knowing how easy it was to distract him and arouse him at the same time. Their relationship should never have happened as long as she was involved with Jennifer's care, but it had been impossible not to fall in love with Eddie.

He had given her a cock and bull story about how he had gotten into trouble. It was never his fault, whatever happened. Even when he was alone, it was always

12

someone else's fault. "No exceptions in special cases?" he asked, wiggling his eyebrows suggestively, causing her to laugh and blush at the same time.

"No exceptions, Eddie." She turned serious then. "Besides, we're the only ones who know how 'special' this is. If my superiors knew about us, I'd be fired for sure. I'm sorry we have to do it this way, my love, but until Jennifer is settled our love will just have to remain a secret."

Eddie pulled her close, nuzzling her neck. "Whatever you say, sweetheart; I'll take what I can get." His easy acceptance masked the elation he felt. As long as no one knows about them, he was home free. No one would suspect him.

~~~

"It'll only be a few more days, Sis." Under the guise of explaining why she had to stay in foster care, Eddie had gone to the home where Jennifer was staying. "I've got plans for taking care of any obstacles in my way." His low voice held its usual taunting measure.

"Whatever you say, Eddie; I'm not going anywhere." She shrugged, sounding resigned to whatever he did. She couldn't let him know how much she dreaded whatever he was planning. Since Miss Jones had told her only the day before that she had to stay in foster care for at least two years so Eddie could get his education, she could only guess at what he had planned for the social worker. It wouldn't be anything good though. Brenda Jones had obviously bought Eddie's snow job. She didn't know that Brenda was sleeping with her brother. If she had, she might have been worried they were planning something together.

That night Jennifer began making plans of her own. Staying put and waiting for Eddie to come collect her, was stupid. And no one had ever accused her of being stupid. *I might be only fourteen*, she thought. *But I'm not stupid*. In fact, it was just the opposite. Jennifer's IQ was nearly off the charts, and she could see the writing on the wall if she stayed around waiting for "the system" or Eddie to do something.

Eavesdropping on a telephone conversation a week later, Jennifer learned of Brenda Jones' "accidental" death. But Jennifer didn't believe it was an accident. She could see Eddie's hand all over it. What idiot took a bath with a radio sitting on the edge of the tub, especially a radio with a frayed cord?

In a matter of hours, as soon as it was dark, Eddie would be there to take charge of her. He did his best work under cover of darkness. If anyone tried to stop him, it would the last thing they did. Maybe that's what had happened with their parents, she thought. Maybe they had tried to stop Eddie from hurting her again. They hadn't been successful before Eddie had been locked up, nor had they tried all that hard, she admitted reluctantly. They knew it was useless to deny him anything; his will was simply stronger than theirs. If they had tried to cross him again, he would do anything to have his way. Just like he had with that poor social worker, she thought. Now she had to get out while she still could.

With only the few clothes she could stuff in her backpack without looking suspicious, Jennifer let herself out the back door. "I'll be at the library until supper time," she called out. "I have a test tomorrow." No one bothered to acknowledge her. Such was the "good" care of foster homes.

Since entering foster care, she'd spent a lot of time at the local library, enjoying the books as well as getting to know the workers. After talking with several people to establish her presence, Jennifer slipped out a side door. She still had several hours before dark. It was doubtful anyone from the foster home would be looking for her before then. If her luck held, she had until ten o'clock before the cops were called in.

Jennifer walked as far from the library as she could before dark. No one paid any attention to her, but she tried to keep to the shadows as much as possible anyway. Sleeping out under the stars wasn't the adventure it had been when she was younger sleeping in her own backyard. Homeless people slept in the park and even at this hour, teenagers were everywhere. She needed to find a secluded place to hide for a while. She couldn't risk having someone report seeing her here alone.

Her plan was simple. If she could make it to their old house without being seen, she could slip in through her bedroom window, and stay there for the night. Even Eddie wouldn't think to look there. Crime scene tape was still across the doors, as if that would keep her or anyone else out if they really wanted in.

Since her fingerprints would naturally be all over the house, she didn't have to worry about leaving evidence behind to screw up the investigation. Besides, the police were looking for a stranger, not someone right under their noses. Unless they took a closer look at Eddie, he had managed to commit the perfect crime.

Standing in the shadows, Jennifer stared at the dark house. Her heart beat rapidly. The house was completely dark as she expected, but she couldn't force herself to get any closer. It wasn't just that her parents had died violently in there. Something didn't feel right. Was someone in there, or was her imagination running wild?

After watching the house for over an hour with nothing happening, she began to relax. Maybe just a little longer, and then she'd go in, she told herself. Sleep was beginning to blur her vision.

Suddenly, she awoke with a jerk, unsure what had happened or where she was. Sitting up straight, she took in her surroundings. The crescent moon didn't offer enough light to see the dial on her watch. She could have just dozed off, or she could have been sleeping for several hours. Judging from the dense shadows, it was several hours.

Looking across at the house, Jennifer's breath caught in her throat. Shadows shifted against the house. The same uneasiness she'd felt earlier settled over her. She couldn't tell if someone was there, or if the shifting light caused the shapes to appear like they were moving. For a long while Jennifer remained motionless, not wanting to give her own position away if someone was really there.

At last, the shifting shadows came together. Jennifer's heart seemed to leap into her throat as Eddie stepped away from the house into the light from the street lamp. Unaware he was being observed, Eddie allowed the evil he normally kept hidden to etch itself into his usually innocent-looking features. *If the police could only see him now*, she thought, *they would have no doubt who had killed her parents.*

Jennifer remained hidden in the bushes for the rest of the night. When he found out she was missing from the foster home, Eddie had apparently guessed she would come to their old house. Somehow he was always one step behind her, sometimes even one step ahead of her. The fact that he had walked away from the house without trying to hide could be a trap to make her show herself. A trap she had no intention of falling into.

Long after daylight, Jennifer continued to scan the street, searching out places someone could hide. Eddie was in none of them. People began leaving for work and school. Rafael Gonzales came out just in time to get on the school bus. Jennifer watched longingly, wishing she could join him, that she could turn back the clock and somehow change what had happened.

After another hour, the street was quiet again. Everyone was either at work or school. Nothing stirred.

Did she dare to leave her hiding place? After sitting on the hard ground all night with nothing to eat or drink and no bathroom, nature finally made the decision for her. She was hungry and thirsty and felt like some of the bugs from the bushes had taken up residence in her clothes. Besides, she had to go bad enough to risk moving.

Staying as close to the houses as she could, Jennifer walked away from her old home for the last time, refusing to look back. If she was ever going to be safe, she had to make a clean break with everything and everyone in this life. She couldn't rely on anyone but herself.

Three blocks away, she went into a Jack-in-the-Box to use the restroom and get something to eat. Eddie hadn't jumped out to catch her; no one had paid any attention to the slightly built young girl who should have been in school. The ease with which she made her get-away was almost anti-climactic.

With a mixture of relief and regret, Jennifer left the restaurant a short time later. From this day on Jennifer Miller ceased to exist. She would use the skills Eddie had taught her to get by.

Twelve Years Later

"What's the matter with you, Judy? Who or what are you running from?"

For the briefest moment her heart skittered in her chest. How much did he know? How had he found out? Then common sense reasserted itself, stiffening her spine. "I'm not running away from anyone or anything, Ted. I'm simply saying I'm not looking for a steady relationship. I told you that when you first asked me out. It seems to me that you're the one with a problem." Her voice turned as cold as the icy gray-green eyes staring at him.

"So this is it? You're just going to walk away from all we could have?" Ted Watson's face turned red with suppressed anger. "I thought you'd gotten past all those inhibitions you were harboring when we first met,"

Judy Masters sighed wearily. "I had no inhibitions then or now, Ted. I'm simply NOT looking for a steady relationship. I don't know how to say it any plainer than that. I see nothing wrong with it either. Guys do it all the time, but if a woman isn't looking for a husband and kids, there's something wrong with her. Well, I don't give a damn what you or anyone else thinks. I'm not going to fall in line just because you want me to." She didn't bother to tell him she had already quit her job and was leaving town as soon as she finished packing.

Reaching in her purse, she pulled out a ten-dollar bill. "For my share of the lunch. See you around, Ted." Before he could stop her, Judy walked out of the restaurant, leaving Ted stunned and speechless.

She walked briskly down the street feeling a sense of Deja vu. How many times had she walked away from everyone she knew, to start over again somewhere else? How many more times would it happen in her life? Ted had no way of knowing she was actually doing him a favor. Now at least he had a chance to live long enough to have the wife and children he so badly wanted.

In spite of the warm sunshine, Judy shivered. Only once had she made the mistake of forgetting her past; of thinking she could have a normal life. *But you can't outrun what you are*, she told herself now. No matter how far you go or how fast you run, who and what you are tags right along.

Back in her apartment, Judy busied herself packing the few things she would take with her, trying to keep unwanted thoughts at bay. But old memories intruded, taking away her breath, and forcing her to sit down on the side of the bed. Since the day she'd left home, she always had the feeling she was only one step ahead of Eddie. There were even times she suspected he'd been in her apartment. No proof, just feelings.

Then four years ago she'd made the fatal mistake of believing she was safe. It had been several years since Eddie had even come close to finding her, lulling her into a false sense of security. Surely he'd given up or been arrested for another crime, she'd reasoned. Besides, she'd changed her name and location, even her looks so often that at times she couldn't remember what name she was using or where she was. Sometimes she was even surprised when she looked in the mirror.

That's when she had met Fred Baxter. Sweet, gentle Fred, she thought, as a sob tore itself from her throat. How could she not fall in love with that gentle man? Fred is the one who paid the price though. And such a high price!

When Fred disappeared, the police hadn't paid much attention. They saw it as a man walking away from his life. Maybe he'd decided at the last minute he didn't want to get married after all. When she reported him missing the officers even smirked when she tried to explain that they were getting married. He wouldn't just take off. Before she would agree to marry him, Judy/Jennifer had told him what had happened all those years ago. She explained about Eddie, and that he was still after her. Fred hadn't cared. He held her, allowing her to cry for the first time for all she had lost. He left her that night with the promise to return first thing in the morning to get their marriage license. They would be married as soon as possible.

But Fred didn't come for her in the morning. No one had seen him after he left her apartment; his roommate said he never came home. His car had turned up more than a hundred miles away in the long term parking lot of an airport; there was no sign of violence or foul play. The police weren't very concerned. They said the only fingerprints belonged to Fred and Judy. She wasn't sure if she believed that or not. If Eddie had done something to him, how did he not leave fingerprints behind? It was just one more example of police incompetence as far as

Jennifer was concerned.

Two days later the mutilated body of a prostitute was found several blocks from Jennifer's apartment, turning the attention of the police to more important matters. The note Eddie had managed to slide under the door of her apartment, knowing only she would find it, had been explicit. That could have been her; she could run, but she couldn't hide. At least not forever. He would always find her. She almost wished it had been her. Then it would all be over. But killing Fred and the prostitute had just been part of Eddie's game. He didn't want this game to end too soon.

She had considered showing the note to the police, but her experience with law enforcement didn't encourage her to trust them. Besides, trying to explain eight years of running and hiding with no real proof that Eddie had done anything wrong would be impossible. The note meant something only to her; the police wouldn't understand his hidden message.

She would never put someone else at risk like that again, she'd vowed. Even if it meant life on the run forever and always alone, she couldn't ask anyone else to put his life on the line for her. Jennifer ran an unsteady hand across her face, surprised by the tears she found there. The confrontation with Ted had resurrected memories she had kept buried for several years.

Since Fred's disappearance not a day went by that she didn't look over her shoulder expecting to see Eddie stalking her. Although he never showed himself, she always knew he was only a few steps behind her no matter where she went, or how many names she used. Sometimes she felt there must be some kind of psychic thread linking them, leading Eddie to her wherever she was.

Jennifer didn't want to believe that, but how else could she explain the fact that he unerringly found her, maybe not immediately, maybe not even each time she moved. But he always caught up with her, leaving her little "love notes" to let her know she couldn't escape. So far he hadn't actually confronted her, but that was just part of his game. Terrorizing her had always been much more fun. But she wasn't a child any longer; she didn't terrorize so easily now.

Forcing herself to resume packing, Jennifer went over her next identity in her mind. She'd been planning her next move for more than a month, and always had several ready to use. The Internet made it easy to become someone else. But she never took the identity of a living person. Identity theft was a big thing now, and Jennifer had tried very hard not to break any laws. She never left behind debts, giving creditors a reason to trace her, or the name she was using. She didn't want to leave a trail for anyone to follow, especially Eddie.

For the first few years, Jennifer had lived by her wits and the street smarts she'd learned avoiding, or trying to avoid, Eddie. She knew the perils facing teenage runaways. After all the abuse she had suffered at Eddie's hands, she had refused to submit to being a teenage hooker. Instead she'd worked in burger joints and anonymous greasy spoons until she was old enough to get something better. Decent paying jobs were nonexistent during those first few years, but things were different now.

At first she had chosen different jobs, in different fields, seldom using the same one twice. *I feel sort of like the character from the movie Catch Me If You Can*, she thought with a wry smile. She could do a host of different jobs, and no one was the least bit suspicious that she hadn't always done that specific job. Learning had always come easily to her, something she didn't have to work at like the other kids in school. After reading a book once, she knew it from cover to cover. Not just the words, but the knowledge those words imparted. Of course, research and book knowledge didn't replace hands on experience. But she had been able to bluff her way through until she gained the experience needed.

Discovering computers and the Internet had proven to be a godsend for her. After a few days at a public library in one of the many towns where she'd lived, Jennifer had discovered not only did she have a photographic memory, but she was also a natural with computers. By studying every computer book she could get her hands on, she could now hack into almost any system without leaving a trace.

The Phoenix Police Department's computer files had been a challenge, but not a very serious one. She now had a duplicate file of everything they had on her parents' murders. Eddie had certainly out done himself that time. Pure rage had been written all over the murder scene. But the police had overlooked that, assuming it was nothing more sinister than a burglary gone horribly wrong. The murders were still listed in the open file, but no one had bothered with them in years. Any leads were now cold or lost.

Of course, Eddie's fingerprints and DNA were all over her parents' house; he lived there. But the police didn't even look in his direction as a suspect. How he had managed to make Fred disappear and kill the prostitute without leaving any fingerprints somewhere still baffled her; he was simply too good at this.

At the time of her own disappearance, the police had questioned Eddie, which had given her a thrill when she'd learned of it. But since there had been no body and no sign of foul play, the police simply listed her as a runaway. *How astute of them*, she thought cynically. They hadn't bothered to find out why she would run away. No one had bothered to challenge the pronouncement of "accidental" in the death of Brenda Jones either.

Altogether, this made the police, at least those particular police, seem rather inept to Jennifer. It also made her want to do something about it. Since the time she hacked the police files of her parents' murders, she had checked back occasionally just to see if there was anything new. The sergeant, who had given her a hard time the day of the murders, had died suddenly just weeks after Jennifer escaped. It was chalked up to a heart attack due to overweight and stress on the job. Jennifer knew better. Eddie had a hand in it somehow. No one treated Eddie that way and got away with it. If he could get away with all of these murders, how many other people in other places had gotten away with the same thing?

She had used her much loved computers to get her GED, take classes on-line, apply for credit cards and buy things. All the things ordinary people did every day. She now had a superb credit rating, and in another year would have a degree in Forensic Science in an identity that was mainly in cyberspace. She could only hope that the trail she had managed to lay so far was so convoluted that Eddie couldn't trace her until she was ready for him.

~~~

The damn bitch had disappeared again! He was getting sick of her little game. Maybe it was time to prove to her once and for all that she couldn't escape him. Whether she liked it or not, she was his to do with as he wanted.

First he had to find her, again. Eddie punched the wall in the dingy motel room. Reluctantly he acknowledged that she was getting more and more clever with each move, each new identity she made for herself. It was taking him longer to find her, and sometimes he suspected he was losing her altogether.

CHAPTER ONE
The Present

Stepping off the frigid bus I drew a deep breath of the hot desert air, almost searing my lungs in the process. I'd forgotten how hot it got in Phoenix in July. An odd sense of homecoming stirred emotions I thought were long forgotten. I hadn't believed I would ever feel that way about Phoenix again. Too many bad things had happened here; I'd lived in too many places since. Nowhere else had given me this feeling of home though.

My stomach churned slightly, and I pressed a hand against my mid-section to still the butterflies. Am I doing the right thing or was this a colossal mistake? I'd planned carefully, meticulously, but was it enough? There'd been no hint of threats, no sense of being watched, in over two years, but I still couldn't let myself relax or get careless. I couldn't afford to. Anyone who might try to get close to me couldn't afford for me to let down my guard either.

Pulling the small suitcase, I walked down the line of cars looking for the one I'd rented. In a few days I'd get my own car. Until then I had to have a way to get around. In most of the cities I'd lived, a car wasn't a necessity. If my research proved correct, that wasn't the case in Phoenix. Public transportation hadn't improved much in the last fifteen years, and left a lot to be desired even today.

My new job starts on Monday. That means I have four days to find a car and a place to live. My stomach rolled again. I'd deliberately cut it close getting here, not wanting any time for second thoughts. *This had to work*, I told myself. If it didn't, my life wasn't worth much anyway so it really doesn't matter if Eddie finds me or not.

At fourteen my world had consisted of a very small

part of Phoenix. Still, I knew the city had changed considerably in the intervening years. Phoenix wasn't the only thing that had changed. Anyone from my past would have a hard time recognizing me, but I wasn't taking any chances.

Colored contacts muted my emerald green eyes to a dull hazel, and the permanent make-up I'd recently had done subtly changed the shape of my eyes and lips. After years of coloring my hair even I was surprised to find my mousy brown locks were now a natural deep russet.

Growing up I'd worn my hair long and pulled back into a ponytail in a vain attempt to control the tight curls. Over the years, I had tried straightening it, letting it curl and everything in between. Last week I had the last of the old color cut off. I was left with a springy cap of curls. Self-consciously, I ran my hand through the curls, fluffing them up. I have to admit it's extremely easy to care for. Maybe I'll let it curl from now on.

I'd used my much-loved computers to build my final identity, using that identity only to get my degree and several part-time jobs in my new field. I now had the references and job experience needed to move forward.

Fifteen years ago Eddie had been crazy, but as cunning as a fox and just as smart. He hadn't known much about computers, but neither had I. What he had learned in the intervening years was anybody's guess. I have to make sure he doesn't find me before I'm ready.

~~~

First-day-on-the-job jitters fluttered in my stomach. I'd never experienced that before, but those jobs had always been temporary. One way or another, this was the final one. I'm not moving on from here. Either I stop Eddie for good, or he finally wins his macabre game, and my life is over. I have to make this work. Passing the lie detector test will be the supreme test. *I am Casey Gibson*, I told myself. I am Casey Gibson.

Drawing a shaky breath, I pushed open the door to the Human Resources office. This was it. "Hi, I'm Casey Gibson." New employee orientation here wasn't any different from a dozen other places. As expected, I had to take a lie detector test. By concentrating on who I am now and everything about my identity, I was able to pass without any problems.

By lunch time, I was ready for this part to be over. I wanted to get started in the lab. "Want to grab a bite to eat?" Tessa Gordon, one of the others in orientation, asked. "It might be the last time we get to relax for the rest of the day. I think they're going to keep us busy right up to quitting time."

"Um, ah, sure. Where do you want to go? I don't know what's around here." Caught off guard, I wasn't sure how to respond at first. Tessa's friendly smile had me relaxing for the first time all morning. She was several years younger than me chronologically, but probably light years younger in experience. Something about her seemed to call to my missed years.

Tessa smiled. "Downtown Phoenix has a lot to offer. What are you hungry for?" She quickly listed several different options, and we agreed on a Mexican restaurant within walking distance.

"It sounds like you know the area pretty well. Have you lived in Phoenix long?"

"All my life. When I was a teenager I thought I wanted to live somewhere else, but now that I can move away, I don't want to go. This is home." She gave a self-conscious shrug. "Where are you from?"

I drew a deep breath. This was it. It was time to start living my new identity. "I've lived just about everywhere in my life. My folks both worked for the government, and we moved around a lot. They died in a small plane crash when I was eighteen. At the time, I thought I'd just stay where we were when it happened, but I guess I inherited their wanderlust, so I kept moving around for a long time. When I got tired of traveling, I was in Fort Collins, Colorado. I decided to finish my Master's degree there, and see where I could get a permanent job." I just about spit out my entire life history all at once, false as it was. Nerves had me guessing whether I should have told her in bits and pieces. Everything I'd said was verifiable, but only online.

"Wow! That sounds exciting. Except losing your parents when you were so young. I can't imagine not having my parents. I'm sorry about that."

The waitress set steaming plates of enchiladas in front of us, and for several minutes we ate in silence. "Where are you living now?" Tessa took a breather between bites.

"I found a small apartment not far from here. On days when it's not hot enough to melt your shoes, I can even walk."

Tessa sighed. "I was hoping to get my own apartment, but my folks don't want me living alone. They think it's dangerous for a young girl to live by herself." She laughed. "Get that? Girl? I'm twenty-three, and they still think I'm a girl. The closest I got to living on my own was while I was in college; I lived in the dorm on campus. Being the baby of the family, and the only girl, sucks. I thought my folks would go nuts whenever there was trouble on campus. They called me at all hours of the night to check up on me. Both of my brothers are married, and have kids of their own. I think my folks just don't want to be alone with each other." She laughed again.

"I think it's sweet that they care enough to be protective of you." I could hear the wistful note in my voice, and hoped Tessa didn't pick up on it.

I couldn't really blame my folks for the way Eddie turned out. He had been as horrible to them as he was to everyone else. Whenever they tried to discipline him, he would either set something on fire or break something. Once when Dad tried to punish him, Eddie had beaten him so badly he couldn't go to work for a week. I'll never understand why they hadn't called the police, except that they were afraid of what he would do if they did. Time had proven them right to be afraid. He'd killed them when they tried to do something he didn't like. Maybe someday I'll find out just what they had done to set him off that final time.

By the time we headed back to the office complex, I knew all about Tessa's family, and she had a thumbnail sketch of the life I'm living now. I'd learned a long time ago that if you're a good listener, most people are willing to talk about themselves without realizing you're giving away very little information of your own.

"Would you like to come over to the house tonight for dinner? I'd like for you to meet my folks." Tessa's perky voice broke into my glum thoughts. "They always enjoy having my friends over."

"Thanks, Tessa, maybe some other night. I know it sounds like a cliché, but I have laundry to do. Really; I didn't have time to do it before I moved, and I've been so busy since I got here I haven't done it yet." I gave a small laugh. "I also have to go shopping for some summer clothes. Summer clothes in Colorado are more like winter clothes here."

"Maybe we can go together. I love to shop especially when someone else is paying the bill." She stopped, looking suddenly self-conscious. "That is, if you want company?" Her bubbly personality was hard to resist, and I nodded agreement.

"That sounds like fun." After I said it, I realized the words were true. I've kept to myself for so long, I've forgotten what it feels like to have a friend. "Let's plan on going Saturday. That way we won't have to hurry home."

Tessa's exuberance was catching, and for the first time in a long while, I felt lighthearted and free. I just hoped it lasted, and friendship with me didn't cost Tessa more than anyone should have to pay.

CHAPTER TWO

My first week in the lab was behind me, and I was feeling pretty good as I stepped out into the still boiling temperature of the parking lot. I'd stayed late to finish a report, and there were few cars left. My credentials were real, and my work had been excellent so far. I'd even helped on a case, pinpointing some missing evidence like Abby on *NCIS*. I laughed at myself. If people knew I identified with fictional characters on television shows they would probably put me in the looney bin. But my life was a work of fiction so maybe my identity crisis made some sense. At least to me.

I wished I could work alone like Abby, then I wouldn't have to interact with the others in the lab. Maybe I was like Abby in more ways than one. She didn't like others working in her lab either. But on *NCIS* the lab really was hers, and here I was just one of many working side by side.

"Rafe Gonzales, you scoundrel, what the hell are you doing here?" Shouts from two uniformed officers brought me back to real life and out of the *NCIS* lab in my mind. A tall, dark man was heading in their direction across the parking lot. They began walking towards him, closing the distance.

I stopped, wondering if there was going to be a gun battle right there in the police department parking lot. Should I go back inside for help? The two officers didn't look intimidated as the man continued towards them. They didn't go for their guns, and I couldn't tell if the man they called Rafe had a weapon. I couldn't hear what he was saying to them, but they suddenly broke out in raucous laughter, wrapping each other in back slapping bear hugs.

My breath whooshed out on a sigh of relief, and I

nearly sagged against the wall. I always saw trouble even when there wasn't any. If my plan works out the way I hope, maybe someday I will be able to relax, and not always be on guard.

The three men continued to joke around as I headed for my car again, and their words carried on the gentle breeze as I drew closer. "Who's the cute redhead? I haven't seen her before." I wasn't sure which one of them asked the question.

"See what you're missing by working in the boonies, Rafe?" one of the officers said. "You need to come downtown more often, man. She's new in the crime lab." I could feel my face burning, and I didn't think it was from the heat. They didn't seem the least bit concerned that I might be able to hear what they were saying.

"She can come to my crime scene any old time," Rafe laughed. "Maybe I'll go over and introduce myself."

"Come on, man. Leave a few of the cute ones for the rest of us." They were all joking around at my expense, and I just wanted to get to my car and get away.

Unlocking my car, I sat down a little too quickly, and I almost jumped back out as the hot seat came into contact with my legs. Not wanting to draw any more attention to myself, I stayed put, but kept the car door open to let some of the stifling heat out.

Sitting there, a long forgotten memory floated to the surface of my mind. It was another Rafe, this one about fifteen and also very good looking. All the high school girls clamored for his attention. But that Rafe was more juvenile delinquent than law enforcement. As I closed the car door and reached for my seat belt, I looked over my shoulder at him. Was it possible they were one and the same?

My heart turned flip flops in my chest at the thought. He was too far away to get a good look at him; besides, more than fifteen years had passed. There was no way to be sure without revealing my true identity. Pulling out of the parking lot, I looked in my rear view mirror. He'd stepped away from the others, watching me drive away. If he was the Rafe from my past, would he connect me with that fourteen-year-old bean pole I'd been? I shook my head, trying to reassure myself. The only reason I'd thought of that teenage boy was his name. *It's probably not the same person*, I told myself. *There must be a lot of men with that name in Phoenix.*

As I drove, I kept one eye on the mirror. He wouldn't try to follow me, would he? I'm just being paranoid. I've been looking over my shoulder for so long; it's become second nature now. Before opening the door to my apartment, I checked to make sure all my warning signs were still in place. Melodramatic, yes, but if it gave me fair warning that someone had been inside my apartment; I'd take melodrama any day. Of course, if it was Eddie, he'd managed to bypass my traps before.

Everything looked just the way I'd left it that morning, and I quickly closed the door behind me, throwing the three locks I'd had installed after moving in along with the chain lock and the lock on the door knob. My third floor apartment wasn't exactly convenient when I had an arm load of groceries, but no one was going to break in easily. The small balcony wasn't connected to the one next door, and they were far enough apart that only an acrobat would be able to safely make the leap.

I sat down on the one piece of furniture in the living room, a secondhand sofa I'd picked up at the Goodwill store. Had that tall, dark haired man in the parking lot been the same Rafe I knew fifteen years ago? I questioned again. If so, what did that mean to me? At fourteen, my figure hadn't filled out yet, and my hair was long and mousey brown. I'd thought I'd reached my full height at five feet three, but apparently not. I now stand at five feet seven.

With all these differences and a new name, there was no reason he would connect me to that long ago girl. Nonetheless, I planned on avoiding him like the plague until I knew he wasn't the same person.

~~~

Shopping with Tessa was an adventure for me. Usually I go into a store, grab what I need and head out again. Not Tessa. She could be a professional shopper. She looks at everything, tries on all kinds of clothes, samples perfumes and lotions. By the time we got back to my apartment it was nearly five, and my feet were killing me. "How do you do it, Tessa? You still look like you just stepped out of a shower."

"Lots of experience," she laughed. "Mom is a master bargain hunter. We used to spend all day Saturday going to all the yard sales and secondhand stores."

"Well, she has nothing on you. We hit few of those today, too." I had to admit I got some wonderful bargains. My closet wasn't going to be bare for long, and neither would my apartment. I didn't know people sold perfectly good appliances and clothes just because they got tired of them. I'd never had that luxury.

"Why don't you come home with me? My folks are dying to meet you. I've told them all about you. I think you'd like them, too. Mom's a great cook."

"Thanks for the invitation, but the only thing I'm going to do tonight is soak my feet in a warm bath and veg out with a good book." Meeting her family wasn't on my agenda right now. I was already out of my comfort zone spending this much time with Tessa.

"Oh, come on," she pooh poohed. "You're on your feet all day at work. A little shopping couldn't wear you out. Besides, you have to eat."

I had to laugh at her. "After the lunch we had, I won't be eating until tomorrow about this time. I'll take a rain check on the invite though." I hoped that would put her off, and she would forget about it for a while. Meeting her over-protective parents with all the questions they would probably have for any friend of hers was even more daunting than starting a new job.

Tessa sighed dramatically. "All right, I'll let you off for now, but I want you to meet my folks. They're going to love you, and I know you're going to love them." I wasn't so sure of that, but I didn't argue. If they were anything like Tessa, they would be sweet and kind. I just wasn't sure they would want their daughter befriending someone with no real background.

~~~

"How had that bitch completely disappeared?" Eddie muttered as he paced around the small dingy motel room. She couldn't just disappear from the face of the earth; there had to be some trace, somewhere. He gave a mean little chuckle. Unless she had the kind of help he'd given that bastard who thought he could get away with marrying her. I'll bet he still hasn't been found. That's what you get when you try to take what's mine. After he disappeared, she took off so fast he hadn't been able to track her, and he'd lost her completely. Where was she?

He continued to pace around the room, the walls closing in on him tighter with each pass. He had to do something. He'd always thought he would be able to find her wherever she went. Each time she disappeared, it was taking him longer to find her again. This time though, he feared she had managed to slip away from him completely. In a fit of anger, he punched the wall, leaving a hole where his fist had landed. The walls in the crappy place were so thin; his fist had nearly gone through to the room next door. What did it matter? One more hole wouldn't even be noticed.

He had to find her. Panic was beginning to settle on him. He couldn't let her get away. If she ever got up the nerve to go to the police, it could be the end of him. But he wouldn't let that happen; he'd die first, taking her with him.

Four years in that hell hole of a nut house had taught him a lot of useful things; he'd been able to refine his techniques until not even the best forensics specialist could find evidence against him. Hadn't he proven that with his parents? Of course, it didn't hurt to have some incompetent detectives working the case. He let out with his mean chuckle again. He'd taught that fat guy a lesson about respecting his betters. Of course it was a lesson he wouldn't have to use any time soon. He'd gone to his reward a long time ago.

Giving himself a shake, he turned his thoughts back to the matter at hand. He had to find Jennifer before she had put so many layers between them that he'd never find her. Ever since she disappeared that first time, she'd been on the move, never staying in the same place more than a year, two at the most. She'd change her name, her looks, but there had always been something leading him to her. It was longer than that since he had any clue where she was now. He always thought they had some sort of connection, something that told him where to look for her next. The pressure was building inside him; he had to do something before he exploded. He couldn't let himself get careless though. There couldn't be anything to point a finger at him.

~~~

On my resume and during the interviews, I had stressed my desire to work on cold cases as well as current ones. My degree and references had impressed people enough to hire me, but so far the powers that be hadn't seen fit to allow me near any cold case. If I could find one piece of evidence that helped crack one of the old cases, it would certainly help move me in the direction I wanted to go. First I had to be allowed to help with one.

In the meantime, I spent as much time as possible in the crime lab. With no family and Tessa the only friend I'd made, my time was my own to do with as I wanted. And I wanted to be at work. It was where I would be able to prove Eddie had killed my parents. Until he came after me again though, proving his guilt wasn't going to help me. As long as he stayed in hiding he was as safe from me as I was from him. It was a two-edged sword. If I could be certain he was either dead or in prison, I could finally relax. Until then, I had to be careful.

I have Eddie's fingerprints from our old house, but I can't run them through the system to see if he's been arrested for a crime somewhere, or if they were on file for a crime he hadn't been caught for yet. Doing that would certainly alert someone that I was looking into something that didn't pertain to a current case.

I've never been able to understand why the police didn't find it odd that there were no strange prints in our house. Since when did junkies looking for drugs, or money to buy them, worry about leaving prints behind? The detective in charge of my parents' murders, Lieutenant Vargas, was still on the force. *She can't be a very good detective if she let that little detail slip by unnoticed*, I thought. I'm just glad I haven't run into her yet. Still it wouldn't be a good idea to get caught running Eddie's prints unless my boss had given me the go ahead to work on cold cases.

"Hey, girlfriend, it's past quitting time on a Friday evening," Tessa bounced into the lab, interrupting my musings. "Let's blow this Popsicle stand. I thought we were going out to celebrate our first paycheck." She was so excited she could barely stand still. "I've waited a long time for this check." She waved it in the air like a triumphant flag.

"Okay, give me a minute to clear things up here." Her excitement was contagious, and by the time we left the lab, I was looking forward to an evening of simple girl stuff.

"You up for another shopping trip tomorrow?" she asked as she sipped her virgin margarita at her favorite Mexican restaurant.

"Oh, please, no." I held up my hands as if to ward off an attack. "I'm not sure I could survive that." I laughed, letting her know I was joking. "Besides, my closet is full, and I haven't decided what other furniture I need. My apartment is pretty small, you know."

Tessa gave a dramatic sigh, "Okay, so what do you want to do instead?"

My antenna tingled. She'd given in a little too quickly. She was up to something. "I have laundry to do, and I need to clean my place. I didn't get around to it this week." I watched her suspiciously, waiting for the other shoe to drop.

"Oh, good, then you can come over for dinner tomorrow night. Mom and Dad are looking forward to meeting you; I've told them all about you."

Well, I walked into that one, I thought with a groan.

"Come on, Casey," she pleaded. "It won't be that bad. My folks promised to put away the instruments of torture until your second visit."

"Okay," I laughed, "as long as you promise no torture."

She gave one bounce in her seat, picking up her glass again. "I don't know why you're so worried. It's not like you're meeting your boyfriend's parents for the first time. Now that can be nerve racking!"

"You sound like the voice of experience. How many parents have you been introduced to over your looong life?" Six years my junior, she probably had a lot more experience with boyfriends than I had.

"Just one," Tessa's expression grew distant for a moment, as though lost in her own thoughts. "It's not something I'd like to repeat any time soon." She drew a deep breath, letting it out slowly. "My freshman year in college I fell hard for a guy." Her voice was soft, speaking more to herself than me. "I thought he felt the same way, but that only lasted until I met his mother. Apparently I'm not fashion model pretty, Einstein smart and Bill Gates rich. She wasn't even polite in her disapproval. Before the evening was over, I knew our romance had gone so far south I could see icebergs forming."

Giving herself a little shake, she drew a deep breath. "Lesson well learned," she said sagely. "But enough of those depressing thoughts. Have you met any of the cute, young officers yet? How many of them make it into the lab? Doesn't seem like a good place to meet men."

"No, most of the people I see are the detectives, and most of them are older and married," I confirmed. My thoughts flashed to the officers in the parking lot last Friday, especially the tall one. From the conversation I overheard, his buddies weren't married, and he was definitely single and on the prowl. Not someone to get interested in, even if I was looking.

"How about you?" I asked. "See any cute guys you'd like to meet?" Girl talk wasn't my strong suit, but I knew how it went.

Tessa grinned, "Just one but I think he's way out of my league. He works in a different precinct, but he makes it downtown every now and then. I think he's a detective, but definitely not older."

"Why do you think he's out of your league? Don't judge all men by that creep in college."

"Oh, this one is scary cute. No, scary handsome." Tessa laughed. "Men or women that good looking usually know just how good looking they are, and expect everyone to fall at their feet in worship. Not for me."

"This scary handsome guy got a name? I'd hate to run into him, and not be prepared." It was a lot easier than I expected to joke around and just be normal. Thanks to Tessa.

38

"Laugh if you want, Casey, but believe me, this guy isn't someone to get serious about. He flirts with every female he comes in contact with, it doesn't matter how old or young they are or if he's just arrested them." She laughed. "He brought this woman in today. She was fighting mad that he had arrested her until he started with the sweet talk. He had her eating out of his hand in no time. She was almost glad to let him book her. His name is Rafe. I never heard his last name."

I must have gasped or something because her head snapped up, her eyes growing big in her pixie face. "You know him? How? Where? Come on, girl, tell all!"

There really wasn't much to tell, I related the scene in the parking lot last Friday in a matter of seconds. "It must be the same guy. He was definitely sure of himself." Of course that wasn't all. I couldn't tell her of my fear that he was the same Rafe Gonzales I knew fifteen years ago.

"He actually saw you? He wanted the others to introduce you? Oh, girl, he's trouble with a capital T. Stay away from him." Tessa was adamant.

"That will be easy. I'm not looking for any kind of a relationship, and especially not with a born flirt." *Especially not one who might know my real past*, I added silently.

For the rest of the evening we avoided all talk of men, and the havoc they could wreak in our lives. It was late when I finally fell into bed. Tessa reminded me of dinner the next day with her folks as she climbed into her car. *How bad can it be*, I asked myself just before sleep claimed me. *After all, I'd passed a polygraph test with flying colors.*

CHAPTER THREE

Monday morning I was grateful for a full schedule. There'd been a stabbing over the weekend and several burglaries. I had fingerprints to run, blood samples to analyze, tire tracks to process. In other words, doing just what I enjoyed doing, and what I'd been trained for. While I worked, my mind replayed dinner with Tessa's family. Her brothers and their families had been there. With three grandkids all under five running around, there'd been little time for a question and answer session. Everyone had been as nice and welcoming as Tessa said they'd be. They all took me at face value, not questioning my background. Her parents had even invited me back anytime, saying Tessa's friends were always welcome.

The break room was empty and blissfully quiet when I entered to eat my lunch. I'd deliberately chosen the latest lunch time so I would have the room mostly to myself. The only people coming in now would be those grabbing something from the vending machines and hurrying back to work. Pulling a book from my bag, I settled on the hard chair, propping my feet on the one across from me. Within minutes I was lost in the mystery unraveling on the pages.

Several minutes later, the hair on the back of my neck bristled, and a shiver traveled down my spine. My stomach knotted. Had Eddie found me, right here in police headquarters? Would he be stupid enough to come after me here? Cautiously, I looked over my shoulder. If it was Eddie, I was trapped well and good. The only exit was behind me. Until I began working for the police department, I had always sat with my back to a wall, facing the door so I wouldn't be surprised. Stupid move not to continue that habit here, I told myself.

But it wasn't Eddie standing in the doorway. Instead, the tall, dark officer from the parking lot was standing there as though frozen to the spot, a confused frown drawing his dark brows together over even darker eyes. "Were you looking for someone?" I tried to act casual, like it was no big deal that he was staring at me.

"Uh, no. I just came in for a soda." He gave himself a shake, fishing his wallet out of his pocket. Watching him out of the corner of my eye, I saw him make several stabs at the slot with his dollar. My presence seems to have unnerved him as much as his presence had me, and he couldn't get his hands to work properly. He finally retrieved the bottle of soda, and turned back to the room. I kept my head down, pretending to be engrossed in my book, but I was acutely aware of him watching me. Why didn't he just leave?

Well, if he wouldn't, I would. Closing my book, I gathered my lunch papers, stuffing them in the trash. He moved in front of me, blocking my way. "Have we met before?" That same confused frown still drew his brows together.

I forced myself to laugh. "Now there's an original line. But I doubt we've met before. I just moved here three weeks ago."

"No, that's not a line." He shook his head as though to clear it. "I just have this weird feeling like I know you from somewhere."

"Well, I've traveled a lot, and lived in a lot of places. Maybe you saw me in one of them. But I don't remember you. Now if you'll excuse me, I need to get back to the lab." He didn't move, and I was forced to slide past him in the narrow doorway. I did my best to avoid any contact. I could feel his eyes on me until I turned the corner at the end of the hallway.

Slipping into the ladies restroom, I sagged against the door. *How could he recognize me? It's been fifteen years*

41

since we saw each other. Time alone should have been enough to make it impossible for him to know who I am. Add in the changes I've made to my looks, and that should have been enough so no one would know me. Apparently it wasn't. Now what do I do?

The rest of the afternoon I kept looking over my shoulder, expecting him to be there watching me. I had no doubt now that this man was the same Rafe Gonzales from my past. I still found it hard to reconcile the hell raising teenager with the accomplished police officer he seemed to be now. I was going to have to avoid him. When that wasn't possible I would need to keep any conversation strictly on business. I couldn't take the chance I'd say something that would click in his memory.

~~~

It had been weeks since that first encounter with Rafe Gonzales in the break room, and I hadn't seen him again. Maybe he was avoiding me as conscientiously as I was avoiding him. At least I could hope that was the case. I was finally able to relax without worrying that I would meet him around every corner or down every hallway.

After three months, Timothy Watkins, my boss, seemed pleased with my performance, and wasn't watching every move I made, double checking my work. "Don't let him get to you," Barb Jenkins told me my first week in the lab. "He watches everyone like they're fresh off the farm when they first start here. It usually takes him a few months to realize he isn't the only one who knows what they're doing." It was good to know it wasn't just me he was watching, but it was a little unnerving all the same. I wanted him to trust me enough to let me work on the cold cases when time permitted.

Until I found out that Eddie was either in prison or dead, I couldn't completely relax. Even then, I would always be Casey Gibson. Jennifer Miller had ceased to exist fifteen years ago. No matter the outcome with Eddie, she wouldn't be making a comeback.

Lost in my own thoughts and the job I was doing, I jumped when Mr. Watkins barked, "Gibson, my office." My heart nearly stuttered to a stop. What had I done wrong? Placing the slide I'd been working on back in the proper case, I joined Mr. Watkins in his office.

"Yes, sir. Is something wrong?" I tried to sound confident even though my knees were knocking together.

"Why does everyone assume they're in trouble when I call them into my office? This isn't the principal's office, and we aren't in high school," he growled. *It might have something to do with the barking tone;* I wanted to tell him, but wisely kept silent. "Anyway," he went on without much pause, "You said you wanted to work on cold cases. Does that still go, or were you just showing off?"

"No, sir. I mean, yes, sir," I fumbled with the right words. "I do want to work on cold cases, and I wasn't showing off." I hoped I was making sense.

"The Cold Case detail has some tests they need run on one of their cases. It doesn't take precedence over what you're already doing, but when you have a few minutes, take a look at it. That's all," he added when I just stood there.

"Oh, uh, sure." I turned to leave, but stopped in the doorway. "Will they bring me the evidence or should I contact someone?" I didn't know how this was handled.

"Someone will bring it to you either today or tomorrow. Those guys work on the cases when they have time." He had already dismissed me, and was concentrating on the file on his desk.

I could have danced all the way back to my work station. This was the break I'd been hoping for. Could I be lucky enough to get my folks' murder case first shot out of the bag? *Probably not*, I told myself, trying not to get my hopes up. At least now, I had my foot in the door.

Every time someone came into the lab I expected it to be for me, each time I was disappointed. By the end of the day, I was frustrated. If they had evidence they wanted me to analyze, why didn't someone bring it to me?

The next day was more of the same. Finally I decided Mr. Watkins had just been testing me. He wanted to see if I really was interested in cold cases or just beefing up my resume. Clearing up my station at the end of the day, I wasn't paying attention when someone came into the lab. "I'll be right with you," I said without turning around. At this time of day I was the only one left in the lab.

"No hurry. I just brought some evidence for C. Gibson. Can you point me in the right direction?"

"That's me." I didn't recognize the deep voice, and I turned to see who was looking for me. My heart nearly stopped for a second. Rafe Gonzales held a storage box ready to hand it to me.

"You're the lab rat working on cold cases?"

"You're the detective working on cold cases?" We both spoke at once. We stared at each other with our mouths hanging open. At least my mouth was hanging open. Finally gathering myself, I answered with as much dignity as I could muster. "I'm not a lab rat; I'm a forensic scientist. I have a Master's Degree in Forensic Science."

"Well, good for you." He didn't even try to hide his grin as he enjoyed my discomfort. "A few of us work on cold cases when we have some spare time. Tim Watkins said to bring this down to C. Gibson. Nice to know you have a name. It's not exactly what I was expecting, but nice all the same. Does the C stand for something?"

Tessa said he was a charmer and a flirt. Flirt maybe, but definitely not charm. He was making fun of me, or trying to. "Of course it does," I answered his question without satisfying his curiosity. "I'll take that." I moved to take the box, but he held it out of my reach.

"It's kind of heavy. Tell me where you want it." That teasing smile hadn't changed in fifteen years, causing my stomach to churn. This man was dangerous on so many levels.

With evidence of any kind, even from cold cases, we had to make sure it wouldn't be tampered with. I pointed to a locked cabinet, opening the door for him to set the box on the shelf. I avoided making eye contact until the silence stretched out for several minutes. When I looked up, that same confused frown he'd worn when he saw me in the break room, rode his dark features. "Is something wrong?" I asked, trying to sound casual.

He shook his head. "I keep thinking I've seen you before, but I don't know where. You want to go get something to eat?" His quick change of subject caught me off guard.

"What?!"

"Eat. You know, food. It's something we all do to survive." His teasing smile was back in place.

"No." Belatedly I added, "Thank you."

"Why not? You have to eat, don't you?"

"I have a rule that I don't date people I work with."

"Technically we don't work together. I'm in the field, you're in the lab."

"Splitting hairs," I countered. "We both work for the police department."

"Okay, so don't call it a date. We're just two people getting something to eat at the same place."

Before he even finished speaking I shook my head. "Sorry, rules are rules."

"I'll bet you just made that up," he argued. "Besides, rules are made to be broken"

"Rules are made to live by." How was I going to get out of this stupid conversation?

"Do you have rules for everything?" He scowled at my stubborn refusal.

"I'm working on it." I would have laughed if this situation wasn't so full of pitfalls. The conversation mirrored one from an episode of *NCIS*. Until now I hadn't realized how many rules I had put in place for myself.

"That's ridiculous! I just asked you to dinner, not to make a life commitment." Thankfully, he didn't make the connection with the television show.

I crossed my arms, staying silent. I wasn't going to argue with him. The longer we talked the bigger the chance he would connect me with that girl from long ago.

"Oh, hell." He stormed out of the lab, letting the door slam behind him.

I let out a pent up breath, a small giggle escaping with it. We had argued like this as teenagers, and part of the time I had even bested him. I'd done it again. I sat down on the stool at my lab table before my legs gave out.

If Rafe worked on the cold cases, that meant we would be working together part of the time. Constant contact would either cement me as Casey Gibson or continue to remind him of that person from his past until he remembered exactly who that was. How did I keep that from happening? "Oh, crap!" I muttered. Who would have thought that Rafe Gonzales would become a cop?

CHAPTER FOUR

What do I do now? he asked himself. Where do I look next? He couldn't let her get away. She knew enough to put him away for life, or worse, set him up for a lethal injection. He didn't worry about being caught by the cops though. He was smarter than them, always had been. Leave your fingerprints and DNA where the cops expect to find them, and they won't consider you a suspect. Make murder look like an accident, and they won't look for fingerprints and DNA. If you can't do either of those, make sure the victim is someone the cops don't really care about, and they won't look very hard for the murderer.

Jennifer was another story. She might be smarter than him, but he'd always be more cunning than her, and until now it had always paid off in big dividends. Now he was afraid he was losing his edge. Where the hell had she gone?

He knew that someday he might run up against a smart cop willing to look beyond the obvious when trying to solve a murder. He couldn't let that happen until he'd finished with Jennifer. She couldn't outrun him forever. Could she? Sometimes he doubted himself, and he couldn't let that happen either. He had to find her and teach her that he was still in command of her life.

~~~

Rafe waltzed into the lab three days later, like he owned the place, expecting and getting the attention of the two other women there. Giving them each a wink, he turned to me like we met here every night. "How's that evidence coming?"

"Well, let's see. We've had two murders in the city, and a rash of burglaries, and an arson fire. I've been rather tied up. Mr. Watkins said cold cases came after the current ones. Things should slow down tomorrow unless someone goes on a killing spree. I'll get to it as soon as possible, and I'll e-mail you with any results." I tried to keep my voice professional, and not let on how much his presence bothered me on so many levels.

"Oh, e-mail isn't necessary. I'll pop in to check on how you're getting along. I've been transferred to headquarters, so we'll be seeing a lot more of each other." That sexy little smile I remembered from years ago flashed at me. Unfortunately I wasn't any more immune to his charm than any other female alive. I was just better at hiding it than most.

"Whatever." I shrugged. "Suit yourself." I turned my back on him, hoping he would take the hint and leave.

Lost in my work I didn't realize he was still in the lab until he spoke, startling me enough that I nearly fell off my stool. "How did you get into forensics?" he asked, unaware that he'd startled me. "It doesn't strike me as something that would interest a woman."

"That's a sexist remark." I avoided looking up.

"Okay, so it's sexist. Now answer the question."

"I love science, and I like solving mysteries. I just combined the two. How did you become a cop?" I needed to keep him from questioning me, and changed his focus turning the question back on him.

A far off, almost haunted look came into his dark eyes, making them even darker. "The area I lived in when I was a kid wasn't a very nice place. Bad things were always happening. One day something really bad happened, and the cops didn't do a very good job solving it. I just didn't want that to happen again."

My heart did a stutter step, and my breath hitched in my throat. He was talking about the murder of my parents! I had to change the subject and fast. But how did I do that without making him suspicious of the swift change? I didn't have to worry about that, though.

48

"How about grabbing a bite to eat when you finish here? It's getting late. There's a great little restaurant not far from here. You do like Mexican food, right?"

"No thanks."

"No, you don't like Mexican food?"

"No, I don't want to grab a bite to eat with you. I already told you I don't date people I work with." I kept my attention on the work in front of me.

"It's not a date. It's just two colleagues eating at the same place. I'll even let you pay for your own dinner."

"No thanks."

"So you don't go to lunch with your co-workers? Isn't that being a little stand-offish?"

"I usually bring my own lunch. It's cheaper."

"Man, you're tough. I'm just trying to be friendly. Do you have a rule about being friends with co-workers?"

"Nope. No rules against friends. I have several here already." Suddenly I realized I was enjoying this verbal sparring. I needed to put a stop to it before he won me over. Something I couldn't let happen. "Now, if you want to stay here while I work on these samples, you'll have to be quiet. You wouldn't want me to be distracted so I make a mistake, would you? I could mess up your case, and you'd never get the conviction you're looking for."

Instead of being quiet, he laughed. "I've been watching you work for the last hour. I don't think there's anything, short of a bomb, that would make you mess up on those tests. I've never seen anyone so intent on her work. I'll bet you're able to juggle a multitude of tasks at once, and not mess any of them up." He was quiet for a long moment, and I was hoping he would stay that way. It was too much to hope for, though. "You just might be the person who can solve the one case that started me in law enforcement. See you tomorrow, Casey." With that, he walked out of the lab without looking back.

I sagged against the counter, resting my head on my

arms. His objective is the same as mine. Solve my parents' murders. Can I risk working with him on that case? It would bring back so many memories of a certain fourteen-year-old girl. *What do I do now?* I asked myself. I couldn't stop working with him on the cold cases. At the same time, could I risk it? What would it mean if he recognized me as that young girl? I didn't know if he'd keep my secret, or turn me in as a fraud. My degree and work experience are real, just not the name attached to them.

~~~

"Hey, girlfriend, what's up? I haven't heard from you all week. I thought maybe you'd left town." Tessa blew into the lab on Friday after work in her usual tornado fashion. She had more energy than ten people.

"You can't get rid of me that easy," I countered. "My boss gave me some cold cases to work on, so I've been busy. I'll be finished with this in a few minutes; then I'll wrap up for the night."

"For the night? How about for the week? Today's Friday, so let's go party. Some of the people I work with are going to a sports bar. I thought we could join them." Maybe she still lived with her parents, but that didn't seem to hinder her social life.

I started to shake my head, but reconsidered. I'd been nearly a recluse for most of my life, and it hadn't gotten me anywhere. Eddie always seemed to find me when I didn't want him to. Now that I was ready to play his game and confront him, he was missing in action. Maybe it was time to start living and hang the consequences. "All right, give me a few more minutes. I'm right in the middle of something, and I have to finish it."

Tessa did a little victory dance, and I couldn't help but laugh at her antics. She was probably the best thing that happened to me since Fred. The thought sobered me a little. Was I placing her life in jeopardy? Would Eddie go after her the way he had Fred? That was assuming Eddie found me again. It had been nearly four years without even a hint that he knew where I was. I couldn't let my guard down completely, but I wanted to enter into life again. I would just have to remain alert.

It was after one in the morning when I finally made it home. My head was spinning, but not from the one glass of wine I'd had. After that I'd switched to virgin margaritas. I didn't dare let myself get drunk and lose control. I couldn't take the chance that I would say something that would give me away. I was tired, but for the first time in more years than I cared to count, I'd had fun. I'd met more people in one night than I usually allowed myself to meet in a year. It felt good.

The last time I'd felt comfortable making friends had been a long time ago, Eddie had been locked up, and I didn't have to worry about what he would do to me or my friends. Until tonight I hadn't realized how much I wanted that again. *How do I speed up the process of proving he killed our parents?* I wondered. Did I dare ask Rafe...Detective Gonzales about the case that had set him on the path to law enforcement?

By Monday I was anxious to be back in the lab. It had been a slow weekend in Phoenix with no murders, which was good for the citizens, but there were several assaults and burglaries, When I wasn't working on the current cases, I still had plenty to keep me busy working on the cold case for Rafe, Detective Gonzales, I corrected myself again. I didn't want to get comfortable with him. That would be a big mistake. I still wasn't certain what it would mean if he realized who I really am. I just wasn't willing to find out at this point.

~~~

I couldn't believe it was October already, and I'd been in Phoenix over three months. Still no sign that Eddie knew I was here, or that Detective Gonzales knew my true identity. In the month we'd been working together he continued to ask me out, and I continued to refuse. Occasionally I would find him staring at me, that same confused frown drawing his dark brows together. Something about me still niggled at the back of his mind. I had hoped with enough time, he'd dismiss any similarities that nagged at him, and accept me for who I am now.

We had cleared two of the cases he'd brought me, but so far no murders or rapes. Each new case he brought in, I hoped would be the murder of my parents, but so far nothing. I couldn't very well run Eddie's prints through the Automated Fingerprint Identification System without a case to tie them to. I wanted to know if there were unsolved cases anywhere in the country linked to his prints. If that happened, other jurisdictions could also be looking for him, not just me.

"We've got a good record clearing these old cases," Detective Gonzales said without preamble when he came into the lab at the end of the day. "Maybe now Watty will trust us with more important ones soon."

"Watty?" I raised one eyebrow in question. I couldn't believe Mr. Watkins approved of that nickname.

He grinned mischievously at me. "Sure, Mr. Watkins is just too formal for coworkers. Just don't tell him we call him that. He can be a stuffed shirt sometimes." He paused for a moment. "Sort of like you calling me Detective Gonzales all the time, ya know? By now we should be on first name basis. Oh, wait a minute; I'm on first name basis with you. It's just you who refuse to call me Rafe. You got something against my name?" When I refused to rise to the bait, he went on. "Some of the guys call me 'Gonzo'. Would you rather that?"

"No, I wouldn't. I just want to keep everything on a professional basis." My tone sounded stilted, even to me.

"Oh, come on," he said, frustration lacing through his

voice. "I know you call the people you work with here in the lab by their first names. I've heard you," he added when I started to object. "You and that young girl in Administration are friendly. I've seen you with her and, bunch of others down at Flanagan's on Friday nights. What's the difference between going out with them and going out with me? Where's your rule for that?" He was starting to get angry.

"You want to go out on a date; I'm just one of the crowd when I'm with Tessa and the others."

"But you and Tessa do things together outside of work, right?"

"We're friends," I stated matter-of-factly. "I'm not dating her." I looked around; hoping everyone else had already left for the day. I didn't want this conversation being spread through the gossip mill in the police department.

He blew out a frustrated breath, trying to rein in his temper. "Okay, how about this. We can go out to eat, and we each pay our own way. We'll just be friends, no dating."

"What difference does this make to you? Why are you pushing the issue?" I could feel my own temper begin to get the best of me.

My question seemed to confuse him for a moment, and then he shook his head. "I don't know why I'm pushing the issue." His words were so quiet I wouldn't have heard him if there had been any noise in the room. He looked up at me like he'd forgotten I was still there. "I just am." Now his words were firm.

"Is it because I won't go out with you, and you can't take rejection? Am I just a challenge now?"

"No! I like what I see in you, and I'd just like to get to know you better. Is there something wrong with that?" He sounded insulted now. His feet were braced apart, his fists rested on his narrow hips. My stomach churned for a long moment. He reminded me so much of the boy he'd been.

He might have been Peck's bad boy getting into all sorts of mischief, but he'd never been a bully; in fact, just the opposite. If someone was being bullied, Rafe had been the first one to defend him or her. "Well, don't you have anything to say?" His question brought me back to the present.

"Uh, um, thank you?" It came out more like a question than a statement. "I mean, thank you. But I still don't date men I work with."

"But we can be friends, get together in groups." What should have been a question from him was a statement of fact.

"That's not what I said."

"Close enough." He turned to leave, walking with a definite swagger now. As he opened the door, Tessa was reaching for the door knob. "Hello there, Tessa." He gave her a courtly bow, touching his fingertips to his brow in a small salute before continuing down the hall, whistling a jaunty tune.

"Wow!" Tessa breathed out a sigh, fanning her hand in front of her face. "He's really something. What was he doing here?"

"Just talking about one of the cold cases." I shrugged nonchalantly.

"I don't think so," she argued. "That was a 'cat that ate the canary' look on his face."

"He's been asking me out." We were alone so I confided in her.

"Are you going to go?" She was starting to give her excited hop.

"Of course not!"

"Why not?"

"Tessa," I said with exasperation. "You're the one who told me to stay away from him. He's nothing but a tease and a flirt. Remember?"

"Oh, I know, but he's just so good looking." She sighed romantically, staring at the door where she had last seen him.

"And that was one of the reasons you gave for staying away from him. A man that good looking knows the effect he has on women, and is always looking for his next conquest."

She sighed again. "I know, but everyone says he's really not like that. Even the women he's dated still think he's the greatest thing since sliced bread. He doesn't dump them in a bad way, just lets them down easily and moves on."

"How many women have you been talking to about him? How many has he gently let down?"

"W... well," Tessa stammered. "I know I shouldn't gossip, even listening to gossip is bad. But everybody thinks he's a great guy. It can't be bad to know that about someone, can it?" She looked so guilty I couldn't help but laugh.

"No, it's not bad to know that about someone. That doesn't mean I need to go out with him. Besides, I have rules against dating men I work with."

"Oh, you and your rules," she tsked. "You don't need to have a rule for everything."

"It makes life a lot less complicated to have rules to live by."

"Of course it does. You just don't have to make up your own. That's what God does," Tessa said sagely. "Live by his rules, and you won't have to make up your own."

This sounded like something I'd heard when I'd gone to the youth group at the local church while Eddie was locked up. Once he was out, we all stopped going. My folks said it wouldn't do to take Eddie there. After what happened to them, I figured God wasn't watching over people anyway, so why bother going to church?

Until I met Fred, that is. He had put so much faith in

God; I tried to do the same. But when he disappeared, I couldn't see how God had protected him, so why should I trust Him? I couldn't tell Tessa this, so I kept quiet. Fortunately, she didn't push it either. I knew her family went to church every Sunday; they'd even invited me to go with them. I just hadn't accepted the invitation. Yet.

CHAPTER FIVE

It was close to the anniversary of my parents' murders. I hadn't been to the cemetery since the day they were buried. I wasn't sure it would be safe to go now, or if I even knew where they were buried. At fourteen, I hadn't paid attention to where we were going. Other things occupied my mind at the time; such as, how to stay out of Eddie's grasp.

Drawing Eddie into the open was my goal now, but first I had to be able to prove he had killed my parents, maybe even the social worker, Brenda Jones. Failing that, my life wasn't worth much. I was never going to let him abuse me again; I would fight him with everything in me. This meant I would die if he caught me, and maybe so would he.

The internet gave up a wealth of information, and I'd been able to locate my parents' graves. With Google Earth, I was even able to see the cemetery, pinpointing the location. For now this was the best I could do. At the time, Eddie hadn't bothered to have a headstone made, and the graves still sat unmarked. If I managed to have Eddie locked up, I would take care of that. Until then, I would just watch from afar. I might even be able to see if he showed up anytime during the year. It would be just like him to be watching their graves to see if I showed up.

~~~

It had become a custom every Friday after work for a group of us to meet at Flanagan's Bar and Grill. They had a good happy hour menu of appetizers that served as dinner. The size of the group and the members were up for grabs depending on who had other plans. Tessa and I and one or two others were the only ones who showed up weekly. What did that say for our social life?

Sitting on the high stools around a small table with a couple of women Tessa worked with, a familiar deep voice spoke behind me. "Mind if I join you, ladies?" I groaned and turned to see Rafe standing close to my shoulder.

"Detective Gonzales!" Tessa and Jill gasped simultaneously. "What are you doing here?"

"Oh, come now, ladies. We're all friends here, and we're off duty. You can call me Rafe. I already know most of you, if not by name at least by sight. And I'm here because I heard a group of you went out for happy hour. I wanted to join the crowd if that's all right with everyone." He looked at me, daring me to deny him entry into our group.

The others nearly fell over themselves to make room for him. Instead of taking the empty chair between Tessa and Jill, he pulled one from another table, squeezing in next to me. None of this went unnoticed by the others, especially Tessa. She elbowed me and gave me a knowing little nod. She seemed so self-satisfied; I wanted to knock her off the high stool.

Others joined us, and soon the tables filled up with police department personnel. Rafe wasn't the only officer to join us for the first time. We were loud, but no one got out of line. Before long everyone in the bar was joining us in conversation. I hadn't realized until then that most everyone in the bar worked for the city. It was like one big, happy family. Some of the people were dancing and Rafe leaned over to me. "Shall we join them?" He nodded towards the small dance floor.

My stomach twisted and I shook my head, almost in a panic. "I don't dance."

"What have you got against dancing?"

"Nothing, I just don't." How could I tell him I'd never danced before without sounding like a complete moron?

Rafe frowned at me, "Is it a religious thing?"

"No." I still couldn't think of a good excuse for not dancing, without telling him the truth.

"Oh, come on. Just think of it as exercise to music. You do exercise, don't you?" He looked me up and down, taking measure of my slim form.

"It's not exactly the same thing," I tried to argue. "When I exercise, I don't have to worry about stepping on a partner's toes." That was as close as I intended to get to the truth.

"Oh, come on," he said again as he stood up. "I'm rough and tough. I promise not to scream if you step on my toes, at least not much." He pulled me onto the miniscule dance floor, wrapping his arms around my waist. He held me close to his lean, hard body. No amount of resisting did any good; he was simply too strong for me.

Bodies were packed so tight there wasn't any room to move around; we were barely able to do more than sway to the music. "This isn't any kind of exercise I've ever done before. We're barely moving," I complained. With all the noise in the bar, I had to put my mouth right next to his ear to be heard. The intimacy of this was more than I was comfortable with.

"I kinda like it." His breath ruffled the hair around my ear, causing a knot to form in my stomach.

Fortunately the music ended, but Rafe still held me close as the others headed back to their tables. I stopped moving and pulled slightly away. At least as far as his iron grip would let me. "The music's over. People are looking at us." I could feel my face turning red. I didn't want to be the topic of gossip in the department for the next week.

"I know. I'm just waiting for the next song to start." He continued to sway slightly.

"Well, I'm not! Let me go, or I'll stomp on your toe for real."

Chuckling, he dropped his arms from my waist only to take my hand as he walked back to our group. "This being just friends is nice. We'll have to do this more often."

"When pigs fly," I muttered. I knew what he was doing, and I wasn't going to fall for it. Rafe Gonzales was a flirt now just like he'd been at fifteen. I had to remember what my purpose was here. If I was able to prove Eddie was a murderer and get him off the street once and for all, maybe then I could live a normal life. Until that day, I couldn't take chances like I had with Fred's life. Rafe might be a cop and able to take care of himself, but Eddie would consider him a challenge the same as he had always considered me.

Fifteen minutes later I decided I'd had enough fun for one evening. Whispering to Tessa, I slipped off the stool hoping Rafe wouldn't notice since he was deep in conversation with another detective. Turning away I walked into his rock hard chest. The man had the uncanny ability to appear out of nowhere, and end up right up in front of me. "Going somewhere?" he asked.

"Ladies room. Are you going to escort me?" I smiled my best innocent smile.

"Sure." He stayed by my side until we reached the Ladies Room.

"This is where we part company. Unless you want to create a riot, of course. I'll meet you back at the table." I pushed the door open, letting it close slowly behind me. "Damn, man," I muttered. "Why doesn't he leave me alone?" Of course, I knew. He didn't like to lose in any game he played, never had. I waited what I considered long enough for him to go back to the table, opened the door just wide enough to peek out. The coast was clear.

I stepped out and headed for the door and escape. It was dark outside, but the parking lot was lit up as bright as day, although shadows still hid around every vehicle. My Jeep was halfway across the parking lot, a ton of shadows to walk through. I hesitated. This would be the perfect place for Eddie to hijack me. Would I be able to defend myself in tight quarters? Would someone come to my defense?

I wouldn't have to worry about it tonight though. "Didn't your father tell you not to walk through a dark parking lot alone? It's not safe." Rafe spoke right behind me.

Under normal circumstances I wouldn't let my mind wander back in time. But with Rafe, that seemed to be happening on a regular basis. Thoughts of my parents must have been obvious on my face. "I'm sorry, Casey. I didn't mean to say anything to hurt you." He took my arm, slowing my stride even more. "I was joking around, but I was serious, too. You shouldn't go out alone. You never know who might be lurking in the shadows." His words mirrored my thoughts of moments ago, but I couldn't tell him that.

"It's fine. I'm tired, and didn't want to break up the party atmosphere. Thought I'd just slip out and head home. Go back in, I'll be fine now. Here's my car."

"Where are your keys? You should have them out before you reach your vehicle. That way you don't have to stand around looking for them, making yourself a target."

"I know all this, Rafe, but you're with me so I didn't get them out. Here they are." I clicked the key fob and unlocked the door. "Go back inside. I'm fine now. Thanks for walking me out." I closed the door, started my car, and backed out. Checking the rear view mirror, he was standing in the middle of the lane watching me drive away.

Sleep was very elusive that night, coming in fits and starts. Finally, at five fifteen I gave up and got out of bed. The sheets were twisted, and pulled out from under the mattress. I was getting too involved with Rafe; he was getting too close to me. I knew that the murder of my parents, and the fact that it had never been solved had affected him, drew him to law enforcement. He was a good man, but I couldn't let him get too close. What would he do if he realized who I am? I didn't want to find out. Did I? That question bothered me the rest of the day.

After another restless night, I got up early again. This was going to have to stop, or I'd be tired even before the work week started. I didn't bother with makeup, and let my hair curl any which way it wanted. Carrying a basket of laundry to the apartment complex Laundromat, I kept a careful eye out for Eddie, or anyone else out for mischief. It had been nearly four years since Eddie had last found me, but he could pop up at any time.

Weekend meals were still hard for me even after all these years. My parents had always had a big meal on Sunday with just the three of us while Eddie was locked up, enjoying the peace it offered. Before that and after he came home, meals were tense, sitting around the table waiting for the next storm to hit. Now I never knew just what to do with myself on any given Sunday. Ron and Gina Gordon, Tessa's parents, had invited me over so often I felt guilty for intruding, though they insisted I was doing no such thing. Their big meal always came after church, and I still hadn't agreed to join them in that endeavor. Tessa was still working on me though. The thought brought a smile now. If there was ever a happier, more outgoing, loving person, I'm sure I didn't know who that would be.

Because Eddie had been so much on my mind and the fact that he hadn't been seen for so long, when someone knocked on my door, my stomach went to my toes, and my heart nearly jumped out of my throat. I tiptoed to the door, almost afraid to breathe. Was this the showdown I'd been waiting for? Looking through the security hole in the door, my breath whooshed out.

"Come on, Casey, open up. I know you're in there." He waited while I did nothing, leaning my head against the door. I didn't want to deal with Rafe Gonzales today. Any day as a matter of fact. He knocked again. "Casey, I know you're there. I saw your shadow in the peep hole when you looked through it."

Reluctantly, I released the two dead bolt locks, the door knob lock and the swing arm privacy lock, or maid lock, leaving the chain in place. "Okay, Rafe what are you doing here?" I spoke through the small space the chain allowed.

"Wow, Casey, four locks?"

"Five," I corrected. Apparently he hadn't heard me release the maid lock.

"Five," he acknowledged, "what are you expecting, the hounds of hell to come knocking at your door?"

No, just one, I thought. "How did you know where I live?"

He laughed. "I'm a detective, so I detected."

I still hadn't opened the door. "What do you want?" He was dressed casually, but still dressed up for a weekend.

"Well, I'd like to talk to you, but not through a small crack in the door. How about opening up?"

I looked down at myself. I had on the ratty old shorts and a tee shirt I'd put on when I got up. I was sweaty from my recent workout. So far I'd managed to stay to the side of the door, not letting him get a look at messy me. "Go away, Rafe. I'm busy."

"It's lunch time. I thought maybe we could get something to eat."

I laughed, "Not likely. Like I said, I'm busy. Go away." I started to close the door. He held up a bag, swinging it just enough to bring the aroma of spicy, hot food into my living room. My stomach growled noisily and he laughed.

"It's just lunch, Casey. We eat, I leave, you get back to your busy life." He raised one dark eyebrow.

My stomach growled again, and I blew out a breath in resignation. Closing the door enough to release the chain, I opened the door to let him in.

As he walked in, I reached for the delicious smells coming from the bag, looking up at him. "Okay, we eat, then you..." I stopped talking. The look on his face froze the words in my throat. "What?" I looked down at my attire. "So I'm not dressed up fancy like you."

When I looked away from him, he seemed momentarily confused. "Your eyes," he whispered. "They're green, really green."

I forgot about being hungry, butterflies now filled my stomach. I didn't have the colored contacts in, muting the green of my eyes. Taking the bag of food, I turned away. "So, they're green." I sounded far more casual than I felt. "What about it?" He had that same look on his face that he'd had when he saw me for the first time in the break room, like something was tugging at a long ago memory. My heart was pounding so hard it's a wonder he couldn't hear it.

Giving a small shake as if to clear his mind of something he couldn't quite grasp, he followed me to the small kitchen table where I placed the bag of food. "Why do you wear colored contacts that hide those gorgeous eyes?"

"They act like sunglasses?"

Rafe laughed, and even I could hear the question in my voice. "Is that an answer or a question?" he asked.

I shrugged and ignored him as I pulled the food out of the bag. Somehow he had picked my favorites, green chili chicken enchiladas with plenty of chips and hot sauce. How did he know exactly what I liked? "Let's eat so you can go, and I can get back to...what I was doing." I couldn't even remember what I had been doing.

He laughed. "Do I make you nervous, Casey? I wonder why that is?"

"Maybe I just don't like pushy men, and you're *really*

He nodded. "Okay, I'll buy that, but when I see someone I like, I just go after them."

"And drop them just as fast when you grow tired of them," I added.

He frowned at me. "Who told you that?"

"You're the quintessential bad boy every woman thinks she can reform, and turn into the ideal husband. By the time they figure out that isn't going to happen, you've managed to turn them into friends, and they no longer care when you dump them as long as you remain friends."

"That didn't tell me who's telling stories about me." His dark brows lowered over his dark eyes. It was probably the same technique he used on suspects to intimidate them into talking.

I shrugged nonchalantly. "It's just the scuttlebutt around the department. No more talk. Let's eat so we can both get back to what we were doing."

"I've already been to church, so the rest of the afternoon is free." His gaze skimmed over my messy clothes. "I'm guessing you didn't make it to church this morning."

I felt my cheeks color, and turned away to get glasses for soda. "I've been busy."

"Hmmm. Anyway, I'm free now, and willing to help you with...whatever it is you're so busy doing."

"Thanks, but no thanks. I don't need help. Now eat so you can leave." He laughed, but let the subject drop.

When he finally left, I collapsed onto the sofa. He was getting too close. I still didn't know what he would do when, no if, he finds out who I really am.

"You're Casey Gibson," I told myself forcefully as if to remind myself of that fact, and reinforce my identity.

Once Rafe was gone, I wandered around my apartment aimlessly, restless for no reason I could pin down other than the fact that he had invaded my personal space. The remainder of the day seemed to take forever to get over.

CHAPTER SIX

By Monday morning, I was a little surprised Tessa hadn't called over the weekend. On any other weekend since we met, we exchanged numerous phone calls in that length of time. But we're not joined at the hip, I reminded myself. She has a big family, and more than me as a friend. What is surprising, I told myself, is that she has time to fit one more friend into her schedule.

I was at the lab early to go over all activity from the weekend when Tessa opened the door. She wasn't her usual bubbly, exuberant self, instead she looked upset or angry or...somewhere in between. My stomach churned. Had Eddie found out we were friends and decided to punish me by hurting her or her family. "Are you all right, Tessa? Your family?" So far she hadn't said anything.

"Of course, why would you think something was wrong with me or my family?" She held herself rigid, not moving towards me.

I shrugged. "You look upset or angry. Did I do something to make you mad?"

"Did Rafe go home with you Friday night?" The question wasn't what I expected, and left me stunned.

"Of course not! Why would you even ask me that?"

She released a pent up breath. "He walked out with you." I didn't know why that would upset her.

"No, he followed me out. I was trying to get away without him seeing me. What difference does it make?" I explained how I had tried to skip out by myself only to have him come up behind me in the parking lot. "He was still standing in the parking lot when I pulled out. Believe me; I made sure he didn't follow me. I drove around for almost a half hour, going through neighborhoods and surface streets before heading home."

Tessa gave her signature giggle, covering her mouth with her hand. "Where did you learn to drive like that?"

"Years of living alone and being a little paranoid about all the bad guys out there," I said. *And the need to make certain Eddie wasn't behind me*, I added silently. "So why did you think Rafe went home with me? Didn't he go back inside?"

She shook her head. "He must have gone home after you left."

"So everyone thought the worst of me, figuring I was sleeping with Rafe," I stated flatly. "I barely know the guy, Tessa. I don't sleep around!"

Her face got red. "No, the others think it's just fine if you're sleeping with him, almost like they expect it. I guess I'm the only one who thought the worst. I'm sorry, Casey. I should have known you weren't like that, but you know how people are. When the others said you were going home together, I just believed it. I'm so sorry." She sounded so miserable; I felt sorry for her. I didn't know what to say to make her feel better. "Can you ever forgive me?" she asked, tears sparkling in her clear blue eyes.

"Of course, Tessa." I gave her a quick hug. "Believe me, I've never willingly..." I stopped, realizing where my sentence was going. I couldn't explain what had happened to me years ago, it didn't go with the life I was living now. I hadn't even slept with Fred. Once he learned what Eddie had done to me, he was willing to wait until we were married to sleep together. Of course that had never happened.

Fortunately, she didn't pursue where I left off. "Lunch today?" she asked. I nodded, and she bounced out, heading to her office.

Alone, I sagged against the counter. Now I'm the latest topic of gossip. This was exactly why I had been reluctant to go out with the others. I didn't want people talking about me. I just want to be left alone.

~~~

"Hi Casey, how's it going?" Rafe walked into the lab at the end of my shift like nothing unusual had happened all day.

"Just fine, Detective. I don't have any results for you." After stewing all day about the things Tessa had told me this morning, I was ready for a fight. I didn't know why I was taking it out on him though. It wasn't his fault that people were talking about us.

"Detective?" He gave me a hard stare. "What's going on?" He looked around the lab. We were the only ones there at this time of day.

"Nothing's going on. I'm just busy. Did you bring me a new cold case to look at?" I was trying hard to keep my voice professional while my temper was simmering just below boiling.

"Hey, what's the matter?" He reached out to touch my arm, and I pulled away like he was trying to burn me. "Everything was fine yesterday when I left your place. What happened since then?"

"Shhh! Keep your voice down." Even though I knew we were alone I shushed him, looking around the empty lab.

"There's no one to hear us, and so what if there is? We just had lunch, we haven't done anything wrong."

"Well, that's not the scuttlebutt that's going around the department," I snapped. "After Friday night everyone we were with at Flanagan's thinks I'm sleeping with you!"

"So?" he shrugged.

"So?" I nearly shrieked. "What do you mean, 'so'? It isn't true."

"I know. What difference does it make what others think as long as we know the truth?" He seemed truly confused by my anger.

"I don't know about you, but I don't want people

gossiping about me. Now please leave. I don't have anything for you, and I don't want anyone catching you here."

"Catching me? You make it sound like we're doing something dirty. All we're doing is talking...well, arguing." He gave me that charming smile that usually gets him whatever he wants. "This is our first quarrel, is it a lover's spat?"

I couldn't believe he was actually making a joke out of this when I was ready to explode. "It's precisely that kind of talk that I'm trying to avoid. Now leave, don't come back unless you have a case for me to work on."

"Casey, you're being unreasonable."

"No, I'm not. I'm being sensible." If he knew the truth, that I might even be saving his life, he would probably thank me instead of arguing and making jokes. If Eddie was anywhere around, and thought for a minute that I was sleeping with Rafe, there's no telling what he would do. I turned my back on him; continuing to work on the slide in front of me. Although it was past quitting time, I still needed to finish what I was working on.

"Okay, Casey, you win for now. But don't think for a minute that I'm going to let this drop. I want to find out exactly what burr you have under your blanket." Without another word, he left.

Tears pricked my eyes, tears that I hadn't shed in years. I didn't know what was wrong with me. It's not like there had really been something between Rafe and me.

When I got home, Rafe was leaning against the wall outside my apartment, his arms crossed over his chest. His stance was casual, but the dark look in his eyes told me otherwise. He was here to continue our earlier discussion. "Go away, Rafe." I opened all my locks, hoping to ease in the door without him.

He reached over my head and pushed the door all the

way open, following me inside. "I want to know why you're so bent out of shape, Casey. Office gossip is just that, gossip." His fists were propped on his hips, his feet splayed apart so reminiscent of the teenage boy I'd known.

"I don't want people gossiping about me. I don't know why you can't understand that."

"Did someone say something to you today?"

I shrugged, not wanting to tell him it was Tessa who brought me the news of what the others had said Friday night. "No one said anything directly to me; I just heard that everyone there Friday evening thought you had gone home with me because we left at the same time." Once said, I realized how lame that sounded.

He chuckled, firing up my temper again, but he held up his hand to keep me from speaking. "Casey, men aren't the only ones who exaggerate their sexual encounters. If I slept with every woman who says I've slept with her, I wouldn't have time to do my job. I don't care what others think I've done as long as I know the truth. They'll have to answer for all their lies someday, and God knows the truth. He always does. I have no intention of getting HIV or any other STD by sleeping around." He looked embarrassed for a moment before he continued. "I'm not saying I'm a saint, just not that big of a sinner. I've slept with women before, but no one night stands with women I barely know."

"All right," I conceded, "but you can't keep coming into the lab just to visit. I still want to put a stop to all the gossip."

"The more you protest, the more people will believe it's true. They'll think you're having morning after regrets. We just need to go about our lives as usual, and ignore all the talk."

Easy for him to say, I thought. He'd feel differently if he knew what Eddie would do to both of us if he heard the gossip. I didn't want any more bodies heaped on my conscience.

"Now, how about getting something to eat?" He thought everything was cleared up.

"No, I still don't date coworkers. You can say all you want that we don't work together, but we do, especially since Mr. Watkins has me assisting you on the cold cases."

He let out a frustrated sigh. "How many rules do you have? Should I memorize them, or are they written down somewhere?" Now he sounded like an episode of *NCIS*.

"I've never counted them," I answered with an offhand air. "When something arises that needs to have a rule to take care of it, I put another one in place."

"So these aren't hard and fast rules?"

"Of course they are. Once a rule is in place, I seldom change it. It's a good way to live your life. Everyone needs rules." I couldn't believe how pompous I sounded, but I couldn't back down now.

Rafe chuckled again as though he'd read my thoughts and agreed with them. "There's a rule book out there with all the rules you need to live by. It will save you a lot of time and energy if you'd just read it." Before I could comment, he opened the door. "Be sure to lock all these, Cas." He flicked each lock in turn. "You wouldn't want someone wandering in here by accident." Then he was gone, leaving me alone with all my thoughts. I didn't know what to make of him, or what to do about him. Something told me he wasn't going to just fade away into the background of my life. He was going to be right there in my face. Great! Just great!

The rest of the week was busy with current cases, and I didn't see Rafe again. If there was any talk going through the department about us, it didn't make it back to me in the lab, for which I was grateful. Friday evening I decided I would forgo happy hour. No amount of pleading on Tessa's part was able to get me to change my mind. "I've been really busy this week, Tessa. I just want to go home, have a glass of wine and put my feet up. Why don't we get together tomorrow? A new second-hand store opened up not far from my apartment, and I've decided I need a couple more pieces for my bedroom. You willing to help me pick something out?" That was a silly question; I knew she was hooked even before I asked.

"You need to ask? Of course I'll help. When do you want to go? I'll bet Mom doesn't know about that place. She hasn't said anything about it. She's always looking for new stores to find new treasures."

Escaping the noise and chaos of happy hour, I stopped at the restaurant close to my apartment, taking home a steaming hot burrito, deep fried, enchilada style. Not what anyone could call healthy food, but certainly my choice of comfort food. Frederico's always added a bag of fresh tortilla chips with their signature hot sauce that is spicy enough to bring tears to your eyes and clear your sinuses.

I didn't even bother to change clothes before sitting down in front of the television with my food, digging in to the still steaming burrito. The news was gloom and doom as usual, and I was only half listening to the latest shooting in town when I saw Rafe in the background behind the reporter. He'd missed happy hour tonight, too. I hoped that wouldn't add to the gossip mill if we were both missing on the same night.

Logging onto my computer later, I pulled up the file from my parents' murders. Nothing had been done with it in years, not even cold case reviews. Why hasn't Mr. Watkins given it to Rafe to look over? It was what we were both waiting for, even if Rafe didn't know it. I felt like I was just spinning my wheels, but I didn't know what to do about it. I couldn't enter Eddie's fingerprints into the system to see if he had committed a crime elsewhere until I had a case to work on. I wasn't certain how much attention Mr. Watkins paid to that kind of detail, but I couldn't risk getting caught and possibly fired. *And if*

Eddie showed himself before then? I asked myself. What would I do? I'm not the weak little girl I'd been when Eddie killed our parents. I wasn't going to run anymore. But Eddie had to show himself first.

CHAPTER SEVEN

"That was fun," Tessa enthused as she sank down on the sofa in her parents' living room. "I love that armoire you bought. If I had my own apartment, you might have had a little competition for it." She raised her voice, just enough for her parents to hear from the kitchen. "I'm still working on them," she whispered. "I wish they would see me as an adult instead a teenager."

"Get yourself settled in your new job, Tessa. Then we'll talk about it." Mr. Gordon walked past her, mussing her hair as he went. "Throwing hints around isn't going to get you what you want right now, Sweetie. You know the bargain we made." Tessa's face turned beet red at getting caught. She hadn't said anything about bargaining with her parents over an apartment, which surprised me. She'd been an open book on everything else.

Doing my best not to pry, I greeted Mr. and Mrs. Gordon, "Thank you for inviting me to dinner." It was only three-fifteen but I was already hungry. The quick sandwich we'd eaten about four hours ago was long gone.

Before they could comment, my cell phone chirped. I frowned and apologized for the interruption, as I pulled it out of my pocket. Only Tessa and work had my number. Since I was with Tessa and didn't recognize the number as one from work, I almost dismissed the call, but a niggling something kept me from doing that. "Excuse me; I think I should answer this." I turned away and pressed connect. "Yeah, Gibson." If it was work, that's all I needed to say. If it was an advertisement, it was probably a recording, and it wouldn't matter how I answered.

"Ah...Casey?" I didn't recognize the voice, and was ready to hang up when he continued. "Who taught you phone etiquette? This is Rafe."

I released a frustrated breath, and walked away from the curious eyes of Tessa and her parents. "How did you get this number?" I hissed. "I don't give it out."

"Well, Mr. Watkins does." His tone was all business. "You might want to talk to him about it. But first, he was wondering if you could come in to give us a hand on some cases. We've been slammed last night and today."

"Oh, ah, sure. If he needs me to come in, I'll be there. Give me thirty minutes or so. I'm not home." I quickly made my excuses to Tessa and her parents and left, unsure what I was getting myself into. This better hadn't be some kind of trick Rafe's pulling.

The lab was bustling when I walked in, and Rafe was nowhere in sight. Jeremy, one of the lab techs, looked up from his computer. "Oh, am I glad to see you! Last night was a bad one, and we can sure use your help." He pointed to a stack of files. There had been several murders, a bad traffic accident, and a bar fight that led to several people being stabbed. The detectives were also waiting for results from numerous tests to clear up a day-old case we'd been working on.

It was after ten when everything was finally in the computer and tests were in the process of being run. Now it was a waiting game as the machines did their work. Nothing is as fast as it appears on television, evidence isn't found, and cases don't get solved all in the space of an hour. Sometimes it takes days and even weeks for the results of tox screens to come back. Different detectives had been in and out all afternoon and evening, including Rafe, hoping to hurry things along.

I still hadn't had anything to eat, and my stomach was beginning to protest. Jeremy and I locked up the lab and headed outside. His stomach rumbled in answer to mine causing both of us to laugh. "I guess it's about time to get something to eat and get some sleep," I said as I headed for my Jeep. "See you Monday."

"How about we all get something to eat first?" Unaware that Rafe and two other detectives had followed us outside, we both whirled around; my heart was racing. Having someone sneak up behind me in the dark isn't my favorite thing. "It's been a long day," Rafe continued. His look clearly dared me to decline because of my rule against dating coworkers. Before I could say no, my stomach rumbled again. Reluctantly, I agreed to go along. I couldn't very well refuse to go when everyone else thought it a good idea without looking like a total idiot.

The restaurant Tessa and I went to our first day with the department stayed open late on Friday and Saturday evenings, so we headed there. Nights were chilly this time of year, and I hadn't planned on being out this late. My thin tee shirt wasn't a good barrier against the cool breeze. Rafe slipped off his police windbreaker, draping it over my shoulders when he noticed me shivering.

I wanted to brush it off, but it still held warmth from his body, and it felt good. Once again, I had the choice of accepting graciously or making myself look like an ungrateful fool. Finally I just nodded my thanks and followed him inside the warm restaurant. As the only female in the group, I felt a little out of place, but the others didn't appear to notice.

Everyone seemed to be well acquainted, and I listened as they talked about their families. Engrossed in their stories, I forgot to eat as fast as they were. I was surprised to learn that Jeremy was married with two small children, something I hadn't known even after three months of working side by side. Admittedly, I knew very little about any of the people I worked with on a daily basis. Was it time to relax and open up a little? Did I dare relax?

One by one the others left as soon as they finished eating while I was still working on my meal. Within five minutes Rafe and I were alone at the table. Before I could think of an excuse to leave without finishing, someone came up behind me.

"Hello, Jennifer." The voice sent chills through my body and my stomach rebelled against the meal I'd just eaten, threatening to send it back up.

Swallowing hard, I looked up at the man as he came up beside me. My heart was pounding so hard in my throat, I couldn't even speak. Pulling out a chair like he'd been invited, he sat down never taking his eyes off my face. "You look good, Jennifer. I like what you've done with your hair."

Eddie hadn't changed much since I'd seen him last. He'd aged of course; maybe he was a little taller. But there was no doubt who he was.

Finally getting my voice back, I looked at him with as much bravado as I could muster. "I'm sorry, but you have me confused with someone else. My name is Casey Gibson." So far Eddie had ignored Rafe who was staring at me with his mouth hanging open, recognition clear in his dark eyes.

"Okay, have it your way," Eddie chuckled, standing up again. "Enjoy the rest of your dinner. I'll see you soon, Jennifer. It's good to see you, Rafe," he said, finally acknowledging him. "It's been a long time. I'll be seeing you again, too."

He casually sauntered off like he hadn't just turned my world upside down.

This was what I wanted, I reminded myself. But not like this. I wanted to confront him on my terms, and in private. Now he'd drawn Rafe into the middle of things. I should have known better than to think I could choose the terms of that confrontation. There's no way to anticipate what his next move will be. How am I going to keep myself, and now Rafe, safe until I can get the proof I need to put him away for good? I had always known I might not survive that confrontation. I just didn't want anyone else getting hurt.

Rafe was still staring at me, but at least his mouth was closed. "You...you're... Jennifer..." he stammered. "From the first time I saw you, something tugged at my memory. I just couldn't grab hold of it. What happened? Why did you disappear?"

"My name is Casey now. I haven't been Jennifer for a long time." My voice shook. It was useless trying to bluff my way out of this. "She ceased to exist the day she left here. Please, forget all about her."

"I can't," he whispered. "You're part of the reason I am who I am, why I became a cop. Your family didn't get justice back then. I've tried to make sure nothing like that ever happened on my watch. Why did you disappear?" he asked again.

By now what was left of my food was getting cold, but I couldn't eat another bite. Before I could think of an answer to his question, the waiter stopped at our table, a frown on his face. "Is there something wrong with your food? Can I get you something different?"

I gave the waiter a weak smile. "The food is fine. I guess I'm just too tired to eat very much. Can I have a box, please?"

"Of course," he said solicitously. "I'll take care of it right away." He disappeared into the kitchen for a take-out box.

"Jen...Casey," Rafe corrected himself. "Why did you disappear? What happened?"

"Can't this wait until we're out of here?" I whispered. "Please. I'll explain later."

With amazing constraint, Rafe managed to wait while he followed me back to my apartment before repeating his question. Once inside, he asked again. "Why did you run away, Casey?"

"To save my life," I answered hotly. "If I had stayed, he

would have killed me, too."

"Who? You know who killed your parents? Why didn't you tell the cops back then?"

"Because they wouldn't have listened to me any more than they will now unless I can somehow get proof of what he did."

"Who are you talking about?" Rafe paced across my small living room.

I threw myself onto my sofa only to jump back up, too agitated to sit still. "Eddie!" I spit out the name like it was poison.

"Your brother? How do you know he did it?" He didn't appear to be questioning how I knew; he just wanted to make sure I was certain.

I sighed. "If you knew everything he's done, you wouldn't ask me that." Feeling suddenly deflated, so tired from running all these years, I sank down in the rocker, hugging my knees to my chest.

"I have all night, Casey. Take your time, and tell me all of it." He no longer had trouble remembering to call me Casey.

It took several minutes, but once I got started, I couldn't stop the words from pouring out, telling everything that had happened from the time I was almost too little to remember until Eddie walked back into my life tonight. The bad stuff was burned into my memory, and I would never forget all that Eddie had done to me, my parents, and anyone else who made the mistake of crossing him.

When I finished, Rafe's face was gray with shock. "My God, Casey, why didn't you ever tell me, tell someone?"

"Fear," I stated simply. "Besides, who would have believed how bad it was? In those days sexual abuse wasn't acknowledged the way it is today. I was ten years old when Eddie was committed to the mental hospital.

Those four years he was gone were the best years of my life. We were still poor, but I felt safe for the first time."

"Why didn't your parents stop him when it first started?" He still didn't understand the fear Eddie had instilled in all of us.

"The first time he molested me I couldn't even verbalize what had happened. After that, we were all in such a grip of fear that..." I paused, trying to think of how to explain. "Eddie had taken over all of us. His threats were real; they still are. When the state released him with the pronouncement that he was 'cured,'" I made little air quotes around the word, "we knew better."

"Did he do anything after he came home?"

"You mean besides killing my parents?" I asked bitterly, and then quickly apologized. "No, but we knew it was just a matter of time. My parents told him if he touched me again, they would call the police, and this time he would go to prison instead of the state hospital. The hate on his face when they said that was scary. I knew he would do something eventually; I just didn't expect him to kill them." When my voice cracked, I drew a deep breath in an effort to steady myself.

"Did you tell the police that you thought Eddie had killed them?"

This made me laugh. "Are you serious? You saw that fat sergeant. Do you think he would have believed me or done anything? Besides, they were all convinced it was some hopped-up druggie or a home invasion, if they even had those things back then. I was fourteen; no one was going to listen to me. Even that social worker was infatuated with Eddie. He probably killed her, along with that sergeant."

"He died after you disappeared. How do you know about that?" He frowned. "Did you look it up after you started with the department?"

Guilt made my face turn red, and I looked away. "Ah,

no." How do I tell him I have a copy of all the records without getting myself in trouble?

"You hacked the department files." It was a statement of fact, not a question. There was a small smile on his lips for the first time since I started explaining. "You always were the smartest kid in school, and you're the smartest one in the lab." He gave a bark of laughter. "When did you get the file?"

"Years ago," I admitted. "At first, I followed as best I could in the newspapers. It took me a couple of years to discover what I could do with computers."

"That's how you've stayed one step ahead of Eddie. Why did you come back to Phoenix? Did you think he'd never come looking for you here?"

"No, I always knew he'd find me again; it doesn't matter where I live. I was just hoping I'd have proof I could take to the prosecutor first. This is my last stand, Rafe. Either I manage to stop him for good, or I die trying. I always knew it would come down to this."

The color had returned to his face during our discussion. Now it drained again. "You can't be serious, Casey. You're going to let him get his hands on you again? It will be over my dead body," he said vehemently. He had stopped pacing, but started up again now. "If I'd been older when your parents were killed, I would have done something then."

I stepped in front of him, laying my hand on his arm. "Like you said, you were just a kid, but thanks for the sentiment. Besides, you didn't know what really happened."

He looked guilty now. "All of us boys knew there was something off with Eddie." he admitted. "I even told my folks that he was evil. I don't know if they believed me. There was talk in the neighborhood about what he did to that elderly woman that got him sent away. There were all the pets that kept disappearing from the neighborhood, too. Why didn't you go to the pastor? I remember you went to the youth group back then."

"Eddie promised he 'would take care' of anyone we told. Besides, he could charm his way out of just about anything. If I had told the pastor or a counselor at school, he would have made them believe I was a liar, and turned it around on me. He had done that for years. We were surprised when the family court locked him up for those four years."

"How did you survive when you left here? You were only fourteen."

"Not the way you're thinking," I snapped. "I'd had enough of someone using me for their own pleasure, I wasn't about to become a prostitute."

Rafe held up his hand in a placating gesture. "That's not what I was suggesting. I'm just amazed you were able to survive on your own. You were just a kid."

All the fire went out of me, and I slumped back in my chair. "Sorry. Don't jump to conclusions," I muttered to myself.

"Another one of your rules, Casey? How did that get started?"

I scooted further down in my chair, embarrassed to admit I'd taken the idea from a television show. "You have to have rules to live by. They've kept me sane and safe for a good many years."

"That doesn't exactly explain how you got started with all these rules," he chuckled. "But I'll let it slide for now. What's your number one rule?" I frowned at him. Was he making fun of me? But he appeared curious, not mocking.

"Keep moving. That one had to be forefront for a lot of years. Not so much now. I came back to find the evidence I need to end all the running." *Or die trying*, I added silently. In the space of a few hours, my relationship with Rafe had taken a hundred and eighty degree turn. I was still Casey Gibson, yet we were childhood friends.

"What are you going to do now that Eddie's here?"

I shrugged. "Keep looking for proof of his guilt. If I can get my hands on the evidence collected at the house, I'll be able to prove it. I'll also be able to run his prints through AFIS to see if he committed crimes elsewhere. My hands are tied until I can do that."

Feeling completely drained yet oddly at peace for the first time in years, I rested my head on the back of the chair. For the first time in a long while, I didn't feel so totally alone. "I know he killed the prostitute at the time Fred disappeared," I muttered.

"From the articles I read at the time, the police didn't try very hard to find out who killed her." Explaining about Fred had been difficult. I have always tried to keep those memories at bay.

"What about his family? Didn't they push the police to find him? Or his employer?"

I shook my head. "He was raised in foster homes. We were both alone. That's how we became friends. He'd been abused as a child. When he told me his story, I couldn't stop myself from telling him what had happened to me. When he disappeared, I tried to push the police, but to them I was the jilted girlfriend he was running away from. Our boss was just mad that he took off without giving notice. He believed what the police said."

"Do you know if they ever found his body?" Rafe the policeman was back in charge of himself.

"I stuck around as long as I dared after he disappeared. The police were convinced he left of his own free will because he realized he didn't want to get married. They didn't even look further after his car was found at the airport. For a while I checked the Kansas City papers to see if they ever found his body. I finally had to give up the same way the police had."

Suzanne Floyd

Rafe shook his head at the incompetence of some of his fellow policemen. "A sociopath is the same as a serial killer," Rafe said, talking to himself as much as to me. "He can't turn that part of himself on and off at will. In the years since he killed your parents, there have to be unsolved murders in every place he's been. Even if he didn't leave evidence at every crime scene, I'm willing to bet he left something somewhere. Because he got away with your parents' murders, and any others he's committed, he's feeling empowered, emboldened. He's bound to get careless, if he hasn't already."

"I am his ultimate goal," I said around a huge yawn. "Now that I know he's here, I can be on guard to make sure he doesn't get me before I can get him." I yawned again. "Right now, we both need to get some sleep. Go home, Rafe, but be careful. You're going to be on his radar as much as I am, especially if he thinks there's something going on between us."

"I can't leave you alone with Eddie on the loose," he argued, sounding shocked I would even think he'd leave. He was in full cop mode now.

"Well, you're going to do just that from now on. We can't be seen together again." He stared at me like I'd just grown another head.

"Casey, I'm not going to let him come anywhere near you."

"This isn't your fight. Now, go home, get some sleep. It's been a long day. Just be careful, and keep your eyes open. If Eddie thinks we're involved, you're as much a target as I am." I was pushing him toward the door, but it was like trying to roll a boulder uphill. He didn't want to leave. "You know all those rules I live by?" He nodded. "Right up there with keep moving, is 'don't involve anyone else in my fight'." I flipped the locks and opened the door. "Go home. I don't want to see you again except at work." I shut the door in his face.

85

"Lock the door, Casey." I could hear him chuckle.

Leaning against the door, I slid down to sit on the floor. Rafe was on my side, he believed me about Eddie. But for some reason, he felt responsible for what happened all those years ago, like he should have known, and done something to prevent it. This was a complication I hadn't counted on.

I slowly stood up, making my way to my bedroom. Like I told Rafe, it *had* been a long day, and each day from now on was going to be more stressful than before. This was all part of Eddie's game. He wanted me to know he was here, that he'd found me. But what he didn't know was now I'm after him. Our game of cat and mouse has begun in earnest.

CHAPTER EIGHT

Sleep eluded me as I tossed and turned all night. Why did Eddie show himself to me? That hadn't been his standard MO in the past. I didn't know what it meant. *What was he up to?* I wondered. Why had he shown himself to Rafe and exposed my identity? I had more questions than answers.

Somehow I had to convince Rafe to stay away from me until I finally managed to put Eddie away for good. I wasn't hopeful of accomplishing that any time soon unless I could run his prints through the system. Could Rafe suggest to Mr. Watkins that we needed to work on the cold case of my parents' murders without revealing my true identity?

Rafe's question about Fred's remains being found kept circulating in my mind. I knew he was dead; I just didn't have proof. It wouldn't be hard to search back papers to see if any unidentified remains had been found somewhere near Kansas City. Computers would make the search easier, and it would give me a reason to stay busy and avoid Rafe.

It was still dark when I finally gave up trying to sleep, and got out of bed. The early morning chill felt good when I opened the window in my bedroom. Even on the third floor, I never felt comfortable with the window open while I slept. If anyone could reach an open third floor window, it would be Eddie. Maybe I was endowing him with supernatural powers, but I knew what he was capable of. I didn't want to take any chances.

I wasn't going to run anymore, but I wasn't going to make it easy for him to catch me either. If Eddie somehow got hold of me, I wanted to make sure that there would be plenty of evidence left behind; enough to convict him, and put him away for the rest of his life.

I couldn't stay cooped up for another minute, and I sat on the small balcony while I waited for the coffee to brew. I had a blanket wrapped around my shoulders against the early morning chill. When someone knocked on my door, my heart nearly jumped out of my chest, and I sat frozen in my chair. Eddie wouldn't just knock on my door, waiting for me to open it, would he? That had never been his style. Nothing was ever straight up and forward with him. He preferred sneaky and devious. Whoever was at the door was persistent as they pounded on the door again.

Slowly, I walked into the living room. When Rafe brought over lunch last weekend, he knew I had looked through the security peep hole when my shadow covered it. How could I look through it without letting whoever was on the other side know I was there? I was standing beside the door when the person on the other side knocked again causing me to nearly jump out of my skin. Until Rafe spoke, that is. "Open up, Casey. I know you're up." He sounded grouchy.

Blowing out of sigh of relief, I flipped the locks and opened the door. "What are you doing here so early?"

He pushed his way inside, glaring at me. "What were you doing on the balcony? Are you inviting Eddie to take a shot at you?" He gripped my arms, giving me a shake. "I thought you had more sense than that."

I pulled away from him. "This isn't any of your business, Rafe. Go away."

"Not on your life. Everything I've done since that day has been about you."

"What are you talking about?" I started at him.

He ignored my question, asking again, "Why were you sitting out there in the open? Eddie could have shot you at any time."

"He's not going to shoot me," I said scornfully, as I pulled away from him. "He wants me alive so he can torture me, even if it has to be from a distance." I stalked across the room. "Now, what are you doing here, Rafe? I told you to stay away from me. It's not safe."

He laughed. "*You're* trying to protect *me*?" He sounded incredulous. "I'm a cop. I carry a gun all the time; I even sleep with it."

I couldn't help but laugh at that. "TMI, Rafe! Seriously though, what are you doing here, and why are you so upset?"

"You can ask that after what you told me last night? Eddie wants to kill you!"

"No, he wants to dominate me. It's always been about power with him. Sure, he thinks he needs to punish me for running away, but I'm not a little girl now, and he doesn't scare me." That last part wasn't the complete truth. He did scare me, but not for myself. I didn't want him going after anyone else in his quest to punish me. That's why I've tried to stay alone all these years. I wasn't sure if he'd go after Tessa and her family, but how could I tell her to stay alert without going into details?

"I'm not going to let him get his hands on you again, Casey," Rafe insisted. "And he's not going to come after me because he's smart enough to know I can and will take him *down*."

"You can't protect me 24/7," I argued. "I don't want you or anyone else involved. This is my problem, and I'll take care of it, and him. I also have a gun, and I know how to use it. I'm not going to let him get his hands on me again."

"To use your own words, or die trying to stop him," he stated flatly. "That's not something I'm willing to let happen. You might as well accept the fact that I'm going to stick to you like a second skin until we get this thing with Eddie settled, and he's resting behind bars. Or in the ground." He held up his hand to stop me from arguing. "You need to tell Tessa that we're seeing each other, so she won't be surprised when I'm always hanging around."

"She's not going to buy that story for a minute. She knows all about my rules." I sounded a lot more confident than I felt.

"Then tell her you've changed your mind about that particular rule. Like I said, I'm not taking any chances that Eddie gets his hands on you."

I stared at him. "Why are you doing this? This isn't your fight."

He looked exceedingly uncomfortable, and cleared his throat several times before giving me a non-answer. "Just suffice it to say that I'm making it my fight."

"Why?" I can be just as stubborn as he is.

He walked over and ruffled the soft curls I hadn't bothered to do anything with this morning. "Because I want to." He laughed at my disgruntled look. "It's about time for church. Want to join me?"

"Ah...I think I'll pass. You go without me."

Ignoring me again, he shrugged. "Okay, we can stay here. I'm sure we'll think of something to do." He waggled his eyebrows suggestively.

"All right," I sighed. "I'll go; anything to get you out of here. But after church, you're leaving me alone. Deal?"

"Don't count on it," he muttered, turning away from me.

It was the same church I'd gone to as a kid, those years that Eddie had been locked up. My stomach churned. How many of the people I knew back then still went here? How many would remember a certain young girl and tap me as that girl? The building was much the same, high ceilings, semi-comfortable chairs, stained glass windows. The interior was cool and crowded. The songs were familiar, tugging at long buried memories. A different pastor directed the service. He was probably in his mid-thirties, full of energy.

Sitting there with the sun shining through the stained glass casting beautiful designs on the carpet, I soaked up the familiar and the unfamiliar. A strange feeling I couldn't name washed over me. I remember the feeling of peace and safety I'd had every time I came here as a kid. I always thought it was because Eddie was locked up. Now I wasn't so sure that was the reason for those feelings, especially since Eddie was in Phoenix, and had made himself known to me.

After the service, Rafe introduced me to the pastor and several others. I remembered the names of several of the older people, but thankfully they didn't seem to recognize me. I half expected to see Rafe's parents and wondered how he would explain my presence to them. Would they remember me? What would they do? Once in his truck, I couldn't stop myself from commenting, "I didn't see your folks. Do they still go here?"

He laughed, "Sure, but to the later service. Mom says one day a week she's entitled to sleep in. Dad still gets up early so he can go golfing, then they come to church and go out for lunch. It works for them, but I'd rather go early, then I have the rest of the day to do something. You about ready for something to eat? We can have a late breakfast."

Arguing with him was useless. He didn't argue back; he just ignored what I said, and did what he wanted. Within minutes we were seated in a small restaurant not far from where I'd spent the first fourteen years of my life. The area had changed in those intervening years. Now it was a mix of commercial and residential. Some of the houses had been torn down; others had been remodeled and updated, or made into small cottage businesses. "What happened to my parents' house?" I asked quietly. Several times I'd been tempted to drive by, always changing my mind before I got close.

Rafe sighed, "It sat empty for several years. I guess no one wanted to buy it after what happened there. Finally someone bought it and tore it down. There's a small medical building there now."

I nodded understanding. I wouldn't want to live in a house where such brutal murders had taken place. Still it made me sad. Rafe reached across the table, squeezing my hands. "Remember who you are now. That's what matters."

Throughout breakfast, he kept up a running commentary on life in Phoenix over the past fifteen years, catching me up to date on kids I'd known back then. He was still friends with several who lived in the area, but he'd lost contact with most of them. "People move around a lot," he said to explain.

"You can't tell anyone about me, Rafe." I couldn't stop the quiver in my voice. "I'm not that girl anymore. I'm Casey Gibson, and that's who I'll be the rest of my life."

He nodded agreement. "I have no problems with that." He was quiet for a moment before finishing his thought, "Jennifer Miller belongs in the past, and that's where she'll stay. Casey Gibson is now, and I kind of like her." He gave me that teasing smile that had even won over teachers when they really wanted to punish him for one of his pranks.

~~~

Rafe pulled into the parking lot at my apartment building just as my cell phone chirped. Pulling it from my pocket, I looked at the read-out. "It's Tessa." I looked at him sternly. "Keep quiet. I don't want her to know you're with me."

"Casey, you..."

My phone chirped again. "Hush! Hi Tessa. What's up?" I frowned at Rafe, silently warning him to be quiet.

"Hi Casey" her chipper voice came through the speaker. "I was wondering how you're doing today. How late did you have to work last night?"

"Tell her," Rafe mouthed to me, and I shook my head,

turning away from him.

"It was a late night. A bunch of us went out to eat when we finished." I laughed, hoping it didn't sound as phony to her as it did to me. "We were starving by then. I don't even know what time it was when I got to sleep." That much was true. I had no idea what time it was when Rafe left and I finally fell into bed.

"You too tired to come over for dinner?" she asked hopefully.

Rafe's intent stare was still locked on me. "I'm just veg'ing out, but thanks for asking. Tell your folks I'm sorry I had to skip out yesterday." We talked for another few minutes before hanging up.

Slipping the phone back in my pocket, I looked at Rafe. "Thanks." I couldn't quite meet his dark eyes though.

"You need to tell her something because I'm not going anywhere. I'm not letting Eddie come anywhere near you."

"Be realistic. We both have jobs to do, and I'm not letting you move in with me. I can take care of myself. I've done it for a long time." I walked into my apartment hoping to shut the door before he could follow me. No such luck though. He was sticking to me like glue, literally.

"I don't want to move in with you...well, maybe," he added in a whisper.

I whirled around to face him, poking my finger in his chest. "What's that supposed to mean? I'm not sleeping with you, so just forget about it! After what I've told you, how could you even think something like that?"

He held up his hands, palms out. "Sorry, it just slipped out. But I'm serious. I'm going to do everything in my power to keep Eddie away from you, so you're going to have to say something to Tessa."

I knew he was right, I just didn't like it. I also knew if Eddie thought I was sleeping with Rafe, he would go after him before he did anything to me. Getting Rafe to understand, that was the problem.

CHAPTER NINE

Tessa came into the lab Monday morning in her usual bubbly, exuberant manner. "Hi there, girlfriend, you get rested up from your late night Saturday?" She plopped down on the stool next to me.

I nodded. "I didn't even do laundry. Now I have to play catch-up this week, or I won't have anything to wear to work by Friday. Sometimes it's not worth taking a day off from everything, and just veg'ing out."

"You just need to go shopping again," Tessa advised happily. "I'll be glad to go with you."

"Shopping will only diminish my bank account further. I did enough damage on Saturday to last a while, and I didn't even buy clothes." I laughed.

"Speaking of Saturday," she changed the subject. My stomach gave a slight roll. Had she somehow learned that I was with Rafe? "When are you going to pick up that magnificent armoire? Do you know someone with a truck, or are you going to rent one?"

I released the breath I'd been holding while I waited for her question, grateful it was an innocent one. "Renting a truck would do further damage to my bank account, and I'd still have to figure out how to get it up three flights of stairs. I'm just glad the owner of the store said I could leave it there until I can figure out how I'm going to pick it up."

"I'll bet some of the guys have trucks, and would be more than willing to get it for you. I keep telling my brothers they need a truck, but minivans are their vehicles of choice with the little ones."

"Who needs a truck?" Rafe had entered the lab without either of us noticing. "Mine's always available to help out a friend." His attention was focused on Tessa, and I remembered he'd always been like that; whoever he was speaking to received his total attention.

Tessa smiled up at him, her cheeks turning a pretty shade of pink. "Casey does. She bought this beautiful armoire for her apartment, but she doesn't have any way to get it home. The store doesn't deliver."

"Why didn't you say something?" He turned his attention on me, kicking my pulse rate up a notch in the process.

"Ah, well, we sort of had our hands full Saturday night. I didn't think to mention it." I could feel my face turning red under his scrutiny.

Tessa's head was turning back and forth between us like she was watching a tennis match; a smile spread across her pixie face. "You worked together Saturday night?" She elbowed me in the ribs. "Did you go out to eat afterward?"

"There were seven or eight of us working, and we all went out to eat. It was late, and we were hungry." You didn't have to be a rocket scientist to know where her thoughts were headed.

Rafe leaned closed to Tessa, and in a stage whisper said, "I think I'm wearing her down. She might agree to have dinner alone with me sometime in the next century." He winked at her and she giggled. I wanted to smack them both. This wasn't funny.

"That worked out well, don't you think?" he asked once Tessa had left for her office. "At least now she won't be surprised when I'm hanging around all the time."

"You're not going to be *hanging around* all the time." I stated. "I told you I can take care of myself." He just smiled that infuriating smile of his. "Don't leave the building at lunch," he called over his shoulder as he walked out of the lab. "We'll go get that armoire after work." By now, several others were there with me taking

95

in the exchange. I could feel my face getting red, but I wasn't sure if it was embarrassment or anger. The man knew just the right buttons to push.

~~~

A week later I still hadn't seen Eddie again. I could feel him watching me though, like I had a target on my back. Somehow I needed to draw him out. If I couldn't connect him to my parents' murders or any others, I needed to get something on him in the here and now.

As long as Rafe was with me whenever I was home, Eddie wouldn't show himself. That wasn't his style. Showing up when I was with Rafe at the restaurant had a purpose, but I didn't know what it was. It had put me on alert, and that didn't seem like a good thing for Eddie, but he never did anything without an ulterior motive. Now he was waiting for an opportunity to catch me alone. So far he hadn't shown up in the middle of the night, and he hadn't figured out how to get into my apartment when I wasn't home.

Rafe was driving me nuts. He never left me alone in the evening unless he was working late on a case. Trying to convince him to let this play out without any interference from him wasn't working. Of course, Tessa was ecstatic. She was convinced we were the perfect couple.

Friday evening, Rafe was tied up on a particularly grizzly homicide, and would be there for several more hours. This was an opportunity for some alone time so I begged off the happy hour get-together. For someone who had spent most of the last fifteen years virtually alone, it took some getting used to, having so many people in my life now.

I had just finished eating my take-out meal when someone knocked on my door. "Oh, Rafe, go away," I whispered. I had been enjoying my solitude. Reaching for the first lock without looking through security hole in the door, my hand stopped in midair. It was like someone had whispered in my ear, "Check first."

Looking through the peep hole, Eddie stared back at me, a wily grin on his face. My pulse jumped in my throat. I rested my head against the door, and prayed for the first time in a long while. "Give me strength, God, and keep me safe."

Releasing the two dead bolt locks and the door knob lock, I left the chain and maid locks in place. "What do you want?" I glared at him through the small space they allowed.

"I just want to talk to you. It's been a long time since I've seen you, Jennifer." There was hidden meaning behind his words just like there always was.

"My name is Casey."

"Okay, have it your way." He gave a particularly nasty laugh. "I'll call you anything you want. For now. Can I come in?" He reached out to the door to push it open until I moved my gun into view. He held up his hands in a phony act of surrender. "You'll let Rafe into your bed, but you won't let your own brother into your apartment?" He raised his eyebrow in a question.

"If I let someone into my bed, it's none of your business, and I don't have a brother. Go away and leave me alone." His face grew dark with anger, making my stomach churn in an old and familiar way. He was getting dangerously close to his boiling point.

"You can't escape me, Jennifer," he growled. "You ought to know that by now."

"I'm not trying to escape from anyone. That's why I'm here, and doing what I'm doing. Now go away!" Before he could say anything else, I closed the door in his face flipping the first lock fast enough to prevent him from trying to reach for me. His fist hit the door hard enough to make it shake, causing me to jump back in surprise. "Go away or I'm calling the police," I shouted.

Sliding down to the floor, I stayed pressed up against the door for another twenty minutes. After several more hits or kicks there was nothing more from the other side. I didn't know if he was waiting for me to open the door, and check to see if he was gone or if he had really left. This was the only way in or out of my apartment. "How stupid is that?" I muttered. "I should have thought of that before I rented this place."

An hour later I was still sitting on the floor, my back pressed against the door. How much longer did I need to stay there to be certain Eddie had left? I had to do something before one of my neighbors came home and possibly walked into a trap. Standing up, I peeked out the security peep hole. From what I could see of the hallway it looked empty. To test that theory, I noisily flipped the first lock, still looking out through the peep hole. Nothing moved; no shadows shifted. I watched as I released each lock. Nothing happened.

Taking my courage in hand, I finally opened the door wide enough to stick my head out and look around. All was quiet, no one was there. I released the breath I'd been holding, and turned to go back inside. "Oh, crap!" There were several deep dents and cracks in the door where Eddie had struck it either with his fist or foot. That was going to have to be fixed and fast. In several places, it would have only taken another well placed hit to be clear through the door.

"Who did this?" The building maintenance man stared at the damage to the door, his displeasure evident on his face.

"Obviously someone was trying to force his way into my apartment." This was going to get complicated.

"Did you call the cops? You work for them, don't you?"

"Yes, I do; but I have a gun, so I can protect myself. I didn't think it was necessary to have someone come out when there was nothing they could do. How soon can you get this fixed?"

Disgruntled, he grumbled." It doesn't look like you did a very good job of taking care of things," he muttered as he turned away. "It's Friday night and late to boot. I'll take care of it Monday."

"That's not acceptable." My statement stopped him from walking away. "As you can see, it wouldn't take much to get completely through this flimsy door. What if this nut job comes back when I'm sleeping?"

"Get your cop boyfriend to spend the night. Management isn't going to like having to replace that door. It's going to cost you extra on next month's rent." With that parting shot, he headed back to his own apartment and another of the beers I could smell on his breath. I'd heard others in the building complain about him, so I knew he wouldn't be in any hurry to fix my door.

With a sigh, I closed and locked my door, for all the good it would do if Eddie came back to finish what he started. *So much for a relaxing evening*, I told myself.

I decided to spend the night on the couch with my gun by my side. It took forever to settle down and fall asleep, and what seemed like only five minutes later I was jerked awake by pounding at my door. Gripping my gun, I jumped up so fast I nearly fell over when my head swam. Before I could get to the door, the pounding started again accompanied with shouting. "Casey, are you in there? Are you all right?"

With a sigh of relief I hurried to the door, throwing open the locks. "Shut up, Rafe, before you awake up everyone in the building." I grabbed his hand, pulling him inside, shutting and locking the door behind us. "What were you thinking? Are you trying to wake the dead?"

"Casey, what happened here? Did Eddie do that?" He

nodded towards the door, ignoring my question. He gripped my arms, and gave me a little shake. "What happened here tonight?" he repeated.

I sank down on the couch, propping my head in my hands. "Of course, Eddie did that. He took offense to the fact that I wouldn't let him in."

"Did you call 9-1-1?"

"No, he wasn't here that long. Besides, what am I supposed to say? My brother stopped by for a visit?" I asked sarcastically. I pointed to my gun. "He backed off a little when I produced that."

"Damn it, Casey, you should have called it in. Why didn't maintenance fix that door? It won't take more than a slight shove to be through in a few spots."

I gave a humorless laugh, "He said he'd fix it Monday, and it's going to cost me to have the door replaced."

"Like hell," Rafe growled. "He's fixing it tomorrow. Until he does you can't stay here with the door like that."

"Rafe, I'm too tired to argue. I'll be fine until morning. Eddie won't be back tonight." I wasn't completely certain of that, but it sounded good.

"No? Then why the gun?" It was his turn to nod at the gun I'd set on the coffee table in front of the couch.

"Just being safe. Go home. You just got off an investigation. You have to be tired."

He sank down in the club chair, laying his head back. "Yeah," he sighed. "I'll sleep right here." He closed his eyes.

"You can't sleep here. Go home." I'm not sure he even heard me. In the space of a few seconds his breathing had evened out, a soft rumble coming from him. *What am I supposed to do now?* I asked myself. I knew he'd been at the murder scene most of the afternoon, and it was after midnight now. Indecision pulled at me. It probably wasn't safe for him to drive home as tired as he was, even if I could wake him. But how would it look if anyone found out he'd spent the night in my apartment? No one would believe he slept on the couch, or chair, I corrected myself.

The dark circles under his eyes, and tired lines etched near his mouth made the decision for me. It would be cruel to wake him now. Watching him sleep, my heart softened slightly, remembering the young boy whose tough talk hid a kind heart. Standing up, I pulled the afghan I'd been using off the couch, gently laying it over his sleeping form. I just had to make sure no one found out he stayed here tonight.

~~~

Rafe was still sleeping when I entered the living room a few short hours later. Sometime after I went to bed, he'd moved from the chair to the couch which had to be more comfortable even though it was too short for his long frame. His legs were hanging over one end, and his arm hung over the side cushion. The dark circles weren't as prominent this morning; the lines around his mouth smoothed out in sleep.

I wanted to let him sleep, while at the same time I wanted him to leave before anyone found out he'd been here all night. I wasn't sure who I was afraid of finding out, although I didn't think Tessa and her parents would approve. Explanations would be difficult. I was feeling guilty even though we'd done nothing wrong.

Coffee was brewing when Rafe stumbled into my small kitchen. Dark stubble covered his cheeks and chin adding to the bad boy look. His dark hair stuck up in all directions. "Oh, man Casey. I didn't mean to pass out like that," he apologized. "I hadn't had much sleep in the last twenty-four hours. You mind if I wash up some before I have a cup of that great smelling coffee?"

I was having trouble controlling my breathing and finding my voice so I pointed the way down the hall, mumbling something about clean towels on the rod. Wow!

Never before had the sight of a half asleep man affected my mental capacity quite like that. *He is one good looking guy*, I silently admitted.

I had myself under control by the time he came back to the kitchen a few minutes later. "How do you take your coffee?" I kept my back to him for another minute.

"Black is fine." He came up behind me, looking over my shoulder. "Are you making scrambled eggs and cheese?"

I took a deep breath to steady myself and was instantly sorry. Even though it had probably been twenty-four hours since he took a shower and used after shave, he still smelled wonderful. "Ah...yeah." My voice squeaked, and I cleared my throat before starting over. "Yes, would you like something to eat?" With him standing this close I could feel the heat radiating from his body, and my voice wobbled a little.

"You all right, Casey? Your voice sounds a little funny." His teasing tone had me stiffening my spine.

"Just a touch of allergies," I hedged. That probably wasn't far from the truth; I figured I was allergic to him being this close.

"Yeah, right," he laughed, stepping away from me before turning serious. "I'll pay your maintenance man a visit before I head to the precinct. Whether he likes it or not, he's putting up a new door today. Did you sign a lease for this place?"

I sent him a glaring frown over my shoulder. "I can take care of this myself. I'll make sure he puts up a new door today."

He nodded without arguing, but he didn't agree either. "What about the lease?"

"What's that got to do with anything?" I turned away from the stove to frown at him.

"This place isn't safe now that Eddie's here, and on the

loose. You need to move to a more secure building." There really wasn't a place secure enough to keep Eddie out. Rafe just didn't understand that yet.

"I'll talk to the complex manager about that when I go to see maintenance about the door," I hedged as I set a plate of eggs and bacon in front of him hoping to distract him. Someone from management was always onsite over the weekend, hoping to rent an empty apartment.

"So will I," he stated flatly, almost daring me to argue.

"I can take care of this myself!" I said again. He started to say something, but I stopped him. "Let me handle this. Please."

"How about if I go with you, as backup?" he added with a question at the end.

Reluctantly I agreed to that arrangement. It couldn't hurt to have someone bigger standing behind me when I went to see Mr. Jackson in maintenance. The man was lazy, but he was also a lech. Right now it was time to change the direction of this conversation. "Were you able to find a suspect on the homicide yesterday? How much evidence was there?"

Rafe sighed, his dark brows drawing together. "There was no evidence. I don't know how this guy managed to pull it off, but he left absolutely nothing of himself behind. Her throat was cut from ear to ear, nearly decapitating her. There was evidence she'd recently had sex, but he wore a condom, so no DNA there. Besides, that guy isn't necessarily the one who killed her." For the next several minutes, he continued to describe the gruesome scene while we ate. I could feel the color drain from my face, my hands beginning to shake.

"Hey, Casey." He looked at me, concern written on his face. "I didn't think it would bother you to talk about the scene. You're into forensics, right?"

Pulling myself together, I drew a deep breath. "It was Eddie." I couldn't make my voice work above a whisper.

"Huh? What are you talking about?"

"Eddie did it," I stated in a flat tone. "It's just like the murder of the prostitute who was killed after Fred disappeared." I described what I'd learned of that murder, echoing what had happened to the poor woman here. When I was finished, Rafe had stopped eating, listening intently.

"Okay, how do we prove this?" He was speaking more to himself than me. "How can he commit two murders and leave no evidence behind? There has to be something."

I shook my head. "No fingerprints, no hair, no fibers. Nothing. It was the same thing when he killed the social worker. His prints weren't anywhere in her apartment."

"I thought her death was an accident."

"That's what the official record says. But it's wrong. Eddie had been trying to convince her to let him have custody of me. When she wouldn't agree to that; he killed her. I know that deep down inside."

"Gut feeling?"

"If that's what you want to call it, yes!" I snapped, thinking he was mocking me. "I don't suppose you've ever had a gut feeling about a case?" I threw my napkin down on the table, ready for a fight.

"I don't doubt you, Casey. I was just asking. I trust my gut; I figure you do, too. Now we just have to find proof." There are plenty of murderers who leave little or no physical evidence behind, why else were there cold cases. Somehow we have to find something to tie this to Eddie.

After talking to the Super of my building about my door, Rafe had to go to work. I tried not to let him know I was spooked after our conversation. *How do I stop Eddie when I can't run his prints? Letting him catch me may be the only way*, I decided. The thought almost made me sick to my stomach.

Grudgingly, Mr. Jackson began installing my new door

shortly after Rafe left for the precinct. I'd lived in the building for four months, and hadn't gotten to know the other tenants except to say "Hi" in the hallway. Some of them stopped now to ask what happened. The best explanation was the truth; just not all of it. "Someone tried to break into my apartment." I didn't think Eddie would do anything to the others in the building as long as they weren't a part of my life, but they needed to be warned all the same.

Tessa called just as Mr. Jackson started putting up my new door. "Do you need any help moving things into that new armoire? I can come over to help." I had trouble hearing her because of the racket he was making. "What's going on over there? What's that noise?"

"It's a little hard to talk right now, Tessa. Maintenance is doing some work here. Can we meet for lunch later, and I'll tell you all about it?"

We agreed to meet at noon. The small Mexican restaurant had become our favorite hangout; the food was good, and the prices just right. "What were you having done at your place that made so much noise?"

I kept my explanation close to the truth without going into details of my past. "My door had to be replaced because someone tried to kick it in last night." She gasped, reaching out for my hand.

"Were you there? Are you all right?"

I patted her hand. "I was there, and I'm fine. He didn't get in."

"Do you know who it was?"

"Remember last week when I had to go in late, and we all went out to eat afterward?" She nodded and I continued. "Some guy came to the table just before we left. He seemed to think I was his sister; he kept calling me some other name. He must have followed me home because he showed up about seven last night."

"What did you do?"

105

I gave a humorless laugh. "I've lived on my own long enough to know how to protect myself. I have a gun." She gave another gasp, and I laughed. "Tessa, we work for the police department. It's no big deal. I know how to use it. When he tried to force the door open, I showed him I had a gun, and he backed off enough that I could close the door and lock it. He hit it and kicked it a few times, enough to put holes it."

"Did you call the police?"

"Ah, Rafe came by. He wasn't happy when he saw the door." I had to chuckle at that understatement. "The maintenance man wasn't going to do anything about the door until Monday. With Rafe backing me up I was able to convince him otherwise."

She smiled. "You called Rafe?" Her eyebrows went up. "You like him, don't you." It was a statement, not a question.

"He seems nice." I let her think I'd called him for help.

"What are you going to do now? Do you think he'll come back?"

"Yeah, I think he will," I sighed. "He's fixated on me. If this keeps up, I might have to move to a more secure building or get a restraining order." I knew neither of those would stop Eddie, but I would do it anyway.

"You can stay at my folks' place," she said. "You'll be safe there." She tightened the grasp she still had on my hand.

"No, I can't do that. If he's stalking me, it isn't safe for you or your parents. In fact, I think maybe you'd better stay away from me for a while."

She was shaking her head even before I finished speaking. "I'm not going to abandon you when you need me. What kind of friend would that make me?" She sat up straight in the booth, looking truly insulted.

"It would make you a safe friend, Tessa. Stalkers are a

little crazy; some more than others. If this guy thinks you're a threat to him getting at me, he might hurt you or your parents. I couldn't live with myself if something happened to any of you because of me. Please," I pleaded. "It's just for a little while. He'll get tired of following me around, and pick on someone else. Or he'll do something that we can arrest him for. I'm sure your parents will agree with that."

She didn't look convinced. "I'll pray about it." That was as close as she came to agreeing with me.

"Believe me, I will, too." This made her smile, but she didn't comment.

CHAPTER TEN

The evidence, rather the lack of evidence, was in the lab when I got to work Monday morning. Since there wasn't much to look at, the techs hadn't done anything with it. Like Rafe had said, there was evidence she'd had sex shortly before she died, but he had used a condom. No semen. The photos were graphic and gruesome, but didn't tell anything that would lead to a suspect. Rafe's report was concise and to the point; explaining that there were no prints where you would expect to find them, leading to the conclusion that the perp had worn gloves. But that didn't explain why there were no fibers, no hair, nothing. It wasn't unusual for a criminal to wear gloves, but normally there was something left behind. Not in this case.

My stomach churned with the certainty that Eddie was behind this murder, same as he was behind my parents' murders and that young woman four years ago. Proving any of it wasn't going to be easy. I wanted to know how he managed to leave no prints, fibers, or hair behind.

~~~

It's been a week since Eddie tried to kick down my door. I'm not foolish enough to think he's given up, and will leave me alone. He's just waiting for a chance to catch me on my own. Until then, I know he'll be keeping an eye on me. Trying to act normal has been a problem. More than ever, I keep looking around in every crowd to see if I can spot him.

I debated all week about going to Friday night happy hour with the usual group. A bar filled with off-duty police officers was probably the safest place to be. Eddie wouldn't be so stupid as to approach me there, especially with Rafe in attendance.

Flanagan's was noisy when we pushed open the door, but it was about to get a whole lot noisier. On any given Friday night fifteen or twenty people from the department joined us. They got loud, but never disruptive, and everyone managed to stay sober. Watching Tessa interact with the others, I was slightly envious, wishing I could be more like her. Until now I'd been telling myself that I was going with them to please Tessa. Now I realized for the first time I had real friends, or at least the beginnings of real friendships. Something I'd missed out on all these years when I felt forced to segregate myself from the rest of the world. These were people who would be there to help me if things went south before I was ready.

"I would gladly beat the living crap out of Eddie for all he did to you, and all he's taken from you." Rafe seemed to know where my thoughts were, his soft breath caressed my cheek, causing my pulse to trip faster in my chest.

"The living crap?" I laughed at his language. "I've heard the other officers using much stronger words than that."

He leaned closer, dropping his voice even lower. "When I was in fifth or sixth grade, there was a girl in the grade below mine. She gave me a black eye for swearing in front of the girls. I can swear with the best of them; but never in front of the female of the species. Lesson well learned."

"You remember that?" I couldn't make my voice work much above a whisper.

"Like I said, lesson well learned." He was so close; I thought he was going to kiss me. My heart was pounding so hard, I was sure he could hear it even above all the noise.

"If you're gonna kiss her, Rafe, do it," one of the other officers called from across the bar. "You've been talking about it since the first time you saw her in the parking lot."

I jumped back, putting distance between Rafe and

myself. Heat spread quickly up my neck to my face.

"Why don't you just shut up, Joe?" Tessa slapped his arm. "You're enough to embarrass the entire department."

"What'd I say?" He seemed truly confused. Joe Adams worked with Rafe in the Robbery Homicide Division.

Tessa shook her head, looking around at the others in our group. "Men can be so dense!"

"What?" Joe asked, and Tessa slapped his arm again.

She stomped over to me to wrap her arm around my shoulder protectively. "These stupid men don't know when to keep their mouths shut."

A giggle bubbled up in my throat. Little Tessa was beating up on this big cop, and he was taking it. "It's okay, Tessa. Just consider the source."

"Humph," she huffed, turning her back on Joe who still looked confused. He didn't know what he'd done wrong. Rafe was grinning like a fool.

He looked at Tessa, "If I promise not to embarrass anyone, will you let me dance with Casey?" he asked, tongue-in-cheek.

She appeared to think about it, but finally nodded. Now I objected. "No, Rafe, I can't dance to that." I could manage a slow dance without embarrassing myself and my partner, but they were playing something fast; that was another matter altogether. The others on the floor were doing something I'd never seen before. There was no way I was going to be able to do that without making a complete fool of myself and, by extension, him.

"We don't have to do what they're doing, just follow me." He kept the steps simple while still in time to the music. I made it through that dance and several others before I could convince him to sit down. Who knew dancing was as strenuous as some forms of exercise? The room was warm with all the people, and I was sweating.

The noise level grew in proportion to the number of

bodies filling the small area. There were more people here tonight than usual, and the crush was beginning to freak me out a little. Eddie could be sitting across the room watching my every move, and I wouldn't be able to see him or sense that he was here. Combining that realization with the noise level, I finally decided I'd had enough; it was time to leave. Rafe was talking to some of his friends, and I thought this was the perfect time for me to get away. "I'm going home, Tessa. I'll talk to you tomorrow." I had to shout right next to her ear for her to hear.

She grabbed my hand. "What about the stalker? You shouldn't go outside alone."

I'd thought about that, and had a plan worked out. "I'm going to have the bouncer follow me out. No one would dare try anything with him by my side." The man was about six feet six inches, and over two hundred fifty pounds. He was also packing a gun on his hip. Impulsively, I gave her a quick hug before heading for the door. "I'll be fine."

Making my way through the crowd was like going through an obstacle course, dodging someone each step I took. Several times someone stepped on my toes or jabbed me in the ribs with an elbow. Just before I reached the bouncer someone took hold of my arm. I let out a strangled shriek, jerking my arm out of the grip holding me, and reaching back to take a swing at the person.

"Whoa, Casey, it's me!" I sagged against Rafe, pounding my fist ineffectually on his arm.

"Damn it, Rafe. You scared me to death. What are you doing grabbing me like that?"

"What were you doing leaving alone when you know Eddie could be watching for just such a chance," he countered, still holding my arm as we walked outside to the relative quiet.

Butterflies attached my stomach, and I looked around the semi-dark parking lot. "I'm not stupid, Rafe; I was going to have the bouncer walk out with me."

"Why not just ask me? I know the situation. I wouldn't let him hurt you." He seemed more than a little angry, or maybe it was hurt I saw on his handsome face.

"I'm used to taking care of myself. Relying on others wasn't an option before. Give me some credit. I'm not going to take chances. I want to put him away for good. I can't do that if I let him get his hands on me first." We'd walked to my Jeep, and once again I didn't have my keys in my hand. This man was a total distraction. Looking around the lot, I made sure we were alone. If Eddie was here, he was staying well hidden for now.

"And what were you going to do when you got to your apartment?" His question confused me.

"Go inside?"

"Walk across a dark parking lot alone, go up two flights of stairs, alone? He knows where you live, Casey. He could be waiting for you. I don't think that building manager or maintenance man would come to your rescue."

My stomach churned. What he said was true. Maybe for now, I needed to rely on someone for a little help. "Okay, I guess I didn't think that far ahead. You can follow me home."

"Home and inside," he stated firmly. "I'm checking to see that he didn't somehow get inside." Now he had me completely spooked. I looked around again, wanting nothing more than to get in my Jeep with the doors locked.

My apartment door was intact and nothing looked disturbed inside. I never knew how Eddie got into my apartments in the past without leaving some evidence behind; but he had. Even with two dead bolts in place, he probably wouldn't find it much of a challenge now.

"Rafe, you aren't going to be able to follow me around. There will be times when I have to come home alone, like after work. We don't always work on the same schedule.

You know I carry a gun, so I can protect myself."

"You carry that in your purse. You need to have something in your hand whenever you're alone. Keep your cell phone in your pocket, not your purse. Neither one does you any good if you can't reach them."

I thought he was being overly cautious, but who was I to argue? I'd spent the better part of my life being that way. Now, when I was ready to become the cat instead of the mouse in this little game Eddie and I have been playing all of my life, Rafe wants me to be cautious. I couldn't help but see the humor, dark humor, in that, and I laughed.

"I don't see anything funny about this situation." He almost snarled at me, causing more laughter to bubble up. "What the hel...heck do you find so funny?" Now he was insulted.

Still laughing, I sat down. "I'm sorry, Rafe, I'm not laughing at you or this situation." The laughter died in my throat as quickly as it started. "I've spent more than half of my life more or less alone and on the run. I'm having a hard time accepting the fact that there are people who not only like me, but they are willing to help me. Only once has that happened, and he's most likely dead because of me."

"Not you, Casey; Eddie," Rafe contradicted. "None of this is your fault."

I sighed, "I'm not at fault, but I am the cause. If it weren't for me, Fred would still be alive."

Rafe sat beside me, taking my hand. "You have to believe that God is in charge of everything that happens."

"So you're saying that God let Eddie kill Fred?" I was incredulous. "That doesn't sound like a good thing."

"God is always in charge, but he lets things happen for the good of all. We can't see His purpose; we just have to trust the outcome will be for good. Maybe it was Fred's time to go home to God. Maybe you were meant to come full circle, and confront Eddie here where it all started, where there are people who love you to help."

"So I'm just supposed to let Eddie have at me, and God will work it out?"

"No, you're missing the point. We all work for good, having faith that God will be with us, no matter what. I think Eddie's time is up. I'll do whatever I can to help protect you. You have to stay alert, and not put yourself at risk. When the moment arrives that Eddie makes another try for you, God will be with us to finish it."

"And what about that poor prostitute he killed? How many other innocent people have to die before we catch him?"

"She chose to put herself in harm's way, not necessarily from Eddie, but what she chose to do with her life. We all make choices, and we have to live with the consequences. Eddie is no different. When the time comes, he will have to live or die with what he's done."

Part of what he said reached me, but it was hard to come to grips with the idea that I wasn't in control. Science and knowledge were what I had always relied on. Tonight I was too tired to wrap my brain around all he was saying.

As if reading my thoughts, he stood up. "All the windows are closed and locked. Lock all of those behind me." He pointed at the array of locks on my door, "If I don't have to go in tomorrow, I'll come over in the morning. I'll call."

"You need to be alert when you leave here. Fred never made it home that night." All this talk was bringing back memories.

CHAPTER ELEVEN

Coffee was the only thing in my cupboards besides a can of tuna, two cans of tomato soup and some vinegar. The refrigerator wasn't much better with week old bread and moldy cheese. I took my last cup of yogurt for lunch yesterday. I hadn't been grocery shopping for a couple of weeks. This morning was the time to stock up.

Walking across the parking lot, I kept one hand in my purse holding my gun; in my other hand I held my cell phone. Rafe's words still rang clear in my mind.

"Hey, Jennifer, wait up."

My heart nearly stopped when I heard Eddie's voice. As long as I was upright, I kept walking, pretending not to know he was talking to me.

He called out to me several more times when I heard his mean, nasty laugh. "Okay, I'll play your stupid little game. Wait up, Casey." Pounding footsteps coming up behind me sent my pulse rate soaring, but I tried not to run. That's what he wanted.

Coming to a sliding stop in front of me, he reached out to touch me. I pulled my hand out of my purse, pointing the gun at him. "Keep your hands off me and stand back."

"Whoa, Jennifer." He held up his hands like this was a stick up. "I just want to talk to you."

"My name is Casey Gibson, not Jennifer whatever. Now, go away and leave me alone. The police are already aware you're stalking me."

He laughed. "Stalking? How do you stalk your own sister?"

"I'm not your sister or anyone else's. Leave. Now!" I held up my cell phone showing I had already pressed 9-1-1; all I needed to do was press send.

"Jen...er Casey, I want to apologize for all that's

happened in the past. I've been in treatment, and know how wrong I was trying to force you to be with me after our folks were killed."

Force me to be with him? Our parents *killed*? I wanted to scream at him, but I needed to remain as Casey. "I don't know what you're talking about. Do you want me to finish dialing this number? They could be here in a matter of minutes."

He backed away, his face growing dark with anger. "Have it your way, Jennifer. But you're going to regret this." He turned and stomped off.

I blew it! I shouldn't have pushed that last time. Or maybe he would have slipped over the edge anyway. One thing is certain, he is furious now. There was no telling what he would do next. My legs held me up until I made it to my Jeep, then I collapsed against the seat.

Should I have finished dialing 9-1-1? If he had stayed long enough for the police to get here, Eddie would have spun such a tale that no matter what I said, he would come out looking clean. Somehow I had to get something on him that would put him behind bars. Then maybe I could start building a case against him to prove he had killed my parents, and any number of others.

~~~

"That damn little bitch! She thinks she can brush me off like a bug or something. She's not fooling me calling herself Casey Gibson. Ha! She's Jennifer and she's mine. I've let her have her own way all these years, but not anymore."

Looking around the dingy motel room only increased his anger. "She's living in a sweet little apartment, and I'm stuck in this dump!" He swung his fist at the lamp on the bedside table, sending it crashing against the wall which shook slightly at the impact.

"I should be living there with her, enjoying all the

Suzanne Floyd

benefits of what she has." His warped mind convinced him she was living the life he should have. She stole it all from him because he'd had to chase after her.

"She's got Rafe sniffing after her now like some love sick puppy," he sneered. "Well, he's not going to keep her. She's mine!" His thoughts spun in his mind almost making him dizzy. That other guy thought he could take her away from me and protect her, but I showed them both. Reluctantly, he admitted that Rafe wasn't going to be so easy to get rid of. Making a cop disappear could bring all sorts of trouble down on his head.

Pacing around the small room wasn't going to diminish the anger and frustration building inside him. Only one thing could do that; getting his hands on Jennifer. Until he could do that, he would have to settle for a substitute, as poor as that would be.

He stopped in front of the only window in his room, staring out between the smudges and dirt accumulated there. He needed to take his anger and frustration somewhere else. Another mutilated prostitute this soon might draw unwanted attention. His eyes lost focus, not seeing the weed filled parking lot outside, but any number of bloody scenes as they played out across the screen in his mind.

"How far do I need to go before they connect the next one with the one here last week?" He knew he was talking out loud, but it didn't matter. Right now he was the only occupant on this side of the U-shaped motel.

He packed up his few belongings. It was time to move anyway. Let her think she was free of him. She and Rafe could get cozy. Maybe he'd catch them together. He chuckled at that thought, planning what he would do to Rafe. He'd make her watch. Then she'd know once and for all who was boss. The thought filled him with power.

~~~

I finally got myself under control after Eddie left, and I

117

made it to the grocery store. Rafe was pacing in front of my apartment door when I returned an hour later. His chest heaved when he saw me walking down the hall, and he stomped up to me. Holding my arms, he looked me over like I was a bug under a microscope.

"Where the hell have you been?"

"Ummm." I lifted my arms where plastic grocery bags were suspended. "Grocery store?" I couldn't stop the chuckle bubbling up in my throat.

He didn't laugh. "You didn't think to let me know, that I might be worried? Where's your cell phone? I've been calling you every few minutes for the last half hour."

"Could we go inside to finish this discussion? I'm not interested in having the neighbors listening in. Besides, these bags are getting heavy, and I have more in the car."

The muscles in his jaw bunched up, and he spoke through clenched teeth. "What'd you do, buy out the store?" He took the key ring off my finger and opened the numerous locks on my door. I headed to the kitchen with my load, Rafe close on my heels. "I thought you were going to keep your phone in your pocket instead of your purse, so you could get to it faster." He pointed to my large hobo bag. "That thing is big enough to crawl in and take a nap. You'd never find your cell phone in an emergency."

I looked down at the tight jeans I was wearing, "Do these pants look like I could put something bigger than a nickel in the pocket?"

My face heated up as his appreciative gaze traveled over my body. "As much as I hate to say this, you need to wear something with a little more room or clip the phone to your waistband."

I turned away from him, and headed for the door. "Excuse me while I go get the rest of my groceries."

"I'll get them; you put these away. When I get back, you can explain about the party you're planning on having with all this food." He was out the door before I could object. This was feeling a little too domestic, a little too intimate for my comfort. I didn't know what I could do about it though. Rafe is a power unto himself.

Within minutes he was back, and helping me put everything away. "Why so much food, Cas? Who are you planning on cooking for?" Did he sound a little jealous? Nah, I shook my head at my own fantasy.

"I'm cooking for myself. I don't like to shop, so I get as much as I can at one time. Then all I have to get is fruits and vegetables when I run out."

"So why did you take off without letting me know?" he asked, jumping subjects.

"Look, I've been taking care of myself since I was fourteen. I'm not used to having to account for my whereabouts. No offense, but I have no intention of changing now." I was beginning to sound like a broken record, repeating myself every time I got in an argument with him.

"What if Eddie had been out there waiting for you?" I turned my back on him, heat rising in my face. "What?" He walked around so he could look at me. "What happened?"

"He was out there, but he didn't do anything." I couldn't meet his angry gaze. "I had my gun, and I dialed 9-1-1, I just didn't hit send. If he had tried something, I would have finished that call."

"Damn it, Casey! He could have killed you or worse before they got here."

"Don't swear at me, and what's worse than him killing me?" My voice was sharp enough to cut.

He ignored my first statement, and answered my question. "He could have abducted you. He'd never let you get away again." I could feel the color drain from my face, and my head spin. He was right. That would be worse than being dead. I would rather be dead than be under Eddie's control again. "Did he touch you? What did he say?" He took my arm to steady me, leading me to the couch, sitting down beside me.

"I didn't let him get close enough to touch me. He said he'd changed, and wants a chance to prove it. I told him my name is Casey, and I didn't know what he was talking about."

"How'd he react to that?"

"He lost his temper, of course, proving he hasn't changed a bit. There's no telling what he'll do now." My breath hitched in my throat at the thought of him striking out at someone else because of me. "You have to be extra careful now," I told him. "The term 'loose cannon' doesn't even come close to describing Eddie and what he's capable of."

"I'm a cop. I carry a gun with me everywhere I go. He's not going to get the jump on me."

I shook my head. "You're underestimating him. You don't know him the way I do. I know in the deepest part of my being that he's killed more people than just my parents." I stood up again, pacing across the room to put distance between us, work off some of the nervous energy. "If I could do a search of his prints through AFIS, there's no telling what I would find. I've got to be able to run his prints." I was speaking to myself as much as I was to him.

Rafe followed me across the room, halting my pacing route. "I'm not going to let him hurt you."

"I'm not worried about myself, Rafe! I'm worried about what he'll do to someone else. I have to stop him before that happens."

"You aren't alone in this anymore, Casey. You have people who care about you, and are willing to help in any way they can. Everyone in the department would do anything to protect you."

"I don't want protection," I snapped. "I want to stop

him. He's a monster!"

"I understand that."

I sighed. "No, I don't think you do. I know you've probably seen a lot as a policeman, but what Eddie did to my parents, and to any number of others..." I shook my head, unable to find the words to convey my feelings. "Go home, Rafe. Right now. I'm not good company. Stay away from me." I wanted to say more, but stopped there.

For a minute I thought he would argue, but he finally nodded. "For now, I'll give you some space, but don't think for a minute that I'm going to let you face this all alone. When we were kids, there wasn't anything I could do for you. But that's changed now. I'm not a kid any longer." Before I could stop him, he placed a soft kiss on my cheek and left.

I stayed inside the rest of the day, not sure what I would encounter if I went out. My thoughts kept returning to Rafe and Fred. They were far different men, Fred, gentle, loving, but naive. Rafe, tough, street smart, yet gentle in his own way. Could Eddie get the jump on him the way he had Fred? Fred disappeared when he left my apartment. Could that happen to Rafe? It was Saturday, and I wouldn't see him again until Monday. If Eddie somehow got the best of him, and no one knew about it for two days, there was no telling if he would ever be found.

Unable to stand not knowing if he made it home, I called his cell phone. After three rings without an answer I was ready to hang up and call the precinct. When he finally picked up, he sounded as worried as I felt. "Are you all right, Casey? What's wrong?"

The breath I'd been holding came out in a sigh of relief. "Nothing's wrong, I just wanted to make sure you made it home okay."

His warm chuckle came through the phone like he was standing right next to me. "No problems here. He's not going to take me."

"I know," I interrupted with more snap in my voice than I intended. "You're a cop. No one is going to get the drop on you. I guess that's why a cop has never been killed in the line of duty before. I was just checking. Good bye." I disconnected before he could say anything, but his chuckle still tickled my ear.

For the rest of the day, I puttered around my apartment. I'm not a neat freak or a germ-a-phobe, but by the end of the day you wouldn't know that. There wasn't a speck of dust in my apartment, no dirty laundry waiting to be washed. The refrigerator and freezer had been washed down inside and out. Even the inside of the windows sparkled. I'm sure if I could have reached the outside of them, I would have washed those, too. Nervous energy always sends me into a frenzy of activity.

I'd checked with Julie Easton, the complex manager, about getting out of my lease early, so I could find a more secure place. Her initial reaction was an unqualified NO, in capital letters; unless of course, I want to pay the remaining rent on my lease. After a little arguing on my part, she said she'd check with the management company and get back to me. I was still waiting. I couldn't afford to pay for the remaining months on my lease along with rent on another apartment.

While I was getting groceries, I'd picked up a magazine listing apartments for rent. While waiting to hear back I hoped to find something close to my price range, and still be close to work. It wasn't going to be easy since most apartment buildings in Phoenix didn't have doormen, and only the large, expensive complexes were gated.

Turns out there were two gated complexes close by, and the rent was only slightly higher than I was currently paying. Too bad I hadn't found them before signing here. Now if only the management company would let me out of this lease.

Rafe gave me the space I needed and didn't come over on Sunday as I thought he might. Instead, Tessa came over to keep me company. I could only hope Eddie wasn't out there watching me. I didn't want her to become his next target.

CHAPTER TWELVE

By Monday I was restless, and anxious to get back to work. I knew I was missing something on the murder of the prostitute, I just didn't know what. I was going over the evidence for the third time when Rafe came into the lab. "What's up, Cas?" He frowned at me when he saw what I was working on. "You've gone over this before. Did you find something new?"

"No, but something keeps nagging at me."

He laughed. "The girl with the photographic memory can't remember something?"

"Shut up," I hissed, looking around the lab. There were two others there with us, and I didn't want anyone to get the idea that we'd known each other before.

"Lighten up. No one is paying any attention to us. Besides, what difference does it make if I know you have a photographic memory?"

"It isn't something I advertise. I don't want people to know."

He frowned. "Why? It isn't something to be ashamed of. In fact, it's something most people would be happy to have."

There was no way to make him understand. As a kid in school, I'd been singled out by the teachers because I could remember everything I read. Some of the other kids would make fun of me. Rafe had always been there to defend me even when I just wanted to be left alone. After I left Phoenix, that ability had served me well, helping me get jobs I wouldn't have been able to get otherwise. Now I just wanted to be able to do my job.

"Go to work, Rafe." I turned my back on him. "I'm busy."

"When you figure out what's bugging you, give me a call. I've got a full schedule, but you can reach me on my cell." He left without further argument.

I felt like banging my head on the counter. All my rules were being thrown out, or stood on end. Depending solely on myself wasn't working any longer. Suddenly I had real friends I could depend on. Rafe kept pushing me, but towards what I didn't know. At the moment I wasn't sure how I felt about all these changes.

For nearly half of my life the people I've most identified with, worked to emulate, have been characters on a television show. How lame is that? How dysfunctional? There are real flesh and blood people who are willing to be my friends, to help me, even protect me, no matter how hard I try to push them away. *Maybe it's time for me to grow up, and stop being so isolated from others.* This wasn't the first time this thought had occurred to me.

Still, I didn't want anyone getting hurt or killed because of me. Eddie was deadly, and he didn't care who he hurt. In fact, the more harm he could inflict, the more he liked it. So how do I accept help from those around me, and keep them safe at the same time? *How would Gibbs handle this?* I shook my head, forcing my thoughts away from that question. I had to stop depending on fictional characters, and rely on real live people. Just how I went about doing that was the question of the year.

While I was having this internal conversation, I continued working on the evidence brought in by the detectives and CSI team, shifting slides around, replacing them with different ones. I started to move the current slide when something clicked in my preoccupied mind.

The smudge was the size and shape of a fingerprint; but there were no whorls, loops or arches, nothing but a smudge. Granted, fingerprints get smudged all the time; sometimes accidentally, sometimes deliberately. Even then, there would be something to indicate it came from a person, just not enough to make a match. Had the tech made a mistake when lifting prints? Going to the report, I shook my head. I knew Jeremy was one of the best; he wouldn't make a beginner's mistake. There were several slides like this one, all with nothing but smudges. According to the report they were found all around the victim, on her wrist, her purse. She'd been wearing a shiny metal belt. There was even a smudge taken from that.

What had caused them? How had Eddie, the suspect, I corrected myself, managed to leave nothing but smudges behind? How do I prove Eddie had killed this young woman and any number of others when he leaves nothing behind? There's no such thing as the perfect murder, I reminded myself. There has to be something here that we can tie to him or to someone.

When Jeremy came in a while later, I stopped him to ask about the smudges. "That's all there was," he said defensively. "I didn't make a mistake."

I stared at him in surprise. "I didn't say you did! You're one of the best techs in the lab, why would you assume I thought you made a mistake?"

"Sorry," he sighed. "One of the detectives accused me of being sloppy, and screwing up the crime scene."

"Rafe...ah, Detective Gonzales?" I couldn't believe Rafe would do that, but what did I really know about him now?

"No, he's one of the good guys. Detective Roberts thinks he's never made a mistake in his life, but everyone else does nothing but make them. What did you want to know about those smudges?" He quickly changed the subject.

"I read the report; they were everywhere you would expect to find fingerprints. Why just smudges? What caused them?"

He shrugged, "I have no idea. The only prints were the vics. I've never seen anything like it before."

My gut, or 'spidey' sense, or sixth sense, whatever you wanted to call it, was tingling. How many other crime scenes were left with nothing but smudges like these? Had other CSI techs in other towns been accused of screwing up when in fact that was all there was to find? I could send out requests for other jurisdictions to search for similar smudges at crime scenes. Would they even save this kind of print? Had anyone tried putting them into the system? I could hear the FBI now if anyone tried to have this put into the AFIS data base. Once again the tech would be accused of screwing up the prints.

At the time Fred disappeared the police said the only prints found in his car belonged to Fred or me. But had there been smudges? What about the poor woman Eddie killed at that time? To date, neither case has been solved. Excitement bubbled through me. Could this be the breakthrough I needed to put an end to Eddie's reign of terror?

Throughout the day, I worked on cases that had come in over the weekend, allowing the smudges to sit in the back of my mind for my subconscious to work on. Before going home, I pulled up the file again, still trying to make sense of them. With digital files, everything was always right at my fingertips.

"You figure those things out, Casey?" Jeremy stopped at my corner of the lab.

I shook my head, feeling defeated. Was I losing my ability to remember everything? I'm not even thirty yet, so what's with that? I asked myself. "Logically, I know there is an explanation," I said. "So far, I haven't found it."

"Well, if anyone can do it, it's you."

"Why do you say that? I wasn't even at the crime scene." I frowned, not sure what he was talking about.

"You're the smartest person I know, Casey, crazy

smart." He gave me a sincere smile. I know he meant it as a compliment, but I wasn't so sure I wanted to be 'crazy smart.' That sounded a little too close to how the psychologist had described Eddie years ago, saying he was smart and crazy at the same time.

"Tell me again where you found these smudges." I shifted the topic of conversation. "I read the report; maybe hearing it will help."

Jeremy slowly went over the crime scene with me, where everything was. He flipped through the file on the computer, bringing up pictures, drawings, everything. I kept my back to the screen. I didn't want anything to influence my perception of the scene.

When he finished with his narrative, I turned back to the computer, flipping to the file I'd been working on earlier, leaving one of the smudges on the screen. "Look at the size and shape of these." I pointed to the new prints on the screen superimposing those over the smudges. The size and shape nearly matched.

"There's nothing but smudges." Jeremy sounded defeated. "I know I didn't screw up when I lifted them. Maybe once, but not every single time. I'm not that careless."

"I know. That's not what I'm saying. These smudges fit exactly in size and shape to any set of fingerprints. If you wanted to wipe out your prints, how would you go about doing that?"

"You think the killer has somehow removed his prints from his fingers?" He sounded incredulous.

"What better way to avoid detection than not leave identifying marks behind? I'm willing to bet E...the suspect," I quickly corrected myself, "has figured out a way to do just that."

"What about hair, fibers? He can't commit a crime naked. People would notice a naked person walking down the street."

"No, but if he shaves all of his body hair, that would eliminate shedding any on his victim. A condom would prevent leaving semen behind during the rape. I haven't figured out how he avoids leaving clothing fibers, but I'm almost certain about the rest."

"See, I knew you'd figure it out." He stared at me, with almost puppy-like adoration.

"Well, if you had ignored these smudges instead of lifting them, we'd still be sitting at the starting gate. I wonder how many other techs have ignored smudges like this at other crime scenes." I spoke the last to myself.

I knew I was on to something significant as I left the lab a short time later. I just wasn't sure what good it would do us. Had Eddie managed to erase his fingerprints? Unless other techs had lifted a similar smudge, we still didn't have anything to compare to ours.

Getting the FBI to accept that smudge into AFIS wasn't going to be easy. They would be disdainful to say the least if I tried to enter it into the database. If Eddie had done something to his fingers, I needed to know what they looked like now.

My mind was so occupied with this problem that I wasn't aware of my surroundings. My body was on autopilot as I walked to my car until I became aware of another presence beside me. My heart almost jumped out of my chest when I turned to see Rafe standing there. I clutched my chest, trying to catch my breath. "What are you trying to do, give me a heart attack? Why didn't you say something?" My legs wobbled so much I thought I was going to fall down until he gripped my arm.

"You were so deep in thought if I'd said anything you would have jumped over the nearest car. How many times do I have to tell you to stay aware of your surroundings? You of all people know the evil that lurks out here." He sounded more than a little frustrated with me.

"I'm in the police parking lot. I don't think even Eddie is dumb enough to try something with cops coming and going. You need to stop following me, and doing whatever it is you're trying to do."

"You mean keep you safe?" he snapped. "Well, I'm not going to stop doing that. *You* need to stop being foolish. Eddie is out there." He waved his arm around indicating everything around us. "What would you have done if it was Eddie instead of me walking beside you when you finally realized you weren't alone?"

My heart nearly stuttered to a stop at the thought. Eddie wouldn't have hesitated to take advantage of my preoccupation. By now, I could be stuffed in the trunk of a car on my way to someplace unthinkable. There was no telling what Eddie would do to me before he finally gave me release by killing me.

"What were you concentrating on so hard?"

"The case. I found something, but right now it isn't doing me any good."

Rafe shook his head. "There wasn't anything to find. The only prints belonged to the victim. Her killer didn't leave anything behind." He sounded as frustrated as I felt.

"Jeremy pulled some smudges."

"Right. Just smudges, not prints. That won't do us any good."

"Unless we can match the smudges to other crime scenes, and find the person who left them," I argued.

Rafe frowned down at me. "Smudges aren't going to help us. There isn't anything there to match."

"But what if the killer has managed to wipe out his own prints?" For the second time I put my theory out there. Jeremy hadn't thought I was crazy. What would Rafe think?

He was quiet as we walked the rest of the way to my Jeep. He leaned against the side door while he continued thinking about my suggestion. "I don't see how that's going to help to us. Even if we find the person who left them, there really isn't anything to match."

"But if we had the person, we'd be able to prove those smudges came from that specific person," I continued arguing.

"How? There's nothing there to match. If Eddie did this, and he's managed to remove his fingerprints, we're going to need something else to tie him to the crime scene. So far, there isn't anything."

I leaned beside him against the car. "There's something; there's always something left behind. I just need to find it. I'm going to see if I can get a copy of the files from the murdered prostitute and Fred's disappearance."

"What do you expect to prove? You said yourself the police didn't take you seriously when he disappeared. If they didn't believe a crime had been committed, they probably didn't collect much evidence or keep what they did collect."

I knew he was right, adding to my frustration. Could Eddie be smart enough to have figured out how to commit multiple murders, in multiple places, and avoid detection?

I pushed away from the side of the car. "I'm going home. You need to do the same. Maybe if I clear my head of this problem, something will come to me." I pushed the remote to unlock the door.

"Let's get something to eat. I missed lunch again. I'm starving."

I shook my head. "I'm tired. I'm going home."

"Tired, or afraid Eddie will see us, and set his sights on me?" He cocked his head in a manner I remembered from years ago.

My breath hitched in my throat, but I pushed on. "Maybe a little of both," I admitted. "I don't want to give Eddie the idea that we're seeing each other as anything more than colleagues."

"Ouch!" He rubbed his chest mockingly as if to ward

off any barbed arrows. "That wasn't even kind. I've always thought of you as a friend."

"That was a long time ago. We don't know each other anymore."

"So, let's change that," he said. "I want to know all about you, everything that's happened to you in the past fifteen years. I want to make up for what you've missed."

As he talked, he stepped closer to me, invading my personal space until I thought he was simply going to devour me. My stomach churned, but this time I wasn't real certain why. Slowly, deliberately, he lowered his head until his lips lightly touched mine. I wanted to stop him, but couldn't seem to make my arms work to push him away. He nibbled at my lower lip, tugging slightly, his tongue running over where he had just nipped.

When he finally lifted his head, my arms were around his neck, and I didn't know how they got there; my heart was pounding so loud I was certain anyone in the parking lot with us could hear it. If Eddie was watching, there would be no doubt in his mind what had just happened, and what was going on between Rafe and me. Even if I wasn't certain what that was.

He rested his forehead against mine as he attempted to get his breathing under control. "Wow!" the word came out on a breathless sigh. Looking into my eyes, he smiled that crooked little smile that had always tugged at my heart when we were growing up. "You hungry?"

Grateful the parking lot was dark; I could feel a blush spreading over my face at the inappropriate thought that accompanied the question. As usual he knew where my thoughts had traveled. "Food?" he clarified. "Something to eat." His explanation wasn't helping much as my thoughts continued to supply other meanings for his words.

"Ummm, I don't think that would be a good idea right now. I need to go home."

Rafe laughed, adding to my discomfort. "Oh, I think it will be a great idea. I know you like Mexican food. And Frederico's is on the way to both of our apartments." Before I could argue further, my stomach growled at the mention of food, giving me away again. He opened my car door, waiting for me to get inside. "I'll be right behind you, so don't even think of not stopping." He shut the door on any comment I would have made.

"Damn him!" I hit the steering wheel with my fist. "How does he do that? *Why* does he do that?"

It was after eight by the time we walked into the restaurant. Monday is normally a slow day, and tonight was no exception. There were plenty of tables available. "Sit anywhere you want, Amigos," Javier, one of the waiters, called out

Munching on chips and hot sauce while we waited for our food, I searched for something to say. Coming up empty, I settled back in the booth, checking out the other diners. Now that I knew Eddie had found me again, I wanted to be aware of who was seated around me. Rafe reached across the table, taking my hand in his much larger one. "He's not here, Casey. You can relax." It was unsettling how he always seemed to know what I was thinking or feeling.

I tried to pull my hand away like I was reaching for another chip, but he tightened his grip. "Relax. I promise I won't bite. At least not too hard." He gave me a devilish grin, sending my mind back to the kiss we'd shared in the parking lot. He had definitely been biting me then. Butterflies fluttered in my stomach.

"Have you heard from the apartment management yet about letting you out of your lease?" He carried on a casual conversation, while I felt anything but casual.

He still wouldn't release my hand, so I picked up a chip with the other one, trying to act as nonchalant as he, dipping it in the hot sauce, and eating it before I answered.

If he was going to drive me nuts, I was going to return the favor. "I was going to call them today, but I've been busy. Maybe someone left a message on my phone."

"The department could put a little pressure on them if you want. I've told you before; everyone has your back." He was careful not to say *he* would put pressure on the apartment management, but I knew that's what he meant.

Javier appeared with our food just in time, so I didn't have to answer. For the next few minutes we concentrated on eating. Until the steaming plate of enchiladas was placed in front of me, I hadn't realized how hungry I was. Breakfast was a long time ago. Sitting back with a contented sigh as he finished the large plate of tacos, beans and rice, Rafe watched me. "I'm glad you came back. I've missed you. I always wondered if you were all right, where you were." His soft voice sent shivers up my spine. This was the first time in a while he brought up the subject of our past.

"Don't, Rafe. I don't want to remember that time." I held up my hand to stop him.

"How can you say that? You live with it every day. I've seen you; you're always on alert. Nothing gets past those watchful eyes. You absorb everything around you, like you're starving for memories, or something. I don't know." He shrugged his broad shoulders.

"I've always had to be watchful, all my life, and we both know why. I just don't want to talk about it. Are you ready to leave? I'm tired." Thankfully, he let the subject drop.

He stepped out of his car when we reached my apartment complex, reaching for the keys in my hand. "I'll just check your place, then let you get some rest."

"That's not necessary." I tried to move the keys away from his reach, but his arms are longer than mine, and he plucked them from my hand.

"Maybe not for you, but for my peace of mind it is. Humor me." He stayed right beside me, his eyes surveying the parking lot as we walked.

Nerves began to jangle as we climbed the stairs to my third floor apartment, something was definitely wrong. When he put the key in the lock, I grabbed his arm. "No, don't go in there." Panic shook my voice. "He's been here."

Rafe looked at me over his shoulder. "How do you know? Do you see something?"

"Evil leaves a footprint, an odor. He was here." I couldn't explain how I knew, I just did. Eddie had been in my apartment.

Rafe examined each lock for any sign of tampering, but I knew there wouldn't be any. He was like a ghost; he could get in where he wanted without leaving a trace. Finally, Rafe carefully turned the key in each lock while I held my breath. I knew Eddie was gone, but I didn't know what kind of surprise he had left for me.

Before he opened the door, Rafe pulled his gun, stepping carefully into the room. A vase of roses sat on the small table Tessa and I had picked out at the secondhand store. He looked at me, one eyebrow raised in question.

"I didn't put them there," I said softly. Eddie was gone, so why was I whispering? Rafe continued through the apartment checking each room thoroughly. Stepping into my bedroom, I couldn't stop the gasp from escaping my lips. I make my bed every morning as soon as I get out of it. Tonight, the imprint of a person was clear in the center of my bed. I pushed past Rafe, grabbing the comforter. "That...that..." I couldn't even come up with a name bad enough to describe the evil that was Eddie. "He was in my bed!" I started to yank the comforter off, but Rafe stopped me.

"No, don't, Casey. Leave it."

"I'm not sleeping in that bed after he's been in it!" I whirled around to face him.

He stepped close to me. Holding my shoulders, he stared into my eyes. "I know, but there might be evidence there. I'm calling in CSI. We have to treat this as a crime scene. He broke into your apartment even if he didn't break a window."

"I want Jeremy to process the scene. He'll know what to look for, the smudges."

"He's not on duty, Casey. Another tech will be just as careful."

"No! Call in Jeremy. He knows what I'm thinking about the smudges. You take this case. I don't want Roberts here. He thinks Jeremy messed up that murder scene, but he didn't." I glared at him, daring him to argue with me.

"It's okay. I'm here; no one else will take this. Let's get out of here, and I'll call it in."

"What's going on? Why didn't you call in the night shift?" I could hear Jeremy as he climbed the stairs a few minutes later.

"I requested you, Jeremy." He hadn't seen me leaning against the wall until I spoke. "I'm sorry I disturbed your evening, but you'll know what to look for."

He stopped beside me, a curious frown on his young face. "Okay, what is it we're looking for?"

Until this minute, I hadn't thought about how I was going to explain how the same smudges found at a murder scene were found in my apartment. "Um, just work this the same way you do everything. I don't want to steer you in any certain direction. I know the other techs are good, but I know you won't overlook anything." He nodded sagely, understanding my meaning, and entered my apartment after snapping on gloves and booties to cover his shoes. "Pay special attention to that vase of flowers, and take them with you."

Before the techs were through several neighbors either

came home from a night out or headed out for a night on the town. "Did someone try to get into your place again?" the burly man from two doors down asked. "Was it the same guy?" He'd been very vocal about the lack of security when Eddie tried to break down my door.

I shrugged my shoulders trying to appear less upset than I felt. "I wasn't home, but someone was in there."

"How'd he get past all your locks?" I shrugged again, but didn't say anything. "Lady, you got a stalker. That makes it unsafe for the rest of us. Why don't your cop buddies do something about him?" His voice was a growl, his tone belligerent.

Rafe stepped out of my apartment in time to hear him. "Her cop buddies *are* doing something. We're getting her out of here. Until then, we're collecting evidence. You have any information to help out?"

The man pushed past Rafe without answering, muttering something about talking to Mr. Jackson and the apartment manager. "Good luck with that," I replied to his retreating back.

It was close to midnight when the teams left. Jeremy stopped to talk to me for a minute. "I got everything I could, Casey. Same stuff here." He glanced down the hall where Rafe was talking to one of the uniforms. "I'll have everything ready for you in the morning. If the guy was on your bed, he didn't leave anything behind, not even a hair from his head. I don't know how he does that. The smudges on the vase look the same. I'm not sure they will help us unless we catch the guy. Even then it might not do any good. There's not much to compare." He looked up as Rafe walked towards us. "See you in the morning." He nodded to Rafe, walking away with the vase of roses in an evidence bag along with my comforter.

"Grab some clothes for tomorrow, and let's get out of here." Rafe's sharp tone brought me around from where I'd been watching Jeremy walk away. "You can't stay here.

Eddie proved he's able to get past all your locks without any problems. Your neighbors don't seem to be all that observant or concerned. No one admitted to seeing or hearing anything before you got home."

He was right; I couldn't, wouldn't stay here. After Eddie had touched my things, had laid in my bed, I would never sleep in that bed again. I tossed clothes haphazardly into a suitcase, not caring if they got wrinkled. Before I wore anything, it was all going to be washed. I didn't know what Eddie had touched. "There's a hotel not far from the department," I said over my shoulder. "I'll stay there until I find someplace else."

"You can stay with me." Rafe's soft voice had me swinging around to stare at him.

"What are you talking about?"

He gave a frustrated sigh. "I have a two bedroom apartment. Everything will be above board."

"I don't care if you have a six-bedroom mansion; I'm not staying with you."

"Why?" His teasing smile tugged at my stomach. "Afraid you can't keep your hands off me if we're in that close proximity?"

After the kiss we'd shared earlier tonight, his question had some validity. I'd die before admitting that to him though. "Don't flatter yourself." I put as much scorn into my voice as possible. "I don't want the department to think there's anything going on between us. More importantly, I don't want Tessa to think anything like that happened."

"Tessa would want you to be safe."

"But would she think I'm safe from something else if I stayed with you?"

"Her opinion means a lot to you, doesn't it?" I could only nod when tears prickled the corners of my eyes. I hadn't cried in years; why were they so close now?

"Okay." He agreed, giving in without any more

argument, and picked up the small suitcase when I closed it.

CHAPTER THIRTEEN

When I arrived at work the next morning it was barely light outside, but Jeremy was waiting for me. "It's just like the other scene," he announced. "The only prints are yours, Detective Gonzales, and Tessa's. The rest are only smudges! This has to mean something." He sighed heavily. "I just don't know what." This last part had him confused and depressed.

Looking at the images he'd pulled up on the computer, my heart rate sped up. I could hardly breathe. Had we finally found something we'd be able to tie to Eddie? I just didn't know how we could prove he was the one that left the smudges behind. He wouldn't willingly let me take a sample of his current prints.

Jeremy was waiting expectantly for my answer. I couldn't let my excitement show. There was no way I could explain about Eddie. "The simplest way to keep from leaving prints behind is to use liquid band aid on your fingers. It covers your prints, leaving nothing behind. There are also ways to actually remove the prints from your fingers. We need to catch this guy so we can see if we can match anything to our scenes.

"Thanks for coming last night, Jeremy. I didn't want someone who might dismiss these smudges. I knew you wouldn't." He beamed at my praise.

Reluctantly, I turned the case over to one of the others in the lab. This happened in my apartment. Any defense attorney would claim the evidence had been compromised if I worked the case.

"Girl, don't you ever go home?" Tessa came into the lab some time later. Like always, she stopped to see me before heading to her office. "I called you last night after nine, but you didn't pick up."

"Oh, ah, well. A lot happened last night." It wouldn't take long for the story about my mysterious visitor to be circulated through the department, so I had to tell her. "The stalker somehow got into my apartment yesterday." Tessa gasped, taking hold of my hand.

"Was he there when you got home? What did you do?"

"He was gone, but I knew he'd been there. I'm staying in a hotel right now until I can find another apartment." I was hoping she wouldn't ask more questions, but I should have known better.

"Did you call it in? What happened?"

"Rafe was there. A CSI team processed the place." I let out a frustrated breath that wasn't a fake. I was truly frustrated. How was I going to stop Eddie if he didn't leave any evidence behind?

"Rafe, huh?" She smiled briefly then grew serious again. "You don't need to stay at a hotel. You can stay with me and my folks. They'll want you to be there."

By staying with them, I could put them all in danger. My stomach twisted at the thought. "I can't do that, Tessa, for the same reason I couldn't stay with you after he tried to break in. I don't want anything to happen to you and your parents." I knew full well Eddie would stop at nothing to get what he wants. And that's me.

~~~

"The department put a little pressure on the management company, and they're letting you out of your lease early," Rafe announced after work. "You can move out this weekend."

By "department," he really meant he pressured them. I guess it didn't matter how it came about as long as I could move. A gated complex wasn't going to stop Eddie, but it would slow him down. The more layers between him and me, the better off I'll be.

Saturday morning all the regulars from Friday night

happy hour showed, and by noon everything was in my new apartment. An eight-foot gate only opened when a certain code was input into the key pad. All tenants had their own code. The door into the building opened to another code or a tenant had to buzz someone in. My apartment had a back door that led to another set of stairs. All these security measures would keep out the garden variety burglar, but I had serious doubts they would keep Eddie out for very long.

~~~

He chuckled as he watched her cop buddies troop out with her meager belongings, loading them into pickup trucks. Did she really think moving would keep him away? Unless she was going on the lam again, all he had to do was follow them to their destination. He doubted she was going to run, though. She was making friends; she had a good job, one that gave him some pause. He had to be extra careful from here on. He didn't know how she managed to get a degree in forensic science without him knowing about it. He shrugged off the questions that occasionally plagued him. It didn't matter. She belonged to him. She just hadn't accepted the inevitable yet.

Anger bubbled up inside him when she came out of the building with Rafe right beside her like a whipped puppy dog. He hadn't left her side all morning. "That damn Rafe has been trouble since he was a kid," he muttered." I'll take care of him later. First I need to get her."

As they pulled out of the parking lot, caravan style, he hung back, but kept them in sight. He chuckled again. This was easier than even I expected. They're so arrogant; they don't think anyone can get the drop on them. He chuckled again, stupid cops.

~~~

Moving is a lot simpler when all you have is clothes

and a few personal items. Adding furniture, a television and dishes made it a whole different matter. Now everyone was sitting around eating pizza and drinking beer in my new living room. It was hard for me to grasp the concept that people would give up their Saturday to help me move. Friends weren't something I'd cultivated in the last fifteen years. Hot tears prickled at the back of my eyes, and I turned away before I made a fool of myself.

"Hey, Casey, stop hiding out in the kitchen and join your party." Joe called from across the room. He was sitting with Tessa, and every time I looked at them, he was a little closer. Now his arm rested on the back of the couch, ready to drop down on her shoulders. Ever since she scolded him for teasing Rafe about kissing me, he's had a giant crush on her.

Once the pizza and beer were gone, most of the group drifted off, but Tessa stayed to help me put things away. Rafe and Joe didn't appear inclined to leave anytime soon. By five, I was ready to call it a day. "Time to pack it in, guys. It's been a long day." For the last half hour Rafe and Joe had been camped out on my couch watching some game on television.

"How about grabbing a bite to eat?" Joe looked up hopefully. "After all the work you've done today, you don't want to cook."

"Sorry, I'm beat. You go without me. All I want to do is take a shower, and sit with my feet up for a few hours, then go to bed."

"Me, too," Tessa chimed in. "Feet up sounds great." I almost laughed at the dejected look on Joe's face. He wasn't ready to leave Tessa.

Rafe playfully wrapped his arm around Joe's neck. "Come on, Buddy. The ladies are bushed. So am I." He released Joe, stepping close to me. "Pick you up for church tomorrow?" He quirked an eyebrow in the manner I was becoming used to.

"Ah, no, I'm going with Tessa and her folks." My answer surprised me as much as it did Tessa. She beamed, but waited until the guys were out of hearing before saying anything.

"Were you serious? You'll go with us?"

"I wouldn't lie about that. I'll see you in the morning."

She was so happy she skipped down the stairs. As soon as the door was closed, my conscience attacked me. I wouldn't lie about going to church with her; just about everything else. I shut off those thoughts, and headed for the shower.

~~~

There was work waiting for me Monday morning, but nothing new on the murder, or the break-in at my old apartment. Of course, only three people believe there really was a break in, Rafe, Jeremy and me.

At Tessa's usual time she came bouncing into the lab. "Thanks for spending the day with us, Casey. It was great fun!" I smiled at her exuberance. "I've always wanted a sister. Now I have one."

"That's so sweet of you." My voice was suddenly thick with emotions I couldn't name.

"I don't know about sweet, but it's true. I have other girlfriends that I'm close to, some more so than others. But..." She paused, growing serious. "I don't know how to explain it, but I've felt a special connection to you from the very first day we met." Now her eyes sparkled with tears as she gave me a spontaneous hug. "Mom says some people are just meant to be your family, not by blood, but by heart. That's the way I feel with you. You're my sister by heart." She patted her chest over her heart.

Hot tears prickled behind my eyes. Until now I hadn't been able to put a name to how I felt about Tessa and her family. She'd just described it exactly.

"I gotta go before we both start blubbering." She gave

144

me another quick hug before disappearing out the door. "See you at lunch," she called over her shoulder.

Guilt heaped on top of guilt. I've lied to her about everything from the moment we met, and now she's calling me her sister. I've spent my entire life on the fringe of society, not really living, just existing. Now Tessa and her folks are pulling me into real life. I was absolutely terrified for them, afraid of what Eddie would do once he realized how important they've become to me. And terrified for myself; I didn't know how to handle this new life.

At lunch, Tessa's cheeks were pink with excitement. "Joe asked me to go out Saturday night," she whispered across the lunch room table.

"I hope you said yes, otherwise he'll be devastated." Laughter bubbled up in my throat.

"Of course I said yes. Will you and Rafe double with us?"

"Rafe and I aren't dating."

"Huh?" She looked confused.

"Rafe and I aren't dating," I repeated.

"You could have fooled me." She smiled mischievously.

"He's just helped me out a few times. I don't date people I work with. He knows that." My tone was more aloof than I intended, but she didn't take offense.

"Well, how about asking him to help you to the movie on Saturday night?"

"Sorry, I don't want to send mixed messages and give him the wrong impression. You and Joe will just have to do this on your own." She didn't argue like I expected. Instead, she laughed.

~~~

Frustration ate at him as he waited for her to come out of the building. She never went out for lunch, cheap little bitch, he thought. Or maybe he had her so spooked she didn't want to run the chance of meeting up with him. That thought gave him great pleasure. Just in case, he watched the building.

It had taken him years to find her when she ran away after their parents died. He'd been afraid he'd lost her for good. When he finally found her, she was all grown up and had changed her appearance so much he almost didn't recognize her. Almost, but she'd never change herself so much that he wouldn't know who she was. After all, she was his. She needed to accept the inevitable. Each time she moved, it took him precious time to find her again, but he always did. It was like she left some sort of cosmic footprint for him to follow. Now he had to bide his time which was so hard for him. He felt like he was in a holding pattern while she lived it up with that damn cop. Once he got her back, he'd take out Rafe. That would be so satisfying.

He looked around at the others sitting in the park. They were just as dirty as he, but they smelled a whole lot worse. He only looked like one of the many homeless who lived on the streets of every town in America. But he wasn't homeless, at least not technically. For now, he was living in one of those hotels where you paid by the week. He paid for it by the generosity of others. In fact, he'd lived most of his life off that same generosity. People were usually a generous sort; some just took more persuasion than others.

He gave a nasty cackle, causing some of those around him to look at him warily and move away. This caused him to cackle again. He enjoyed putting people on edge.

Waiting until he was sure she wasn't just taking a late lunch, he finally gave up. He'd come back at the end of the day. She had to leave sometime. She didn't sleep here.

~~~

"You want to take in a movie tomorrow night?" Rafe was sitting beside me at our usual Friday night happy hour.

"Did Tessa and Joe put you up to this?"

146

"What are you talking about? I just thought we could see a movie tomorrow."

I wasn't fooled by his innocent act. I knew what he was up to. "Sorry, I still don't date anyone I work with."

"Who said anything about a date?" He tried to look shocked. "I just want to see a movie with a friend. I'll even let you pay your own way."

"Nice try. The answer is still no." I had to laugh. He looked so dejected, but I still wasn't fooled. Give him an inch, he'd take a mile.

~~~

He was watching in the shadows when she arrived with her groupies, including six or eight burly cops. They were all laughing and joking around, and didn't even see the "homeless" man sitting against the next building. Being homeless means being invisible, at least to the beautiful people. Now she was inside having a good time with all of her little buddies while he sat out here in the dark and cold. Someday, and soon, she was going to pay for all she'd put him through. Until then, he'd watch and wait.

Maybe he'd get a job in there, in disguise of course. He could watch her; make sure she was behaving herself. He chuckled at that. She never misbehaved. Even as a kid she was the perfect one. Their folks thought she never did anything wrong; she got straight A's in school, she kept her room clean, she helped their mom out around the house. When she told them what he was doing to her, they tried to punish him. But in the end, he showed them who was boss. They'd never punish him again. Now he would punish her.

It wasn't long before she came outside. She never stayed as long as some of the others. But of course, she wasn't alone. That damn Rafe was right beside her. He had no right being with her. In the two weeks since she'd moved, he still hadn't been able to get near her apartment. Security was a little tighter than he expected. Most of the time security measures were just for show, and he'd been able to get past them without any trouble. Those apartments had some of the best prizes, and he was able to persuade their owners to "donate" to his upkeep. Again he gave his nasty chuckle. He liked to think of it that way. They were just helping to support him.

He turned his attention back to the couple walking across the parking lot. Rafe opened the door of her shiny new Jeep, checking the back end before allowing her to get inside. "How sweet," he sneered. "The ever vigilant cop and lover."

He didn't bother following them; he knew where they were going. Besides he didn't have nice wheels like they did. His crappy pile of junk would stick out like a sore thumb in her neighborhood. He couldn't get past that stupid gate anyway. He'd have to work on that.

~~~

"Rafe, you don't have to check out my place every time I come home. He hasn't been here, or I'd know it." Of course, he didn't listen to me. He moved through each room, looking in the closets, and even under the bed. For a minute, I thought he was going to start looking in the kitchen cupboards.

"Are you satisfied?" I glared at him, my hands braced on my hips.

"Yes, for now. Don't get too comfortable, Casey. The security at this place is only as good as the people living here. All it will take for him to get in is for one person to get careless, and he'll sneak through."

"Don't lecture me, Rafe! I know better than anyone how evil Eddie is, and how easy it is for him to get in somewhere. Eddie's been slippery enough to get away with murder for a long time. The only way I've stayed alive as long as I have is by being very careful. I came back to Phoenix for the express purpose of making certain he doesn't get away with this any longer. If that means I get hurt in the process, so be it."

"No! I'm not going to let that happen." He gripped my arms, giving me a little shake before pulling me to him. His dark eyes sparked fire for a long moment before they began to smolder with something more than anger. "If keeping you safe means I have to park outside your apartment for the rest of my life, that's what I'll do." His voice softened, and he slowly lowered his head, his lips capturing mine in a kiss that went from gentle to passionate at Mach speed.

When he finally came up for air, we were both breathless. My heart was pounding so hard I thought it would jump out of my chest. "I've had a crush on you as far back as I can remember. When you disappeared, I thought my life was over. If you think I'm going to let Eddie get his hands on you, you're mistaken." He kissed me again. Just as quickly, he released me, stepping away. "Lock your door when I leave. I'll see you tomorrow."

"Don't come over tomorrow. I'm busy."

"Uh huh. Lock the door." He walked out leaving me simmering on more than one level. "Lock the door." His voice came through the thick partition.

I clicked all the locks with a little more violence than was called for, making sure he heard them click. "Damn you, Rafe," I whispered. "Leave me alone. I don't need this."

~~~

That bastard has free access to her apartment, and probably her bed, but I'm stuck out here, watching. Well, I'm about to change that. "You're going to pay, Jennifer, you're going to pay," he muttered before driving off in his clunker, smoke billowing out of the tail pipe. He couldn't resist driving past the fancy apartment building even though he knew he couldn't get to her just yet.

~~~

I had just stepped out of the shower Saturday evening when the buzzer by the door went off. Someone wanted me to buzz them in the front door of the building. I grabbed my robe, and hurried to the intercom. The person spoke as soon as I clicked on.

"Hey, Babe, release the door. My hands are full. I can't reach the key pad."

"Excuse me?" I was hoping I sounded confused at who would be calling me 'babe', but I sounded more indignant than confused.

"Come on, Casey, you know who this is. Just release the door."

"What are you doing here, Rafe?"

"Can we talk about this once I'm inside? I don't want the food to get cold."

"What food?"

"Casey!" His voice growled through the speaker.

"Damn you, Rafe," I muttered, but released the door. I was waiting for him as he came up the last few steps.

"Wow! This is a reception I'd like every time I come to visit."

Until that moment, I'd forgotten I was standing there in my short robe and nothing else. I almost slammed the door in his face. Reading my intentions, he slipped his foot in the doorway to stop me. "Just joking, Cas. I never thought I'd say this, but why don't you go get a few more clothes on while I set out the food?"

Ignoring him, I stood my ground even though I could feel my face flaming, with embarrassment or anger, or some combination of the two. "What are you doing here?"

He held up a warming bag with the logo from a local pizza joint on it. "Since you didn't want to go to a movie tonight, I thought we could just hang out here. You know; two friends eating, having a few drinks, watching a movie

150

on TV."

"I've told you be..." He cut off the rest of my sentence.

"I said just friends. I hang out with my friends all the time to watch movies. Now, go get a few more clothes on before I think you want to be more than just friends. Our pizza's getting cold."

I stomped out of the room, slamming my bedroom door. What am I supposed to do with him? He won't listen to me, or take me seriously. I considered locking myself in my room, and leaving him in the living room by himself. But the mouthwatering aroma of cheese and pepperoni began to fill the room making my stomach growl, reminding me that all I'd had for breakfast was a dry piece of toast. I needed to go shopping again.

"Pizza's getting cold," Rafe called out.

I grabbed a pair of jeans with holes in them and a faded tee shirt. 'Just friends' didn't have to worry about impressing each other by dressing up. My hair had dried into a curly mass, and I didn't bother trying to tame it. This was how I dressed when I hung out.

When I walked back into the living room, Rafe looked up from putting the movie into the DVD player; his hand stopped in midair. His warm gaze traveled over me, taking in my mode of dress, and he started laughing. "What's wrong?" I asked innocently. "Isn't this how friends dress when they're just hanging out?"

"I know that's how my friends and I dress to just hang." He swiped his hand over eyes to wipe away the tears his laughter had produced. "So friend, let's eat before it's too cold, and we have to nuke it." He pushed the DVD into the player, and sat down with a plate piled high with two big slices of pizza, liberally sprinkled with crushed red peppers.

Reluctantly, I picked up my own plate. *I can do this,* I told myself. *We can just be friends like we were back in school.* I'm not sure who I was kidding.

The movie was several years old, but I hadn't seen it before. When you're running from your past, and can only hope for a future, you don't spend money on movies. The only movies I saw were on television. Comedy/action pictures are a lot more fun than I realized, and watching with someone who will laugh along with you adds to the enjoyment.

By the time the movie was over, I can honestly say I felt closer to Rafe than I had to anyone since Fred disappeared. I quickly shoved that thought aside. I didn't want to take what I'd felt for Fred and transfer it to Rafe. I was also feeling very relaxed. While Rafe only had two beers the entire evening, he'd made sure my wine glass never made it below the half way mark.

"Church tomorrow?" He quirked an eyebrow as he headed for the door.

I shook my head. "I'm sorry, Rafe. I can't go to that church. Even if no one remembers me, I remember them. I'm going with Tessa." His understanding nod calmed the uneasy feelings stirring in my stomach.

"See, we can be just friends," he teased. Then he spoiled the 'just friends' by pulling me close for a long, thorough kiss. Before I could object or scold him, he released me and walked out. "Don't forget to lock your door," he called over his shoulder. I could hear his laughter in my mind long after I heard the door to the outside click shut behind him.

Tessa was waiting for me in the parking lot of the little neighborhood church she went to when I got out of my Jeep. "How was your date?" I didn't need to ask. She positively glowed.

"Great! Joe's a nice guy; he didn't even object to meeting my folks."

"Why would he object?" I was confused.

"That's for teenagers on a first date, or when you start

getting serious with someone. It's embarrassing to still be living with my parents. I'm twenty-three, for crying out loud. When my brothers were this age they had their own apartments."

"They love you, and want to protect you. There are a lot of evil people in the world."

"Protective is one thing, but this is overly so." She took a deep breath, letting it out slowly. "At breakfast this morning, I told them I was going to start looking for my own apartment."

"How did they take it?" We started walking through the parking lot to the church.

She laughed. "A lot better than I expected. I think they were relieved. Maybe they're ready for some privacy of their own. You want to help me look this afternoon?" Before I could answer, she gasped, gripping my arm almost painfully. "They're here." Her whisper was awestruck.

She couldn't be talking about her parents, they were here every Sunday. "Who's here?"

"Joe," she whispered. "Rafe."

"Where?" I was panicked now. I wanted to run for my car while Tessa was trying to maintain some semblance of decorum, walking sedately forward.

"Why are you *here*?" I hissed, keeping my voice down while I tried to lead Rafe away from Tessa and Joe.

"Well, I imagine the same reason everyone else is here," he said solemnly, but his lips twitched, giving away the smile he was trying to hide. "I'm here to go to church."

"This isn't the church you go to. Why are you here at this particular church?"

"Is there a reason I shouldn't be here?" One eyebrow lifted in question.

I drew a deep breath, trying to calm down. "No, there isn't." I walked off, doing my best to ignore him. But that was impossible with his chuckle following me.

"I thought we were going to look for an apartment for you," I whispered to Tessa an hour a half later as we left the church.

"We are, just not until after lunch. We can't very well tell them we're busy when they made the effort to be with us." She was floating on air, her feet several inches off the ground. I, on the other hand, was fighting conflicting emotions. I didn't want Rafe with us all day, at the same time I was enjoying myself. He always made sure I had a good time.

At the restaurant both men sat with their backs to the wall so they could see anyone coming at them. It must have something to do with being a cop, I thought. Tessa and I sat across the table from them. Once we'd given our orders, Joe reached across the table, taking Tessa's hand. "What do you ladies have planned for the rest of the day?" he asked.

"Casey is going to help me look for an apartment." She sounded hopeful that he would suggest they help us. I wanted to stomp on her foot or kick her or...something.

Rafe hadn't said anything except to place his order, but his eyes hadn't left me the whole time. Now he burst out laughing. "What?" I asked indignantly. I knew he was laughing at me.

"Don't ever let anyone talk you into playing poker."

"Why?" I frowned, unsure what he was talking about.

"With your expressive face, you'll telegraph your every thought to the other players."

I gave what I hoped was a disdainful sigh, only to have him laugh at me again.

Without any input from me, they agreed to leave the cars at my complex, and go apartment hunting in one car. There were several empty apartments in the complex, so she started her hunt there.

"I didn't realize apartment hunting was such hard

154

work," Rafe commented several hours later. "Did you find what you were looking for, Tessa?"

"I'm sorry to put you guys through this," she apologized. "I didn't know it would be so hard either." She sighed with pent-up frustration. "I like the first one we looked at best, and I'm sure my...I like it because of the security." She changed the direction of her sentence, but I knew what she was thinking. With the security, her parents would feel better about her moving out of their house.

"Well, that settles it," Rafe said. "Let's celebrate. Anyone up for Mexican food?" He put the question to Joe and Tessa, ignoring me knowing I would decline. I wondered if they ever ate anything besides Mexican food.

Tessa didn't give me a chance to say no. "That sounds great, right, Casey?" She gave me a hard stare.

What was I supposed to say to that? "Um, ah sure." I tried to sound gracious, but knew I fell far short of the mark when Rafe laughed.

At Frederico's we settled into our regular table, the men again seated with their backs to the wall. When Joe reached across the table, Tessa gladly placed her small hand in his. A teasing grin tilted the corners of Rafe's full lips, and I knew what he was thinking; what would I do if he reached out for my hand? I looked away, keeping my hands safely clasped in my lap.

A few minutes later, Rafe tensed, sitting up straight in his chair, his dark eyes growing even darker. I wasn't the only one who noticed. "What's wrong?" Joe whispered, looking around the room for any indication of foul play.

Rafe ignored him, his intense stare on me. "Casey, look at me, only me. Don't say anything."

"Good evening, folks. I brought you some chips and salsa."

I couldn't have said anything if I wanted to, but I know I let out a small gasp at the sound of Eddie's voice right behind me. He placed a bowl of chips on the table in front of me along with several small dishes of salsa. His evil laugh drifted back to me as he walked off. He was working at my favorite restaurant!

Somehow my hands ended up in Rafe's, and he gave them a squeeze. "Look at me, Casey. Focus on me and breathe." Until that moment I hadn't been aware I was holding my breath. Doing as Rafe commanded, I focused on him, taking in several gasping breaths, clearing my head of the dizziness Eddie's presence caused.

"Casey?" Tessa stared at me, unsure of what just happened. "Do you need to go home?"

"No," Rafe answered for me. "She's fine. Right?" He gave my hands a hard squeeze.

I knew what he was silently telling me. Don't give in to the urge to run, don't give Eddie that kind of power. Drawing another steadying breath, I looked at Tessa, trying for a smile. "I'm fine. It was nothing."

"Hello. This little group is quickly becoming my best customers." Frederico himself waited on us almost every time we came in. "Do you want the usual, or are you going to be adventurous tonight?"

Everyone opted for their regular, but when it came to me, I couldn't bring myself to order anything. "I think I'll pass. I had a big lunch."

"Give us a minute, Frederico," Rafe frowned at me, waiting for him to walk away. He stared at me for several seconds, but I didn't budge.

"I'm really not that hungry."

"Casey, what's wrong?" Tessa touched my arm, and Rafe tapped my foot under the table. His silent message said I needed to tell them something.

"That busboy." I had to draw a deep breath before I could continue. "He's the one who tried to break into my apartment." That was as close to the truth as I could get.

Tessa gasped, and started to look around, but Joe held

156

her hand tight, keeping her in place. "Don't look at him, Honey. That's what those guys are after, the attention."

I was grateful they accepted that explanation. I still couldn't eat anything he might have touched. There's no telling if he added something to the food. I didn't want anyone to eat it. What if Eddie put something in the salsa before bringing it to the table, or the water? My stomach rolled at the thought.

"Babe, don't give him that kind of power." Rafe brought my attention back to him. "He isn't going to do anything here. Just act natural. I won't let anything happen to you."

Tears I had refused to let fall in what seemed like forever suddenly threatened to spill over. There were people here who would do their best to protect me. I wasn't on my own anymore. I nodded, but couldn't say anything around the lump in my throat.

Eddie didn't come back to our table, but I knew he was around. When I finally managed to get myself under control, I realized this might be the perfect opportunity to get his prints, or his lack of prints. I wanted to take the dish he had placed on our table back to the lab. Sneaking it into my purse wasn't exactly practical. I didn't want salsa dripping all over the inside of my purse. I didn't want to get arrested for shoplifting either.

Before I could make up my mind how to get away with taking the dish, Eddie began clearing the table next to ours. Trying to watch him without seeming to do so, I realized it wouldn't do any good to take any of the dishes he'd handled. He was wearing clear plastic gloves, the kind used in doctors' offices and hospitals. It would be interesting to find out what excuse he gave for using them.

~~~

Watching them leave he chuckled to himself. The look on Rafe's face when he noticed him for the first time was priceless. Too bad he didn't have one of those cell phones that take pictures. I'll bet she has one of those, he thought, resentment filling him. She's going to pay for all I've missed because I had to keep chasing her all over the country.

He put those thoughts aside for now. The fear when she heard him rolled off her in waves. She was so spooked she barely touched her food. She was probably afraid he'd put something in it. He couldn't help himself; he laughed out loud just thinking about it.

"What are you laughing about? You think my restaurant is funny?"

He cursed himself for letting the boss man sneak up on him. He had to stay focused. "No sir. Just thinking about a funny story I heard."

"Think about it on your own time. There are tables that need to be bused. Get to work." Frederico glared at him.

"Yes, sir." He ducked his head, pretending to be cowed. No one was waiting for a table; what was the hurry? It might be fun to teach him a lesson someday, he thought. First I have to take care of Jennifer and Rafe.

~~~

"Are you going to be okay here by yourself?" Tessa whispered when we got out of the car at my apartment building. "Would you like me to stay with you?"

I gave her a hug. She was truly more like family than I'd ever had in my life. "I'll be fine. Even if he gets through the gate, he won't be able to get in the building." I sounded more confident than I felt. Given enough time and incentive, Eddie would be able to get in anywhere he wanted to be.

As usual Rafe insisted on checking my apartment before he would let me go in. "You know he isn't here," I argued. "He was still at the restaurant just a few minutes ago."

"That doesn't mean he wasn't here earlier, and left

158

behind a little surprise like he did before." He certainly knows how to set a mood, I thought.

"All clear," he announced a few minutes later. "Are you sure you're going to be okay here by yourself?" He repeated Tessa's question.

"I'll be fine; he can't get into the building unless someone buzzes him in."

"Exactly my point, people aren't as cautious as they should be." He took my hand pulling me close to him. "You do believe I'll do anything to keep you safe, don't you?"

"It's not your place to protect me. I can take care of myself."

"When are you going to understand you aren't alone anymore? There are a lot of people who care about you and number one on that list is me."

"Rafe, you're remembering the young girl I was, not who I am now."

"I had a crush on that young girl. I'm in love with the woman she is now." Before I could think of anything to say, he pulled me closer, his lips claiming mine in a crushing kiss. When he finally lifted his head, he smiled at me. "I would like to see those green eyes again sometime." He released me, and opened the door to leave. "Lock this behind me."

CHAPTER FOURTEEN

After a restless night where dreams were more like nightmares and Eddie stalked my every move while Rafe chased after him, I was more tired than when I went to bed. Work was a relief. I was tired of thinking about Eddie, and what he might or might not do.

My mind kept returning to Rafe and his declaration that he was in love with me. How could he say that? He doesn't really know me anymore. What am I supposed to do now? The only other person who has said that to me disappeared, never to be seen again. How could I let Rafe into my life, or anyone else for that matter? Would Eddie decide to go after Tessa because she's my friend? I kept asking myself that question. Just thinking about something happening to her struck my heart with fear.

Immersed in work several hours later, I gave a startled jump when the phone rang at my elbow. Picking it up, I was still preoccupied with my work. "Yeah, Gibson."

"I got a message to call a C. Gibson. That you?" The caller snarled in my ear.

"Yes, who is this?" The number of messages I leave in a day can be staggering. This could be from any number of people.

"You called me, lady. Don't you know who you called?"

Whoever this guy was, he wasn't very professional. "I call a lot of people every day. Please identify yourself so I know who I'm talking to. Then I can tell you why I called." My patience was wearing thin.

"This is Detective Billings with the KCPD," he snarled again. "What's the Phoenix crime lab doing looking into one of my cold cases?"

160

My heart shuddered in my chest. I remembered this guy well, and I hadn't called *him*, just someone who worked on their cold cases. He'd been the detective who supposedly looked into Fred's disappearance. I'd called to talk to someone about the prostitute who was murdered right after Fred disappeared. I'd been hoping to talk to someone other than the incompetent fool who had handled, or mishandled, both cases.

Trying to mask my frustrated sigh with a cough, I answered with as much patience as I could muster up. "We recently had a murder similar to one of yours about five years ago. I was hoping to get a copy of your cold case file. Maybe we can clear them both up."

"That case was a long time ago. I've had a lot of cases since then. I can't remember every little detail about all of them. What exactly are you looking for?" His tone was slightly suspicious. The man hadn't changed in the years since I dealt with him except to become even more belligerent.

This conversation wasn't going as I'd hoped it would. He wasn't going to make this easy for me. "Look Detective, I'm just trying to solve a murder, maybe two. I was hoping we could help each other."

"How did you find out about this case? It's been in the cold files for years." My experience with the man told me he hadn't worked the case very hard at the time it happened. He probably didn't consider it important enough to pursue beyond a few weeks, if that long.

I avoided answering his question directly. "Don't you enter unsolved cases into the national data base, hoping to find similar cases to find other leads?" Of course, that isn't how I knew about the case, but I couldn't tell him that. I also couldn't tell him I'd hacked their system years ago. "I'd just like to know what prints or fibers were found at the scene. Are you going to help me, or not?"

He was quiet for so long I thought he'd hung up on me,

but he finally answered. "Not. I have enough cases of my own without trying to solve a case for some stupid lab rat in Phoenix."

"I'm not a lab..." I started to explain that I'm a forensic scientist, but he'd already slammed the phone in my ear. So much for inter-agency cooperation, I thought. He might not be willing to help me solve my case, but if I could get my hands on his case file with all the evidence, especially any fingerprints, or lack of prints, I might be able to help solve his case. Somehow I doubted he'd kept copies of any smudges though. Like Detective Roberts, this man probably blamed the crime scene tech for any smudges, and threw them out. I'd been hoping to have someone better to work with.

I could still hack into the Kansas City PD system to see if the information I wanted was there, but that could cause a whole different set of problems, and I didn't need the hassle. More importantly, any information I got through hacking wouldn't be admissible in court. First and foremost I wanted to nail Eddie for any and all crimes he's committed. I needed to know when and how he had removed his fingerprints. If indeed, that's what he has actually accomplished.

~~~

Mr. Watkins brought another cold case for me to work on in my 'spare' time, but unfortunately it wasn't the one case both Rafe and I wanted. Requesting a specific case though would pose more questions than I could answer. Rafe's captain might let him pick the cases he wanted to work on, but I knew Mr. Watkins wouldn't be as accommodating. I'm also sure he wouldn't be happy with me if he found out that I'd called the KCPD about one of their cases. He jealously guarded his authority, and he would see my call as usurping it.

By Friday I wasn't close to solving that cold case or

proving Eddie killed my parents. The case was almost as old as me, and several of the witnesses had passed away since the crime took place. Rafe was as frustrated as I was, but it looked like this was one case that wasn't going to be solved. It made me feel totally incompetent.

Tessa was moving into an apartment in my complex, but in a different building. The Friday night gang, along with her parents, was helping her move the next day. She had even less to move than I did since she had always lived at home. "I'm so excited about tomorrow," she whispered as we walked into the bar for happy hour. "But I'm embarrassed, too."

I was confused. "What are you embarrassed about?"

"All these people are helping me move my stuff, but my folks and I alone could do it in an hour. All I have is my bedroom set, the couch Mom is giving me so she has an excuse to buy a new one, and my clothes. These people are going to think I'm such a dork."

"Buy the pizza and beer, and no one is going to complain. The less you have to move, the less work they have to do." She still looked so dejected I laughed. "Tessa, do you remember the first time you came to my apartment? What did we sit on?"

She laughed with me at the memory. "All you had were two big floor pillows. You were still waiting for the delivery guys to bring your bedroom set."

"I wasn't embarrassed, Tessa, I was ashamed," I admitted. "I'm twenty-eight years old, and that's all I had to show for my life so far. You didn't care how much furniture I had. You just wanted to be my friend." Hot tears prickled behind my eyes again, and I gave her a quick hug. I understood what she had meant when she called us sisters by heart. I'd never felt this close to anyone in my life.

"Look at it this way," I had to change the subject or we'd both end up in tears. "Now we have an excuse to go shopping again. You're going to need to do a lot of that to fill your apartment."

She linked her arm through mine, a big smile spreading across her face. "Shop 'til we drop, girl."

"We'll have all afternoon Sunday," I laughed.

"What are you two cooking up?" Rafe come up behind us, putting an arm around each of us as we joined the others already there.

Butterflies fluttered in my stomach. He'd kept his distance this week. I didn't know what he was going to do now. Why did he have to complicate things by saying he's in love with me? Just thinking about it made my stomach hurt.

"We're going shopping on Sunday for all the stuff I need in my new home." Tessa's answer had me cringing inwardly. I was hoping she wouldn't invite the guys to go with us. I should have known better. As if reading my thoughts, she immediately posed the question when Joe joined us. He looked a little wary about spending the afternoon shopping with two women, giving me hope that he would decline, and Rafe would follow suit. I was doomed to be disappointed though. He wrapped Tessa in a bear hug. "Maybe I can give a little masculine advice," he teased, trying to sound enthusiastic. "How about it, Rafe? You game?"

Even before he spoke, I knew what his answer would be. "Sure, why not? Sounds interesting."

His blatant lie made me laugh. Shopping with two women wasn't exactly his idea of a fun Sunday afternoon. "We won't hold it against you if you have something else to do. Tessa and I can handle it on our own."

She poked me in the ribs. She wanted the guys to go along as much as I didn't want them to go, and poor Joe was torn. Shopping wasn't his idea of fun anymore than it was Rafe's, but he wanted to spend the afternoon with

Tessa.

"How about a compromise," Rafe suggested. "You girls go shopping, and we'll meet you later for dinner. Sound good?"

Tessa was a good sport and agreed. It was my turn to want to decline. Spending all this time with Rafe wasn't a good idea. I just didn't know how to wiggle out of it. Maybe something would come to mind before Sunday.

Tessa was ready to leave when I did, and of course Joe and Rafe followed us out, but for completely different reasons. I thought it was sweet the way Joe wanted to be with her. Rafe was just irritating me.

"Casey, you can stop right there," he started before I could even say anything when I got out of my Jeep. "We don't know where Eddie's been all day or what he's been up to. I'm checking your apartment, so get over it." His tone was tired and world weary.

"Okay, just do it. I'm tired, and I want to go to bed."

"Someone of lesser character could take that as an invitation." He laughed when I swatted his arm.

"You know exactly what I meant, and it wasn't an invitation. Just get it done, and leave me alone." I waited at the door as instructed.

He chuckled, but made a thorough search of my apartment. Joining me at the door again, he stepped close, invading my personal space, something he took delight in doing. "Why are you resisting so hard? You know how I feel about you even though you don't want it to be true. I'm trying to be patient, and I'm trying to keep you safe. I just wish I could go back in time, and protect you when this first started." He was so close I could feel his warm breath on my face.

I tried to step away, but I was already leaning against the door. There was no place for me to go. "You couldn't protect me then, and you can't put me in bubble wrap to keep me safe now. The only thing that will do that, is putting Eddie away for good."

"You think I don't know that?" He ran his fingers through his hair causing it to stand on end. An unexplainable urge had me reaching up to run my own fingers where his had just been to put his mussed hair back in place.

He took my hand, bringing it to his lips, kissing my palm and rolling my fingers over the spot he'd just kissed. The simple act was more intimate than the few kisses we'd shared so far. My stomach fluttered. I was still backed up to the door unable to get some breathing room between us. "Back up, Rafe; let me move." My voice was just a breathless whisper, but it was all I could muster up right then.

"I'm not going away, Casey. You might as well get used to it. I'll see you in the morning." He gave me a quick kiss, and was out the door before I could come up with a response. "Lock the door," he called as it clicked shut behind him.

~~~

As expected, it didn't take but a couple of hours to move Tessa's things the next morning. Ron and Gina Gordon were good sports, letting the guys do all the work. I'm certain they were secretly pleased with all the friends Tessa had, and they obviously approved of Joe. As soon as the pizza and beer were gone, most of the guys wandered off leaving Joe and Rafe behind with Tessa and me. Wishing Rafe would leave with the others didn't do any good. He wasn't going anywhere.

I stayed as far away from him as possible while Tessa and I arranged her few pieces of furniture, and made a list of all the things she needed to make this her home. The list was long. "Why don't we get a jump on our shopping, and do some today?" I suggested. That would serve two purposes; Rafe and Joe didn't want to get roped in on that chore, and I would be rid of Rafe, at least for a few hours. "We can hit the secondhand stores today, and make it to the *Ikea* store tomorrow after church." Going to church had become important to me again.

I could see the looks of horror the guys shared and couldn't stop the small smile of victory from tweaking my lips upward. "You can't get rid of me that easily," Rafe whispered a few minutes later as we all left Tessa's new apartment. The guys had agreed secondhand stores might hold some interest for them, and had decided to join us.

"Let's take separate trucks," Joe suggested. "That way we'll have plenty of room for all your bargains." They could have been plotting this for all I knew. Joe wanted to be alone with Tessa, even if it was in his truck as we drove to all the secondhand stores.

My stomach churned. Being with Rafe in a group was bad enough, but to be alone with him in the confines of his truck was a different matter. I would be a captive audience if he started to get romantic. Fortunately his truck had bucket seats, and the console would be between us. Even at five feet seven, the high step into his truck was a stretch. Before I could attempt to climb into the high cab on my own, his big hands came to rest on my waist, easily lifting me up.

Goosebumps tingled along my spine when his warm breath whispered against my neck, and he placed a kiss below my ear. This was exactly why I didn't want to be alone with him. He was always doing something like this. Little touches, a peck on my neck, holding my hand when we walked. I couldn't get him to stop. I could hear him chuckle as he walked around the front of his truck. He knew exactly what he was doing to my nervous system each time he did this. I didn't want to become addicted to his touch.

Three hours later we made it back to the apartment complex with Tessa's treasures. She'd found some lamps to go on the end tables she'd found in one of the antique stores in downtown Glendale. They weren't exactly antiques, but they were sturdy and in good shape. "I was hoping to find an armoire like yours, Casey. I'll have to keep looking. Things change all the time in these stores." The prospect of more bargain hunting thrilled her, and disappointed the guys. There was a plus after all. It was my turn to chuckle when they both groaned. I guess they'd had their fill of secondhand stores for a long time.

"Shopping makes me hungry," Joe announced. "Let's get something to eat. How about Frederico's?" We'd finished moving all of Tessa's treasures into her apartment. She was still shy of dishes, silverware and some small furniture, but we'd take care of that tomorrow.

"Sounds great!" Rafe took my hand. "I'm starving."

I held back. I didn't want to go there if there was the possibility of seeing Eddie again. I didn't know his schedule, but the chance that he would be working on a Saturday evening was pretty high. "Why don't we try something different?" I suggested. Declining all together wouldn't work. Rafe would just sweep me along with the rest of them, overriding my decision.

Tessa tugged on Joe's hand when he started toward the door. "That sounds like a good idea. We don't want to get into a rut, always going to the same place. There are a lot of different restaurants in town. Let's give them a try." I sent her a smile of gratitude. She knew exactly why I wanted to go somewhere else, but didn't put it into words.

By the time we finished eating, I was ready to call it a day. After years of a solitary life and having little interaction with other people, the flurry of activity that surrounded me since moving back to Phoenix still wore me down. I gave Tessa a hug, promising to see her for church the next morning; I headed outside with Rafe right beside me. My building was just next door, but he insisted on driving me there instead of letting me walk.

"Until we know his schedule, and just how secure this parking lot is, I don't want you walking around alone, especially after dark." We both knew Eddie could be out there waiting for his chance to confront me again. How that confrontation would turn out was anyone's guess. Frustration must be building up in him, and there was no telling where that would lead. The fact that I hadn't been back to Frederico's since I discovered he worked there would only add to his frustration.

The next morning the guys were waiting for us when Tessa and I arrived at church. She was thrilled; I wasn't sure how I felt about it. Rafe was inserting himself into every part of my life. After a quick lunch, Tessa and I took off for a round of shopping like none other while the guys headed somewhere to watch sports. By five o'clock we were ready to meet up again to show off all Tessa had bought.

"I don't know how you did all this in just a few hours." Joe shook his head in wonder. "Are you through now?"

"Well, there are still a few pieces I want to get, but it's going to take time to find just the right thing," she hedged. She was also going to have to stop spending in order to pay the rent. She'd confided to me while we were out that her parents hadn't expected her to pay them rent even after she started working full time. This was the first time she had real bills to pay. That was going to be a learning experience for her.

"So how about some food? I don't know about you girls, but I'm starved." Rafe could out-eat anyone I'd ever seen, and didn't seem to gain an ounce. "You up for some of Frederico's enchiladas?"

I started to shake my head, but he stopped me. "He won't be there," he whispered as he moved me away from Tessa and Joe. They were caught up in their own conversation and didn't notice us.

"How do you know?" I whispered back, my lips a little too close to his as he'd bent his dark head near to mine.

"Joe and I went there for a beer while we waited for our ladies," he explained. "Eddie wasn't there. It must be his day off."

My stomach churned. Was it because he called me 'his lady' or something else? "You didn't say anything to Frederico, did you?" If Eddie thought we were causing him trouble at work, it could be disastrous for all concerned.

Rafe gave me a look that said he wasn't that stupid, and I let myself relax. Rafe is a good cop; he knew better than to let a suspect know he was a suspect.

"Whenever you two love birds get through making out over there, could we go get something to eat?" Joe called out. My face turned all shades of red causing them to laugh.

The evening was fun, and I even forgot about Eddie working at my favorite restaurant. Now if I could only find out what his schedule was, I wouldn't worry every time someone suggested we go to Frederico's.

CHAPTER FIFTEEN

A crime wave of sorts hit Phoenix over the weekend; burglaries, robberies, muggings, even a carjacking. I would think Eddie had something to do with this except for one thing. There was no violence involved. Even the muggings and carjacking were violence free. That certainly wasn't Eddie's MO. The more violent, the better he liked it.

The car that had been jacked turned up at the Mexican border two days later. Border Patrol had been alerted to watch for it. Stolen cars either ended up in chop shops and were sold for parts, or were driven across the border and sold there. Either way, the owner was out a lot of money, and so was the insurance company. The guys driving the car were illegals, so I wasn't sure if they would be tried here or just deported. Immigration is a touchy subject all around the country, but especially in the Border States.

As the week went on so did the crime wave hitting Phoenix and the surrounding towns. By Friday night there were two murders to investigate. Even though the murders in themselves were violent, they weren't of the caliber I'd come to expect from Eddie. Evidence was even collected leading back to the suspects. I couldn't believe Eddie had gone this long without committing some atrocity.

My search of back papers for any information about Fred had been fruitless so far. There were a lot of papers in Kansas, and it had been years since Fred disappeared. Even searching the internet was proving to be time consuming, and my evenings were no longer free. I was still trying to decide how I felt about this Friday night as Tessa and I entered the bar for happy hour. Rafe and Joe wouldn't be there until later since they were tied up with the latest shooting.

I planned on putting in an appearance, staying only long enough to have something to eat, and then head home. This could be the night to do some internet searches as long as I wasn't called in to work on the murder that had taken place earlier in the day.

An hour and a half later, I'd had a virgin margarita, a diet coke and all the appetizers I could handle. "It's been a long week, Tessa, and I'm tired. I'm going home." I had to shout to be heard over the noise in the bar.

"No! You can't leave." She gripped my arm like her life depended on it.

"Why can't I?" I looked at her suspiciously. She'd never acted like this before.

"Well, I, ah, they..."

Guilt was written all over her face. "Let me guess, Rafe. What did he say?"

"Ah." She looked around wildly, hoping he would materialize out of nowhere. When he didn't, she looked at me again. "He just didn't want you leaving alone. Joe didn't want me to either."

"Fine, we can leave together." I stood up, hoping she would follow me.

"No!" She grabbed my arm again to keep me from moving. "That's not it. He, ah, well, they didn't want us leaving until they got here."

"Is that so? What happens if they end up working all night? Are we supposed to stay here that long? I'm tired. I'm not going to sit here waiting for some man to escort me home. I am fully capable of taking care of myself. I'll have the bouncer walk me out, not because Rafe said I should, but because it's the sensible thing to do." I slid off the stool. "I'm going to strangle him," I muttered, only to have Tessa take my arm again, this time gently.

"Don't be mad, Casey. He cares about you. He doesn't want to see you get hurt."

"Why would he think I would get hurt?" Just how much had he told her and Joe? I wasn't just going to strangle him. I was going to torture him first.

"That guy who's stalking you. What if he's watching? He could follow you." Her voice shook with barely concealed fear. Somehow the noise level had tapered off while we talked, and she didn't have to yell.

"He can't get past the gate at the complex, so once I'm through there, I'll be safe." I knew this wasn't exactly the truth. If he was quick, he could sneak through when the gate was open for a car. There were many ways he could get into the complex. I just hoped he wouldn't try, but in case he did, I always had my gun. I wasn't afraid to use it either.

"Please, stay a little while longer," she pleaded. "If they don't come soon, I'll leave with you. I promise. I know you're tired, but Joe said he would try to be here before eight, at the latest."

A glance at my watch told me he still had a half hour before that deadline. "Okay," I relented. "I'll stay until eight, but then I'm going home, with or without my bodyguard."

With two minutes to spare, the men walked through the door looking tired and a little grim. Joe's face lit up when he saw Tessa sitting at the near empty table. Rafe wasn't as luminous as he pulled up another high chair and plopped down beside me with a sigh of relief.

"Are you through at the scene? Do I need to go in?" I wasn't sure what had happened. If there was going to be a backlog of evidence to be processed, I'd rather get started now. The sooner we got it going the faster the suspects would be caught.

He shook his head. "Not necessary. We got them all. In fact, the ones directly involved are in the morgue, and there were enough eyewitnesses to close the case. There won't be any trial."

I sat up straighter. "What happened?" This wasn't exactly the place to be discussing an ongoing investigation, but if everyone was dead, I guess it didn't really matter.

"A bar fight escalated, pouring out into the parking lot. First guy shot the second guy. Then that guy's friends pulled their guns. It was like 'The Gunfight at the O.K. Corral' all over again. Only this time we don't have many survivors. Five dead, at least ten wounded, the bar nearly wrecked in the fight, and multiple cars full of bullet holes." He gave a tired sigh. "It all started because the first guy took exception to his girl flirting with someone else. Now they're all resting in the morgue along with two of their friends. It could have been worse; the bar was full when it started. Most of them took off when it escalated. From what we could gather, this isn't the first time the three main characters have gotten into it. Just the first time there was any gun play."

He picked up my hand, bringing it to his lips. "Thanks for sticking around. I wasn't sure what we were going to find or how long this would take, but I didn't want you going home alone."

My heart pounded with the intimate kiss he planted on my palm curling my fingers over the spot like he'd done before. He didn't make a public display of affection, knowing I would object. Only those closely watching us would even notice. "Rafe, I don't need you to walk me home every night. I know better than anyone what he's capable of, and I don't take chances." I couldn't make my voice work much above a whisper, and he had to lean close to hear.

He was still holding my hand, drawing circles on the back. "Well, I'm just learning all he's capable of, and it scares me to death. I keep telling you that you aren't alone any longer. We're all here to help you. That's what friends are for. If you walk through any parking lot alone after dark, you're taking chances."

I was having a hard time concentrating on what he was saying, and coming up with a credible argument. "I don't want anyone else involved and possibly getting hurt." My voice was more breathless than I would like, but there was nothing I could do about it as long as he continued to play with my hands.

He didn't bother to hide the small smile playing around his full lips. "As long as others are aware of the circumstances, they'll be on alert, and no one will get hurt."

I tried to pull my hands away from him, but he tightened his grip. "How can you even say no one will get hurt after the carnage you saw tonight? All those people involved knew each other, and what could happen, and they still died."

"They died because they were playing with fire. That girl...woman," he corrected when I raised an eyebrow. "She knew her boyfriend was the jealous type, but she flirted with the other guy anyway. He knew her boyfriend was jealous, but flirted anyway. And the boyfriend knew she was a flirt, and the other guy wouldn't stop her from flirting with him. It's unfortunate that two friends stepped into the middle of it and had to pay with their lives. Not one of them used any kind of caution. Do you really think a bunch of policemen and women will be that stupid?"

"Of course not, but that doesn't mean they will be on alert full time. Besides, Eddie isn't going to pick a fight in front of a bunch of police types. Do you really think *he's* that stupid? He's going to wait until he can pick me off without any risk to himself."

He squeezed my hands. "You just made my point. You have to stay in a crowd. That way he can't get at you." He was so smug I wanted to bop him upside the head.

This time he let go of my hands when I tugged at them. "Happy hour is long over, and everyone is tired. Can we leave now?" I stood up to emphasize my intention. Most of the others had already left. Tessa and I could have left with any number of them, and not been alone in the parking lot. The guys just wanted an excuse for us to wait for them.

~~~

He pounded the steering wheel with his fist. "How'd he make it here so fast?" He watched as the two men entered the bar. "My timing was off. No! This isn't my fault. It was a good plan, and it should have taken them longer to clear the scene. Unless of course, he's as sloppy as every other cop I've ever seen." He chuckled at that thought. It was his experience that cops were generally lazy, taking the easy way out to solve a crime. He didn't think Rafe would be any different. That had always been to his benefit, until today. He hit the steering wheel again.

"I'm getting damn tired of waiting, Jennifer," he muttered in the empty car. "I'm getting tired of this game you're playing, and you're going to be sorry you put me through this." He waited some more, hoping she'd come out soon although it probably wouldn't do him any good. Rafe would be right by her side. He'd taken time off from that stupid job hoping to catch her alone. He should have known better. Now the boss man was going to be on him for calling in sick on a busy Friday night, all for nothing.

A few minutes later, Jennifer walked out of the bar with Rafe and two other people, another cop and the young woman he'd seen with Jennifer several times when he'd been watching her.

"He'll follow her home then go inside with her." He was talking to himself more and more lately, and sometimes it worried him. "But who else am I supposed talk to? Jennifer won't let me get close to her."

He drove slowly out of the dark parking lot, following them, but not close enough to draw attention. Parking along the street, he watched as the four cars went through the gate. It closed so fast each car had to stop to enter a code. He wasn't sure what would happen if a big truck tried to get through. Would the gate close when it was half way through? Someday he'd have to test that theory. First he had to get the gate code. He didn't know if each apartment came with its own code, or if it was one code for everyone. Maybe he needed to bring binoculars sometime, and try to see what each person punched in.

That was for another night. Right now he was heading home to his little slice of heaven. He chuckled. The extended living hotel was as close to a home as he had for now. "She'll pay for that, too." Everything that had happened to him was all her fault, and she was going to pay.

~~~

I'd given up trying to stop Rafe from searching my apartment every time he came home with me. I'm not sure what he thought I did when he wasn't there, and I didn't want to ask. I waited as patiently as possible until he joined me at the door again, stepping close enough that I could feel the warmth from his body reaching out to me. Except for the years Eddie was locked up, I'd never felt as safe as I did when Rafe was with me. *What's with that?* I wondered.

Putting my hand on his chest with the intention of pushing him away, I surprised myself when that hand wrapped itself around his neck. Lowering his head, his full lips claiming mine in a heart-stopping kiss. When he finally lifted his head, I could feel his heart pounding against mine, matching it beat for beat. He rested his forehead against mine, looking at me with those usually unreadable dark eyes. There was no doubt what he was feeling at the moment. "I'm sorry it was so late when we got to the bar, Cas." His voice was slightly breathless. "I know you wanted to get home early."

With my back still braced against the wall, I was glad

for its support. After that kiss, I wasn't sure I could stand on my own. How had he wormed his way through the barriers I'd always thought were firmly in place? I just nodded, temporarily unable to find my voice.

Drawing a shaky breath, he stepped away, letting his hand slide down my arm capturing my hand in his. Sitting down on the couch, he pulled me against him, leaning his head against the high back. Dark whiskers shadowed his firm jaw giving him a rakish look that tugged at my emotions. Rafe was nothing like the soft-spoken, gentle Fred, but I couldn't deny the pull he had on me.

"What are your plans once we've got Eddie behind bars?" He didn't bother to open his eyes when he spoke.

I must have taken too long to answer because he gave my shoulders a little squeeze. "Are you sleeping?"

"No, just thinking about your question. I haven't thought that far ahead. I've never had that luxury. I always had to concentrate on staying one step ahead of him. This is my last stand. I've never thought beyond this."

"Would you think about it now? I don't want you to leave." He tilted my face up to his, placing the gentlest kiss on my lips. "When I told you I'm in love with you, I meant it. I want..."

I placed my fingers over his lips to keep him from saying more. "I can't think about anything else until Eddie is made to pay for everything he's done; everything, not just my parents, but that young social worker, Fred, the prostitute in Kansas City, and the one here. Even that police sergeant, and all the ones we know nothing about yet. He needs to pay, and until he does, my life isn't my own."

"Are you still hoping Fred is alive? Are you still in love with him?" He was actually holding his breath, waiting for my answer.

"I know he isn't alive, Rafe. I knew that when he

178

disappeared. I'll always love him, but I'm not in love with him. He was the first person I told what had happened to me, and he didn't look at me like I was some kind of freak or wounded animal. I'll always be grateful for that."

"Okay, I won't press for anything else right now. Just think about what you want to do when this is over. Because it's going to be over," he emphasized. The silence stretched out, but not uncomfortably. Something had changed in our relationship, and I wasn't sure how I felt about it. I just knew that Rafe was becoming more and more important to me with each passing day.

I was still hoping to do a computer search for any human remains found in the Kansas City area, but I was so comfortable I didn't want to move. When I opened my eyes later, blinking against the bright lights in the room, it took a minute for things to register. Moving slowly, I lifted my head from Rafe's shoulder, sneaking a peek at him. His dark head rested on the high back of the couch, his eyes closed. His soft snores could barely be heard.

The clock on the wall in the kitchen read two-fifteen. How had that happened? We'd fallen asleep almost five hours ago. Standing up carefully so I wouldn't wake him, I picked up the afghan I kept on the end of the couch, and covered him. I was afraid to move him or take off his shoes. He looked so peaceful, I didn't have the heart to wake him up and send him home. If Tessa discovered he'd slept here, I wasn't sure what she'd think, but I had a clear conscience. We'd done nothing wrong. I quietly closed the door to my bedroom. Another five hours of sleep would be good for both of us.

CHAPTER SIXTEEN

I was just stepping out of the shower when my cell phone chirped on the night stand beside my bed. Before I even looked at the display, I knew it would be Tessa. She must have seen Rafe's truck in the parking lot. The explanations would come now, but I refused to feel guilty for something I hadn't done.

"Are you okay?" Her panicked voice caught me off guard when I was expecting recriminations.

"Of course. Why?"

"Oh, thank you, God!" She sighed in relief. "I was going to go for a run on the track here in the complex when I saw Rafe's truck. I was afraid that stalker had somehow gotten in, and you called Rafe for help."

"No, he fell asleep on the couch while we were talking. I didn't have the heart to wake him." I waited to see if she would jump to the wrong conclusion. I should have known better. Leave it to Tessa not to think the worst of any given situation.

She gave another sigh of relief. "That gave me a scare. You want to join me in a run?" That was it, no questions, or accusations. If only everyone was as sweet as Tessa, this would be a wonderful world.

"Thanks, but I just got out of the shower. I don't even know if Rafe is still sleeping. He was really tired last night." I still had a towel wrapped around my head, and another one around my body, dripping water on the bathroom floor where I'd taken the phone to answer it.

"Yeah, Joe was tired, too, and didn't stay long last night." She sounded disappointed. "I guess it was a hard week for everyone, but he said he'd be over this morning. What do you and Rafe have planned for the day?"

"Nothing, he's going home as soon as he wakes up." At least I hoped I could convince him to leave. I needed time to think about his questions. I really didn't know what I was going to do once Eddie was put away for good.

"Okay, I'm going for my run so I'll be ready when Joe comes over. See you later." I laughed as I put down the phone. She took everything at face value.

By the time I was dressed I could smell coffee brewing in my kitchen. Rafe was up. I didn't bother with makeup or the colored contacts. He knew the true color of my eyes, and I didn't need them to see. I was still fluffing my hair as I walked out.

"Don't you keep food in this place?" He closed the refrigerator door as I entered the kitchen. "You don't have anything to eat." When he turned to look at me, he gave me a broad smile, his dimples winking at me. "There are those beautiful green eyes I love so much."

Ignoring his comment, I tried to avoid the kiss he aimed at my lips. "I haven't been shopping for a couple of weeks. I'm going today." Unable to completely avoid him, I submitted to one of his magnificent kisses.

When he finally lifted his head, we were both a little breathless. "Sorry I fell asleep last night." He didn't sound the least bit sorry. "I guess I was more tired than I realized. Let's go to breakfast then we can go shopping." He reached for my hand, but this time he let me sidestep him.

"*I'll* go shopping," I emphasized. "I have things I need to do today."

"Yeah? Like what?" He relaxed against the counter, while the coffee finished brewing.

I took two cups out of the cupboard, setting them beside the pot, and got the flavored creamer from the fridge. "Just some computer research I want to do," I hedged. "Nothing to do with a case. I also have to clean around here," I quickly added when he started to volunteer to help with the research. I didn't think he'd volunteer to

181

help clean.

"That's why I pay a cleaning lady," he said cheerfully. "She even picks up groceries, when she sees the empty cupboards and fridge. I could have her come over once a week."

"Stop trying to take over my life," I said crossly. "I don't need a keeper." I crossed my arms over my chest and scowled at him only making him laugh.

"There's that feisty fourteen girl I was so fond of. She wasn't going to let anyone push her around or tell her what to do."

"That fourteen-year-old girl is long gone, but she's the only reason I've survived this long."

He grew serious. "I know. I'm sorry I caused those green eyes to cloud over with thoughts of the past. That's not what I was trying for." He pulled me against him, ignoring my feeble attempt to stay out of his reach. "You are so much more than that young girl, and I love you all the more for it." He kissed the tip of my nose.

"I wish you would stop saying that! You don't even know who I am now. You can't be in love with me." I stomped my foot barely missing his bare toes. Sometime in the night he woke up long enough to shed his boots and socks.

"Each day I learn a little more about you and it only makes me...you know." His teasing grin set the butterflies in my stomach fluttering.

"Damn it, Rafe. You have to stop this madness. There can't be anything between us."

"There certainly can and is." He was just as stubborn as me. "I'm not afraid of Eddie for myself, but for you he scares me to death. He is evil personified, and I don't want him anywhere near you. I just want him put away for good."

"Then we have the same goal in mind. Let's work

together towards that end, and let the chips fall where they may with the rest of it."

"My goal has a lot more to do with you than him," he said. "It's a long term goal, very long term. I told you last night I don't want you to leave Phoenix once he's behind bars, and I meant it. Please think about it." When he dipped his head this time, I let him capture my lips washing all thoughts of Eddie from my mind. The man certainly knew how to kiss.

Several minutes later, we were both gasping for air, and he stepped away from me. "I think I need a shower." He gave me a crooked smile bringing only one dimple into play.

"Then go home. I'll see you tomorrow."

"Last time I fell asleep at your place you let me shower, you even had a new toothbrush I could use. Why not now?" He lifted one eye brow, making that question mark above his dark eyes.

This was getting much too intimate for my wellbeing. "Give me a break, Rafe."

He laughed, heading for the door after picking up his boots. "Didn't I hear your phone earlier? Something come up at work?" He turned to look at me.

I shook my head. "Tessa saw your truck when she went for a run."

"Uh, oh. That isn't good. Does she hate us now?"

"Of course not. She was afraid my 'stalke'" somehow got in during the night, and I had called you."

"What did you tell her?"

"The truth. We were talking, and in a moment of silence you fell asleep. Unlike most people, Tessa is very trusting, and she believed me."

He'd walked up to me while I was speaking, lifting my face to his. "I'm glad. I know you don't want her to think badly of you, and I wouldn't do anything to bring that about." He placed another kiss on my lips, then turned to leave again. "Tell Tessa not to run while it's still dark. It isn't safe. I doubt Joe would approve." Before I could let him know he and Joe weren't our keepers, he was out the door. "Lock this," he called with a chuckle. I could hear him bounding down the stairs.

"Grrr." Somehow he always managed to get in the last word. A smile spread across my face in spite of my frustration. He sure knew how to kiss a girl crazy.

~~~

Washers and dryers were included in each apartment, so I put in a load before heading for the grocery store. Rafe's suggestion of a cleaning lady who also bought groceries sounded next to heaven, but as yet I didn't want to spend the extra money. After so many years living on a shoestring, that was all I knew. I didn't want to end up in debt.

Sitting in the grocery store parking lot, I examined the few cars there this early in the morning. This had been my habit for so long it was second nature. If anything had seemed suspicion, I would just drive away, and choose another store. I didn't shop at the same store each week, especially now that I knew Eddie was in town. Why make myself an easy target? All looked normal.

An hour later it wasn't as easy to check the multitude of cars in the parking lot to see if anyone was lurking inside. It would help to know what kind of car Eddie had, or if he even had one. Something I needed to check out. I made a mental note to myself.

After scanning the lot and close to the building, I headed for my Jeep, my head swiveling like I was at a tennis match. "You having a party or something?" I let out a yelp when someone spoke right behind me.

I whirled around to face Eddie, keeping the grocery cart between us. Somehow he'd managed to sneak up on me just when I thought I was being so careful. As though

184

reading my thoughts, he laughed. "Don't be too hard on yourself, Sis. It's purely accidental that I saw you. Of course, I was looking for you."

Ignoring him, I turned my back, and continued walking to my Jeep. I didn't think he'd try anything in a parking lot full of people. I told myself that my yelp was simply from being startled, not because I was afraid of him. My pounding heart said something else.

"Oh, that's right; your name is Casey now, isn't it? Jennifer is a much prettier name, but I'll call you Casey for now. I asked if you're having a party." His voice hardened. "That's a lot of groceries for just one person. But maybe you're feeding Rafe now, too?" He made it sound like a question.

"Go away and leave me alone. I don't know you." My voice was loud enough that a couple heading for the store stopped, the man giving Eddie the evil eye.

"You all right, Miss? He bothering you?"

"She's my sister, so butt out, mister." Eddie glared at the man, and his wife gripped his arm. I could read the fear in her eyes.

I shook my head at the couple. "He's delusional. I don't know him." I had my cell phone in my hand as I pushed the cart to my Jeep. "I'm calling 9-1-1 right now."

Eddie whirled around. "Someday you're going to pay for this, Jennifer," he hissed. "You're going to be sorry." He disappeared around the corner of the building. I was hoping to get a glimpse of the car he was driving, but I only heard a loud engine, probably with no muffler, rumble to life.

"Are you going to be okay?" The couple walked over to me, looking worried. "You really should call the police. Someone should follow you home to make sure he doesn't try to follow you."

"Thanks for your help. Like I said, he's delusional, but probably harmless." I nearly chocked on those last words.

"I'll watch to make sure I'm not followed." I loaded my groceries in the back end of my Jeep as fast as I could; hoping Eddie wouldn't be waiting for me somewhere. He probably already knew where I lived though.

I was still shaking a few minutes later when I watched the gate swing shut behind my car. It closed swiftly, but I always made sure no other vehicle tried to squeeze through behind mine or a pedestrian tried to sneak through while the gate was open. I hoped the other residents were as watchful. I told myself the reason I was shaking was an overdose of adrenaline, but I knew better. As much as I wanted to put Eddie away, that was how much he terrified me.

For the rest of the day, I jumped at every little sound. I wanted to go for a run, but couldn't force myself to go outside. The encounter with Eddie had set my nerves on edge. I wanted to get his prints, but I didn't want to let him get his hands on me, at least not yet. First, I had to have some evidence of all his crimes.

CHAPTER SEVENTEEN

Rafe and the other detectives were called in on Saturday and Sunday to re-interview witnesses and customers at the bar where the murders had taken place when cell phone pictures and videos had turned up on the Internet and television. They thought they had confiscated all of them, but of course some had squeaked through. Apparently there was another participant in the initial argument, but no one knew who he was, and there were no clear pictures of him. He wasn't a regular at the bar, but had instigated some of the confrontation.

It was almost four by the time Rafe came into the lab Monday afternoon. He looked tired, but his smile lit up his face when he saw me. If we'd been alone, I know he would have kissed me. As it was, he stopped just short of doing that. I'm not sure how I felt about either action, but the butterflies were attacking my stomach.

"Have you been able to figure anything out on those pictures and videos?" he asked.

"The computer techs are still working on them, but the guy you're looking for was either extremely lucky or knew when someone was pointing a cell phone at him. Right now, we mostly have pictures of his back. Unless we get lucky ourselves, we aren't going to be able to identify him from anything we currently have."

"Figured as much," he sighed. "It was worth a try anyway." He changed the subject. "I'm sorry I couldn't make it back Saturday afternoon, and that I missed church yesterday. You do anything exciting? I hope you got groceries, otherwise you're going to starve this week. Speaking of starving, I am. How about dinner?"

With so many questions thrown all together I could pick and choose which ones to answer; he'd never know the difference. "I understand you had to work. You don't have to spend every moment with me." There was no way I was going to tell him Eddie had been at the grocery store.

"So how about dinner?" This time he waited for me to answer.

"Rafe, you've worked all weekend, and you're tired. Go home, and get some rest."

"I still have to eat, and I don't feel like cooking. And I'm starving. I didn't get lunch again today. I think I could eat just about everything on Frederico's menu. Come on." He gave me a teasing smile putting those dimples into play. "Don't make me eat alone." He tried to play on my sympathies.

My stomach twisted. A piping hot bean burrito sounded great, but I didn't want to run into Eddie. I was certain he would say something about Saturday. Guessing my hesitation, he leaned closer. "If he's there, we'll just get takeout. How does that sound?" He kept his voice down so the others wouldn't hear.

"All right, but I can't leave yet. I still have to finish up here."

"No problem. I'll be back at five thirty."

"Ah, no. I'll meet you there."

He'd started to walk out, but came back now. "Why?"

"People are going to start talking about us if we always leave together."

"So?" He frowned.

"I don't want that." Even now I could feel some of the others in the lab watching us.

"Why? We're not doing anything wrong. What are you afraid of?"

Oh boy, where had I heard this before? But there was no anger in his words as there had been in others who said them in the past.

"People always find things to talk about whether we

188

like it or not. When they're talking about you, they're giving someone else a rest." Without another word, he walked out, whistling a jaunty tune.

"Grrrr. He always comes out on top in any argument." I looked around at my coworkers, but they didn't seem to be as interested in this little episode as I'd imagined.

Pouring myself back into my work, the next hour and a half slipped by, and so did the people around me. There was always more work to be done than people to do it. I liked it that way. There wasn't time for unwanted thoughts to intrude.

"Hey, Babe, why are you still working? It's long past quitting time."

I yelped, whirling around and holding out the pen like it was a weapon. Rafe seemed to have appeared out of nowhere to stand beside me. I sagged against the counter.

Taking the pen out of my shaking fingers, he led me to the stool. "Why so jumpy suddenly?" he frowned. "What happened?"

Since Eddie had been able to sneak up on me Saturday, I'd been jumping at shadows, but I wouldn't admit that to him.. "Nothing, I was just concentrating on my work." A guilty expression had to be written all over my face.

"Right. Are you ready to leave? It's six o'clock." Thankfully he let the subject drop.

I looked around the lab, surprised to find we were the only ones there. "Give me a minute to clean up. I thought you were going to be here at five-thirty."

"Got tied up with work. Guess you did, too." He was as hungry as I was, and he hustled me out the door..

Pulling into the parking lot at Frederico's behind Rafe's big truck, my stomach churned uncomfortably. The restaurant wasn't as crowded on a Monday evening. This was only the second time I'd been here since Eddie started working here. I was hoping we'd just get takeout and go home.

Marisol, Frederico's wife, was playing hostess. "Oh, Rafe!" Distress was written on her normally smooth features when she saw us. "You heard what happened to my Frederico?"

Rafe took her hands, starting to lead her to one of the cushioned seats in the waiting area, but she led us through the restaurant to the office in the back instead. "Okay, Marisol. Tell me what happened."

"He was mugged last night when he took the deposit to the bank." She drew a shaky breath. "The person hit him so hard he has a concussion, and he's in the hospital."

I gasped. My first thought, of course, was Eddie. This was right up his alley, fast money, and if someone was hurt, so much the better. Rafe sent me a warning glance before quickly concentrating on Marisol again.

"Where did this happen? Right outside here?" His question convinced me we were thinking the same thing; Eddie did this.

"No," Marisol shook her head. "At the bank. He is always so careful, checking to see if there is anyone around before he opens the car door to put the deposit in the night drop. He said the man came out of nowhere, and hit him over the head. He was unconscious when another customer found him." Tears sparkled in her dark eyes, and she wrung her hands. Her slight Spanish accent grew deeper in her distress. "He didn't have to hit him; Frederico would have given him the money."

"What did the guy look like? Can Frederico identify him?"

She shook her head. "He didn't see the man. He was hit from behind. The man didn't even speak to him, just hit him, and took our money. I don't care about the money." Tears now streamed down her pretty face. "I just want my husband to be okay." She lowered her head to her hands, sobbing softly.

190

My stomach twisted. This was just Eddie's style. How did I prove it though? Like all the other crimes I was certain he'd committed, there was no proof, and no witness to identify him. Someday he had to slip up.

"Is he going to be all right?" I spoke for the first time, reaching out to touch her arm in an effort to comfort her.

"The doctor said yes. He can come home in the morning." Gaining control of her emotions, she looked up. "I'm sorry to burden you with our troubles. Thank you for listening to me blubber." She looked slightly embarrassed now.

"I'll talk to the investigating officers, and we'll stop by tomorrow night to see how Frederico's feeling." Rafe's voice was tight as he held his own emotions in check. "If there's anything we can do, let us know."

She gave a small laugh. "We are short on staff tonight with Frederico in the hospital, and our best waitress refusing to work with..." She stopped for a minute, a dark shadow crossing her face. It disappeared so quickly, I thought maybe I'd imagined it. "Frederico had to fire one of the new busboys," she continued. "But we will manage for tonight, tomorrow Frederico will be home and Stacy will to return to work."

"What was that about?" I whispered, once we were seated at a table. I looked around the sparsely filled dining area. Eddie wasn't among the servers and bussers moving among the tables. "Which busboy did they fire and why? I'm betting it was Eddie."

"You're thinking he's behind this." It was a statement rather than a question.

"Of course, aren't you? If Frederico fired him, Eddie wouldn't think twice about attacking him, and taking his money. Frederico's just lucky he lived through the encounter. Others haven't been so lucky."

~~~

"Over two thousand dollars, not bad for a few minutes

191

work," he gloated. "Better than I made bussing tables for him. Serves him right for firing me just because I missed one busy Friday night, and that stupid waitress didn't like the way I looked at her. She ought to be flattered. Most women are, at least at first." His evil laugh filled the small room. "Too bad it wasn't his old lady who took the deposit to the bank. I would have enjoyed hitting her over the head. She told the old man he shouldn't hire me. She didn't like the way I looked." His lip curled, and his voice was a snide imitation of hers.

Again he realized he was talking to himself more and more all the time. "Maybe I should get that little waitress to come keep me company for a while. She complained about me, but after a while she'd come to like me."

His mind shifted back to the scene at the bank the previous night. It was sweet how easy it had been to sneak up on the old man. Even if he'd seen him, he wasn't worried about being identified. Jennifer wasn't the only one who could use disguises. Besides, he made sure the old man didn't see him. If there had been any other cars around, he would have waited for another night. Most people are creatures of habit, and Frederico was no exception. He always went to the bank right after closing. Maybe I even did him a favor; now he'll be more careful, even get a safe for his place. He chuckled to himself. "I did the old man a public service," he said out loud, his chuckle turning evil again.

Frederico and Marisol weren't that much older than him, but he always thought of anyone older than himself as old. It helped him stay detached. "Nothing personal, old man," he sneered to the image in his mind.

~~~

I paced around my small living room while Rafe searched the rest of my apartment for any sign that Eddie had been there when I already knew he hadn't. "All clear,"

Rafe sat down on the couch, making himself comfortable. "I can't let this go on, I have to stop him." I continued pacing until he stepped into my path.

"We're going to catch him."

"How? When? How many more innocent people have to suffer or die before we do?"

He tried to pull me close, but I was too agitated to let him. I pulled away, continuing my circuit around the living room. "Casey, you have to be patient. We will catch him."

"I've been patient for fifteen years. Isn't that long enough? I can't let this go on just because I'm too much of a coward to let him get his hands on me."

Rafe grabbed me by the shoulders, giving me a little shake. "If you're suggesting what I think you are, you can just forget it!"

I shook my head. "I always knew it could come down to this. If I have to risk my own safety to stop him permanently, then I'm prepared to do just that."

"Do you realize what you're saying?" Now Rafe was pacing. "He'll kill you, but not before he tortures you. You didn't see that young prostitute he killed."

"I've seen every crime scene photo of every person I suspect he's killed. I've experienced firsthand some of the things he's capable of doing. I can't let this go on." My voice was soft, shaking slightly as I relived those horrible years before Eddie was put away.

Rafe pulled me into an embrace, resting his forehead against mine. "You don't know what you're asking me to do," he whispered. "I'm in love with you, and you want me to let that monster get his hands on you?" Before I could say anything his lips closed over mine, soft and intense at the same time.

For just a second I resisted, then let myself go, sinking into him. My arms made their way around his neck, pulling him closer. That was all the invitation he needed. He deepened the kiss, his tongue dueling with mine. Easily lifting me off the floor, he carried me to the couch, cradling me on his lap, never breaking the kiss. When he finally lifted his head, his dark eyes were clouded with passion. "Promise me you won't do anything stupid. We'll figure this out." I wanted to argue, but with him looking at me like that, I couldn't find the words.

Without making that promise, I rested my head against his chest. His heart beat a steady tattoo against my ear. I don't know how long we stayed that way, the whole time my mind racing over possible scenarios that would help us catch Eddie without putting me in the line of fire. There didn't seem to be any way to accomplish that. Eddie wanted me under his control, and he wouldn't give up until that happened. I could only pray that when the time came, I could stop him from hurting me or anyone else ever again.

CHAPTER EIGHTEEN

It was late when Rafe left. We'd stayed on the couch with only the automatic night lights that came on after dark to illuminate the room. I couldn't let him stay all night, even to sleep on the couch, and I finally sent him home. There was no way I could convince Tessa that everything was on the up and up if he stayed over too many times. Innocent or not, appearances could ruin a reputation.

Refusing to let thoughts of Eddie intrude on the peace generated by Rafe's presence, I took a hot shower before climbing into bed. I wondered how 'Gibbs' on *NCIS* would handle Eddie. I couldn't help but laugh at myself. It had been several weeks since I'd compared my life to an episode of my favorite TV show. "I guess I'm evolving," I whispered as sleep claimed me.

By the time I headed for work in the morning I had made up my mind that the next time Eddie confronted me, I would talk to him instead of avoiding him. My cell phone is programed to record conversations, so maybe I could get him to admit guilt for one of his crimes.

Marisol was right; there was no evidence of any kind for the investigating officers to follow. I was ready to leave right on time that night. Rafe was going to see Frederico, and I wanted to go with him. I was shutting down my computers and machines when Tessa walked in.

"You're ready to leave?" She sounded shocked. "I don't even have to beg you not to work overtime?"

I wadded up a piece of paper and threw it at her. "Okay, smart mouth. I don't work overtime every day."

"No, just every other day." She laughed, tossing the paper into the trash, then she grew serious. "Joe told me what happened to Frederico. We're going with you to see how he's doing. He doesn't know who robbed him?"

I shook my head. "No, but maybe talking about it will jog something in his memory. I'm not sure what Rafe and Joe can do, but I know they want to try anyway."

The large gauze patch on the back of Frederico's head was the only sign of what happened. Marisol was keeping a close eye on him and wouldn't let him work. He was moving through the tables, greeting the customers. A broad smile curved his lips when he spotted us. "Welcome, Amigos." He leaned close. "Thank you for listening to my Marisol last night. She was very upset by what happened. Talking to you helped her very much." He kept his voice low as he led us to a table. The mugging hadn't been made common knowledge to most of the customers.

"Can you take a minute to sit with us?" Rafe asked. "I'd like to ask you a few questions."

Instead of a table for four, Frederico changed directions taking us to a larger booth, more separated from the other tables. Once we were all seated, he looked at Rafe and Joe, waiting for their questions. It took several minutes before the staff left us alone. Finally Rafe asked softly, "Have you been able to remember anything more about the robbery? Anything about the person?"

Frederico shook his head, his hands shaking slightly. "I am sorry; all I remember is driving to the bank, and looking to see if there was anyone around. The rest is a blank. The doctor said it's because of the head injury. Whoever did this, hit me very hard. It's a good thing my head is so hard." He tried to make a joke, but quickly grew serious again. "I should have listened to Marisol. She's told me we need to get a safe here, so we can lock up the money, and go to the bank in the morning. She doesn't like me going after dark."

His hands were shaking more now, and Tessa reached across the table, laying her hand gently on his. "No one is blaming you for what happened, especially Marisol.

Maybe it will come back to you when you're well. Right now you need to take care of yourself." At her soothing touch, he began to calm down; his hands stopped shaking.

"What about any employees?" Joe asked. "Marisol said you let one of the busboys go. Have you fired anyone else, any disgruntled employees?" Because Joe had been with us when we saw Eddie was working here, Joe knew he was my "stalker," but had Rafe told him more than that?

"Most of my employees are like family. They have worked for us a long time." He paused; a worried shadow crossing his features. "Because we were shorthanded when Juan was hurt in a car accident, I hired someone I didn't know." He shook his head, a small smile tilting the corners of his mouth. "Again, I should have listened to Marisol. She said not to hire this man; she got a bad feeling from him. I had to let him go, he just wasn't working out." He didn't explain what he meant, but I could guess.

Tessa gasped. "Do you think he's the one who robbed you? Just because you let him go?"

Frederico shrugged. "Anything is possible, but I couldn't swear to it in court. I didn't see who hit me." He sighed in frustration. I wanted to ask him why Eddie always wore gloves when he cleaned up the tables, but couldn't bring myself to discuss him. When the waitress brought our food, Frederico left us to our meal, and conversation turned to lighter matters.

I had to chuckle when Joe led our little caravan heading for our apartment complex. As we went through the gate, each car stopping to put in the code, I watched carefully for any other cars trying to squeak through. Some of the residents grumbled about the gate closing so fast that two cars couldn't get through, but I was glad.

Sitting in Tessa's apartment, Joe looked at Rafe. "What about the bank's surveillance tapes? Did they show anything?"

Rafe shook his head. "Whoever this guy is, he knew

where the cameras were. He kept just out of range; the only thing captured on the video was his hands when he hit Frederico. Most likely he had on some kind of disguise in case someone did see him."

My heart rate stepped up. "You could see his hands? His entire hands?" This could be the break I'd been looking for.

"I suppose so," Rafe shrugged. "Why? What are you thinking?"

"If the flat of his hands show, I might be able to see his fingerprints or a palm print. He also has an odd scar on the back of one hand that we might be able to use as identification."

"Are you talking about the guy Frederico fired?" Tessa frowned at me. "How do you know he has a scar?"

Uh, oh, I'd spoken without thinking. "I saw it when he tried to get in my apartment." That much was true. "That also could explain why he wanted to wear gloves when he worked at the restaurant. He has a long scar across the back of his hand that looks like a bolt of lightning." Eddie had always had a fascination with knives, even if it meant getting cut himself. I couldn't wait to get to work in the morning to see what I could do with the surveillance video.

Rafe walked me to my apartment, taking my hand in the dark. It seemed natural to curl my fingers around his larger ones. "I almost blew it tonight," I said. "I was so excited about maybe being able to have something on Eddie that I just blurted it out about that scar." I shook my head. I was becoming too comfortable; I had to be more careful.

"It's okay, Babe." He squeezed my hand. "You need to think about telling Tessa the truth though."

"The truth is I'm Casey Gibson!" I bristled, trying to pull my hand out of his, but he tightened his grip.

"Yes, you are. That will never change, but there is a

whole lot more to you than you let others see. Tessa won't think less of you if you tell her, and she will understand why you couldn't tell her before. She loves you, and so do I." He dropped his voice seductively with the last words, making my stomach roll and goose bumps travel up my spine.

Any argument I could give was a rehash of those I'd given before, so I remained silent. As always, Rafe insisted on searching my apartment for any sign that someone had been there while I was gone.

"All clear. We're alone at last." He walked out of the bedroom, his dark eyes resting seductively on me. He was standing so close I could feel his warm, spicy breath on my face, the warmth from his body against mine. Within seconds I was practically hyperventilating. He really played a number on my nervous system. With his dark eyes trained on mine, he lowered his head, his lips capturing mine in a slow, exploring kiss. I don't know how we ended up sitting on the couch, but that's where we were when I finally surfaced through a sensual fog.

I was just getting used to him holding my hand, touching me whenever he was close, hugging me every chance he got. His kisses threw me another curve. Holding my gaze captive with his, a small smile tilting those inviting lips upward, when he whispered, "When this is all over, and we have Eddie safely dealt with forever, will you marry me?"

My body jerked like I had just stuck my finger in a light socket, but he wouldn't let me move away. "Just think about it," he whispered. "Now I'd better leave before I get carried away." He kissed me again until there wasn't a coherent thought in my head. It was several minutes, or an hour later, when he finally left, my mind filled with the possibilities Rafe's proposal had presented. I wasn't sure I could do it, but it was certainly tempting.

~~~

Sleep evaded me for a long while, my mind replaying the evening over and over. Could I enhance the bank video enough to see Eddie's fingerprints? If not, would the scar be enough to identify him? Would that even hold up in court? I didn't have the answers. Overriding these questions was the one Rafe asked. I didn't have an answer for that one either.

When my alarm went off in the morning, I felt like I had just drifted off. My eyes were gritty, and my mind was processing at half speed. If I was going to accomplish anything today, I needed to be in top form. A steaming hot shower helped, along with coffee. I stopped on my way to work for a mocha latte. Caffeine was the only thing that was going to keep me going after the fitful night I'd had.

I was playing with the video from the bank when Tessa joined me in the lab. "Girlfriend, when are you going to start working regular hours? You don't have to be here before the sun comes up." She was still trying to get me to car pool with her, especially since we lived in the same complex now.

"I wanted to get a jump start on this video," I answered, keeping my eyes trained on the computer screen.

"Are you able to pick out any prints or the scar?" She joined me in front of the computer.

I let out a frustrated breath, ruffling my bangs that were beginning to get long enough to hang in my face. "No. Surveillance tapes need to be upgraded to hi-definition to really do any good. I can make out the scar, but I doubt it's clear enough to use as any kind of identification. I've tried to clean up the video, but so far it hasn't helped." I stepped back, rubbing my already tired eyes, looking at Tessa for the first time since she came into the lab.

I thought her eyes were going to pop out of her head. "Wow! Your eyes are beautiful! Why haven't I noticed them before?"

My stomach rolled. Still half asleep when I was getting ready for work, I'd forgotten to put in the colored contacts. "Oh, ah, I guess I was in such a hurry to get here this morning, I forgot to put in my contacts."

She laughed, "I never have to worry about forgetting mine. If I don't have them in, I can't find my way out of the bathroom. Why do you wear colored contacts instead of letting people see how beautiful your eyes are?"

On some things I was going to have to stick to the truth. "My eyes are so green people stared at me when I was growing up. It always made me uncomfortable. I decided to tone them down some." That much was the truth. As far back as I can remember, people have commented on my bright green eyes. After I left Phoenix, I didn't want people to remember me. It took a while before I could afford to buy colored contacts to disguise them.

"Well, girlfriend, stop doing it. If my eyes were that color, I'd never want to hide them. With your dark auburn hair and bright green eyes, you look like a lit up Christmas tree."

"Great. Just what I always wanted to be," I laughed. "Maybe this Christmas I can just put on some tinsel, and I won't have to get a tree." She was still laughing a few minutes later when she left for her office.

For a few minutes I considered the upcoming holiday season. Thanksgiving was just around the corner. Would Eddie try something? Before he'd been sent away, holidays had been just as tense as every other day. We never knew what he was going to do. The four years he was locked up, Christmas had been a happy time. We had all tried to put him out of our minds. I'd even succeeded for a while.

Looking back over those years with the eye of an adult, I wonder why my parents never stopped him when he first started acting out. Was there nothing they could do? The law is a funny thing. Until a person commits a crime, the police have their hands tied, even when threats are made. But Eddie had been committing a crime every time he raped me, or broke into a neighbor's house, or tortured and killed an animal. Were they ashamed to admit their son was a monster? Did they think it was just a phase he was going through, that he'd outgrow it?

By the time he'd been committed, my parents were as terrified of him as I was. They tried to convince the doctors not to send him home, that his behavior would start all over again. But the doctors insisted he was 'cured'. He'd been a model patient. We didn't believe them, but there was nothing we could do. For the short time he was home before he killed our parents, we had lived in constant fear. Tension filled our house while we waited for him to explode, and do the unthinkable. That's exactly what happened, too. I often wondered if the doctors ever realized their mistake in releasing him.

Holidays had meant little after I left Phoenix all those years ago. One day was the same as another, just something I needed to survive. I had no family, no friends, until Fred. But he hadn't lived long enough to celebrate any holidays with me. Rafe was trying to talk me into spending Thanksgiving and Christmas with him and his family. The same with Tessa. I still hadn't met Rafe's folks again. Would they recognize me? Like I told Tessa, people always remembered my bright green eyes. Would that trigger their memories? Would they connect me with that young girl? I didn't want to take that chance. Jennifer Miller had ceased to exist a long time ago. Casey Gibson is who I am now and will be forever.

Pushing these thoughts aside, I turned back to the computer screen. No matter what I call myself, until Eddie is put away for good, my life isn't really my own.

CHAPTER NINETEEN

Three days later my heart nearly stopped beating when I drove into the parking lot at my apartment to see Eddie strolling around with Carole Sanders, the complex manager. An evil smile curled his lips, and he gave a slight nod in my direction. His timing was impeccable, as though he had known the exact time to walk through the parking lot so I would see him.

What is he doing here? He could no more afford to rent an apartment here than I could rent a mansion. Would the manager leave him alone to wander around the complex? She was usually very careful with prospective tenants. I hoped she was just as conscientious today.

Locked safely inside my apartment, I rested my head against the door. What would I do if he managed to rent an apartment here? In all these years I had no idea how he had supported himself. I couldn't picture him being frugal, and saving his money. I couldn't even picture him working to support himself. His style was more smash and grab.

Standing at the balcony door, I wished for the first time that my balcony faced the parking lot instead of the common green. Carole always drove prospective tenants around in a golf cart to see the vacant apartments. I wanted to know which buildings had vacancies, and where she was taking him. I had deliberately parked several buildings away from mine, walking through two buildings to get home. If Eddie didn't already know exactly where I lived, I wasn't about to show him.

Things were coming to a head; Eddie was growing bolder by the day. He was intent on getting me under his control again. But I'm no longer a little girl, I reminded myself. I know how to defend myself, with a gun or physical combat. I've always known it could, and probably would, come to this before I could prove he's guilty of any of his crimes. I couldn't make it too easy for him though, or he would know it was a set-up. I couldn't do it as long as Rafe was around either. He would do anything to stop Eddie from getting his hands on me, including putting himself in danger. I couldn't let that happen. As long as it was in my power, no other innocent person would be put in harm's way because I was too much of a coward to let Eddie get me.

As long as it had been an abstract thought, I hadn't worried about talking to Eddie, even in a public place. Now the thought of running into him every day in my own apartment complex brought tremors throughout my body. I was going to have to face him sooner or later. With every fiber of my being, I wanted it to be later. Like never. I wished he would just vanish.

I wasn't going to say anything to Rafe about Eddie looking at apartments in the complex, but I didn't have to. I could hear him long before I could see him. He began screaming my name before he was even out of his truck. His thundering footsteps pounded up the stairs.

"Rafe, what's gotten into you? Be quiet." I could see him taking the stairs two at a time when I opened my door. He nearly flew up the last flight of stairs, his feet barely touching the steps. Neighbors were looking at us like we'd lost our minds.

"Thank you, God," he whispered when he saw me, pulling me into his arms, crushing me so tight I couldn't draw a breath. He finally released me enough to look down at me. "What was he doing here? How did he get through the gate? He didn't do anything to you, did he?" His rapid fire questions didn't give me time to answer. Just as quick, he pulled me close again, his face against my neck, lifting my feet off the floor. "I was so scared when I saw him driving out of the complex. He even had the nerve to send me a jaunty salute as he drove past. I'll break him in two if he laid a hand on you."

Finally, I put my hand over his mouth so I could get a word in edgewise, and pulled him inside my apartment. We'd put on enough of a show for the neighbors. "He was walking around with the complex manager when I got home," I said. "Telling her he was interested in an apartment is the only way he could get through the gate."

Once the door was closed behind us, he pulled me against his chest again, burying his face in my hair, drawing a deep breath to calm himself. "Give me a minute. I was afraid he'd gotten hold of you. I nearly died right on the spot." I could feel his rapid heartbeat against mine.

"He never came close to me. He timed his arrival and departure perfectly so we'd both see him, proving he's been watching us. He got the reaction he wanted. We're too predictable, too comfortable. I never let that happen before."

"What do you mean?"

"No matter where I lived or worked before, I didn't come and go at the same time every day. I would take a different route to and from work. Leave home at different times, come home at different times. Sometimes I'd go to the mall for a few hours after work, just to be different." I brought my thoughts back to the room and to him. "You have to stop coming over here every night after work."

"Not gonna happen," he interrupted. "I'm not going to let him dictate what I do, or when I do it."

I pulled away, not letting him hold me this time. "Be sensible. As long as Eddie knows where we are at certain times, we're vulnerable. His whole game is to terrorize his victims."

"I'm not his damn victim, and I'll make damn sure you never are again either!" His voice was still rough with an overdose of adrenaline.

"That's not the way Eddie sees us. To him we're both

his victims as long as he can terrorize us. And no matter what we might say," I spoke over the objection he started to make, "that's exactly what he did today." He released a frustrated breath, throwing himself onto the couch. The adrenaline hadn't completely left his system yet, leaving him so jumpy he was up again within seconds.

I sat down now, watching him pace around my small living room. "When I saw him in the parking lot with the manager, I was scared. Just the thought of him moving in here was terrifying. When you saw him leaving, you were afraid he had me. That's exactly how he wanted both of us to feel. He's probably laughing at us right now."

He was quiet for several moments before nodding. "Okay, how do we prevent this from happening again? He can't really get an apartment here, can he? How does he support himself?" He sat down, wrapping his arm around my shoulders, and pulling me close.

I tried to keep some distance between us, but he wouldn't let me. I finally gave up, settling comfortably against his warm body. "I have no idea, but I can't see him working at a steady job."

"What about life insurance from your parents? Do you know if they had any?"

I gave a humorless laugh. "You knew my family. We were dirt poor; we barely had money for the essentials, let alone a luxury like life insurance. Mom worked part-time as a checker at the grocery store, and Dad stocked the shelves. Looking back I don't think he was overly ambitious. I think Mom wanted to make a better life for us, but just gave up because she knew whatever they got Eddie would take it away from them."

"What about life insurance through work? Most companies back then offered a certain amount, even to part-timers."

I shrugged. "They never talked about money or

insurance. I knew we didn't have much. If they did have any kind of life insurance, it's a safe bet Eddie wasn't the beneficiary. When he was first sent away, Mom wanted to move, change our names, anything to get away from him. She didn't want him to find us when he got out."

"So why didn't you move? You would have been safe then."

"I don't know; it just never happened. The longer we stayed there, the longer Eddie was gone, we pretended he was going to be gone for good. Those four years went by so fast, and suddenly they released him." I gave a fatalistic shrug. "I think they somehow felt responsible for the way he turned out, that whatever happened to them, they deserved."

"But you didn't!" He stated vehemently. "You were an innocent kid. Why would they let him get his hands on you?"

That was a question I'd asked myself many times when I was little. I had given up wondering a long time ago. "That's another question I never asked them," I whispered.

If I couldn't convince him to stay away from me, maybe I could convince him to help me. "The whole reason for coming back to Phoenix, for getting a job with the police department, was to prove Eddie had killed my parents. Failing that, I'd get evidence on other crimes he's committed." I was purposely vague on which crimes. If not the ones in his past, then I would settle on the current crime of kidnapping me. I knew Rafe wouldn't go for that, so I didn't spell it out. "I need you to help me."

"Isn't that what I've been doing?" He frowned. "Exactly what are you proposing?"

I stood up to put some distance between us, so I could think coherently. "I'm hoping I can get him to admit his guilt. I want to talk to him in a public place minimizing the risk as much as possible."

"NO!" He came off the couch as though he'd been shot

out of a cannon. "I'm not letting him get that close to you if I can help it."

"You can't be with me twenty-four/seven. If we can control when he has the opportunity to get close to me, making sure there are other people around, I'll be as safe as possible. Until now we've both been avoiding confrontation, hoping to get evidence against him. That hasn't worked. I want to be more proactive, and that means talking to him."

He raked his fingers through his hair. "Do you know what you're asking of me? You want me to risk your life."

"I'm willing to risk it to get evidence against him, and get him off the street permanently. Until then my life isn't my own. I can't move forward; I'm stuck in limbo."

"Casey, you have always been the love of my life," he said softly. "When we were kids I didn't understand those feelings, but once you were gone, you were always there in the back of my mind. No other girl or woman satisfied that part of me. Don't you understand I want to marry you, spend the rest of my life with you?"

"I can't marry you, or anyone; I can't risk having children." My voice was cracking, the same as my heart. Somewhere along the line, he had come to mean a great deal more to me than I ever expected or wanted.

He frowned at me. "What are you talking about? Why don't you want to have children?"

"You know my family history. Eddie is a psychopath, a sociopath. What if it's hereditary? I can't risk passing that on to another generation."

He shook his head. "How can the smartest person I know, say something that dumb?"

"They don't know why someone turns out like Eddie. I can't take a chance on something like that happening," I reemphasized.

"Okay, if that's really how you feel, we can adopt.

There are hundreds of kids in this country alone who need families."

"Why are you doing this? You know I'm soiled goods." I whispered the words that have been bottled up inside me for most of my life.

He gripped my shoulders, giving me a little shake. "How can you say such a thing? Would you tell a rape victim she was soiled goods?"

"Of course not."

"Then why are you saying it about yourself? What Eddie did to you wasn't your fault. Why would you blame yourself? If you want to blame someone other than Eddie, blame your parents. They should have protected you, done something about him when he started hurting animals before he ever touched you." He paused before asking his next question. "Did you make love with Fred before he disappeared?"

My face started to burn. "No. He said we would wait until we were married, and if I still wasn't comfortable, he would understand. I don't even know if I can." I whispered, too ashamed to say the words out loud.

He cradled me close, resting his chin on top of my head. "There is a difference between making love with someone, and what Eddie did to you. There was no love involved in that act. Rape is all about power and violence."

"But what if I can't do it? What if it terrifies me just to try?"

"Does it bother you when I kiss you?"

"Oh, I'm bothered, but not the way you're saying." The words slipped out before I could stop them.

His chuckle rumbled deep in his chest. "I'll take that as a positive thing. When you're ready, you'll say yes to the rest."

I pulled away from him. "I'm not sleeping with you," I snapped, "or anyone else for that matter, unless I'm married." I didn't realize I had just contradicted myself until he laughed out loud. I could feel my face turning red, but at least he didn't pursue the topic.

His only comment was mild acceptance. "When we're married, you'll see the difference. Until then, we'll stick with the preliminaries." He lowered his head, placing a gentle kiss on my lips.

When he stepped away from me, his breathing was as ragged as my own. No, kissing Rafe didn't terrify me. Just the opposite in fact, which was almost as terrifying. I felt like I didn't know myself anymore.

"Do you have any food in the house, or should we call for takeout?" It seemed like we'd come to some sort of a tacit understanding. Rafe was in my life to stay. I couldn't say I was unhappy about that either.

"There's food. I went shopping on Saturday." I still hadn't told him about seeing Eddie in the parking lot, and I wasn't going to now. "What would you like?" He wiggled his eyebrows suggestively making my stomach wobble and goose bumps travel all over me.

"Whatever you feel like fixing." He kept his words neutral while his look had my blood boiling.

My kitchen was small, but somehow we managed to move around each other like a well-choreographed dance team. Mom hadn't been an imaginative cook, but I had taught myself a few things in the intervening years. I enjoyed trying new recipes or inventing my own.

In contrast, Mrs. Gonzales, Rafe's mom, had been a wonderful cook. I remember the tamales she would bring over at Christmas. My favorites were the green chili cheese tamales. My mouth watered just thinking about them. I wondered if she still spent days preparing the traditional Mexican dish.

Am I inviting trouble? I asked myself. What would his parents think of him marrying me? I would tell them who I am before I agreed to marry him. If they had any objections, I wouldn't go through with it. He's close to his family; I wouldn't do anything to damage that relationship. My heart skipped a beat. I couldn't believe I was actually thinking these thoughts. Was it possible for me to have a normal life after all that's happened?

When I left Phoenix all those years ago, I put everything and everyone behind me. I had to in order to survive. Was it possible now to pick up with Rafe? It was more than anything I could ever have hoped for.

A memory from a long ago Sunday School lesson floated in my mind: Bad things happen to good people because the devil is loose in the world. But in the end God wins because He is Supreme. I'd looked the devil's minion in the face, and his name is Eddie. Rafe and Tessa would say that God works for good for those who love Him. Maybe it was time for me to put some of that faith into action in my own life.

CHAPTER TWENTY

The dynamics between Rafe and me had shifted. He didn't feel the need to keep pushing me at every juncture, and I no longer fought if he did push. I knew deep down that I was going to have to face Eddie sooner or later. He was the textbook example of a sociopath, and nothing was going to stop him from killing again. I'm not sure there was anything short of his own death that would keep Eddie from getting his hands on me. Just thinking about that made me sick to my stomach. To protect other innocent people from getting hurt though, I may have to let that happen.

First though, I'm hoping to talk to him, maybe record an admission of what he's done all these years. I just never know when or where he'll show up next. It's been two weeks since he was at my apartment complex, and I haven't seen him again.

Thanksgiving was a week away, then Christmas. Tessa's family asked me to join them, so has Rafe. What will Mr. and Mrs. Gonzales say if they recognize me as that fourteen-year-old girl? Thinking about that gives me a headache.

"What time does Rafe's family have dinner on Thanksgiving?" Tessa asked. We were jogging around the running track at the complex after work. Rafe and Joe would be over later in the evening. Joe and Tessa were getting serious, but she said it was too soon to know for sure. She had a few issues of her own to work through. Meeting his family would be an ordeal for her.

"I don't know. I haven't asked. I think I'll just stay home." I did my best to keep from rubbing my stomach in an effort to quiet the butterflies.

Turning around and running backwards in front of me, Tessa gave me a fierce frown. "You'll do no such thing! I thought the two of you were getting along so much better."

"Just because we're getting along doesn't mean we're joined at the hip. Rafe has a large family, a brother and sister, in-laws, nieces and nephews. Both sets of grandparents live here. I don't need to add to the confusion."

"Why would one more person add to the confusion? I'll bet you aren't the first girl he's brought home for a holiday dinner. Another bet I'm willing to make, and I'd win, is you'll be the last." I could feel my face turning red and she laughed. "Do you think you've been able to hide your feelings for each other? A person would have to be blind not to notice."

"You'd better turn around before you trip yourself and fall." She was still running backwards, and I was hoping to divert the conversation. "Your folks would have a fit if you ended up in the hospital just before Thanksgiving."

She moved back to my side, but she wasn't distracted from one of her favorite topics, Rafe, me, Joe or all three of us. "Joe's family doesn't live in Arizona, so he's coming with me to Mom and Dad's. We always have dinner at six so my brothers can go to their in-laws earlier in the day. You and Rafe are welcome to join us. You know Mom and Dad would love to have you. Maybe Rafe's family eats early. Then you can go to both places."

Those pesky butterflies started attacking my stomach again. This time I had to rub at them to settle them down. "I don't know, Tessa. That's a little more than I'm used to. Besides, I couldn't eat two big meals that close together."

She laughed. "That's part of the fun of holidays. There's always more food than any group can consume, but we always try to put a big dent in it anyway. Everyone brings a dish, and they end up taking home more food than they came with. This will be my first time to take home leftovers." She looked a little dreamy at the prospect before bringing her one-track mind back on line. "I'm sure Rafe's family is the same way, and I know he would love to show you off to his folks. If they eat at the same time as my folks, you can stop over before you go see his family, and we can all get together in the evening for dessert."

"I'll think about it," I hedged. There was still the chance Eddie would pull something to disrupt any plans I made. I didn't want him to involve Rafe's or Tessa's families.

"I don't know what it is with you and Rafe," Tessa continued, growing serious. "It's like you've known each other all your life. The sayings 'soul mate' and 'you complete each other', certainly apply to the two of you."

I frowned. "What are you talking about?" She was a little too close to the truth for comfort. Even though we hadn't seen each other for fifteen years, we seemed to know what the other was thinking part of the time.

"You've known Rafe just days longer than I've known Joe, yet sometimes you know what the other is thinking," she echoed my thoughts. "I can only hope Joe and I get that same thing eventually." She sounded so young, so wistful. Neither of which I had ever been. Two more things I could lay at Eddie's doorstep.

~~~

The day before Thanksgiving, I worked late, hoping I could have a four-day weekend. As long as someone didn't commit mass murder, I would probably get those four days. It was fully dark when I pulled up to the gate at my apartment complex. There weren't any other cars at the gate, and out of habit I looked around before lowering my window to put in the code to open the gate. Apparently I didn't look close enough, because as my window slid down a dark-clad figure stepped out of the shadows. He didn't have to say anything for me to know who it was.

"Hi there, Sis. How's it going?" His cocky attitude was typical. "You going to invite me over for Thanksgiving dinner tomorrow?"

"The only place I would invite you is to jail."

He gave a small laugh. "You never could bring yourself to cuss. I wonder if Rafe still remembers the black eye you gave him for cussing."

It wasn't a question, so I didn't comment. Faced with him now, my mind was blank. How do I get him to admit anything? I had remembered to thumb my phone to begin recording the minute I saw him walking towards me.

"How about inviting me up to your place, so we could talk in comfort? Even in Arizona it gets a little chilly after dark in November."

"If you want to talk to me, you can stand right there, and say whatever it is you have to say."

"At least let me in the car with you." He reached for the door handle but stopped, holding his hands up in phony act of surrender when I lifted my gun up. "Okay, okay, don't shoot me." He gave a nervous chuckle. "I just want to talk to my little sister."

"The only thing I'm interested in hearing you say is how and why you killed my parents." I was baiting him, but I didn't care. That might be the only way to get him to admit something.

"They were my parents first," he snarled.

"Is that why you killed them? Because I was born, and displaced you?" I couldn't believe all that he'd done was in a fit of jealous rage that lasted for years.

"Of course not," he smirked. "I didn't kill them. Don't you remember, the police said it was some junkies looking for money to buy drugs?"

"Riiight." I drew out the word in a sarcastic response. "Junkies always rob people in the poorest neighborhoods because that's where they'll find the most money."

He laughed like I'd made a joke. "No one ever said the

police were the sharpest knife in the drawer. I always thought you were one of the smartest people I knew, but then you started working for the cops, and I had to rethink that. Why would you go and do something like that?"

"Maybe I wanted to add my smarts to theirs, so I could help catch the bad guys. I still intend to catch the person who killed my folks and a whole lot of others. Like Fred in Kansas City."

He laughed again. "He ran off, remember? Didn't want to get married after all. That's what those smart cops said. Cops are a lazy bunch of dummies."

How did he know what the police had said? Was he able to hack into their computer systems the way I had? I couldn't let him see his knowledge disturbed me. "Just because some cops are lazy doesn't make them all lazy." I tried to appear nonchalant or flippant in my answer.

"I suppose you mean your lover and his buddies," he sneered. "Well, they aren't any smarter than any other cop, so don't go getting your hopes up."

"There's no such thing as a perfect murder. You'll pay for what you've done all these years." Before he could answer, another car pulled up behind me, impatiently honking his horn. As silently as he appeared, Eddie faded into the shadows. With a shaking hand, I put my code into the box, and watched the gate slide open. Once on the other side, I watched to make sure Eddie wasn't able to sneak through. The driver of the car behind me didn't want to wait for the gate to close so he could put in his own code. He tried to slip through behind me, only to have to back up, and wait for the gate to finish closing. I was still watching when he zoomed past me after he finally made it through. Even in the dark I could see the glare he sent my way for holding him up the few minutes it took to wait for his turn.

Pacing around my small living room, I listened to the

recorded conversation with Eddie. "A hot lot of good it did," I muttered to myself. He hadn't said anything incriminating. Would I ever be able to trick him into admitting something?

~~~

Reluctantly, I had agreed to have dinner with Rafe's family at one, then we'd both go to Tessa's folks' at six. I wasn't comfortable with large gatherings, and now I had two in one day. "I'll meet you at your folks'," I told Rafe, planning on arriving just before one to avoid the inspection I figured I'd receive. I should have known better.

He shook his head before I even finished my sentence. "Are you trying to get me skinned alive?" He barked out a laugh. "I'm not joking either. 'A gentleman always picks up his date.'" He made air quotes around the statement. "That's a direct quote from Mom. When she's through with me, Nita will finish filleting me. She and Juan never miss the chance to let me know how spoiled I am, how I've always gotten away with so much more than they did because I'm the baby of the family. They feel it's their job to keep me in line if Mom and Dad go easy on me."

Anita and Juan are seven and five years older than Rafe. I'd had very few dealings with them when I was a kid. That's a plus for me now. They wouldn't easily remember me, but I figured big brother and sister were going to scrutinize me very carefully anyway. That's exactly why I didn't want to get there too early.

"Why are we going so early?" He was at my place before eleven.

"All the good food is put out first."

"Good food?" I raised an eyebrow.

"Sure, the junk food. We don't want to miss out on that."

"Tell me again why I'm not bringing a dish." He was propelling me down the stairs.

"I'm bringing our dish. It's in my truck."

"Our dish? What's that supposed to mean?" I stopped walking, giving him the evil eye. "What exactly have you told them about me?" He tried to move me along, but I stood my ground, gripping the banister and refusing to move until he answered. "Do they know who I am?"

"Mom and Dad know all about you. Now can we go? If we're late, Nita's kids will get all the good snacks." He applied a little pressure on my back to get me to move, but now my feet were rooted to the floor.

"What do you mean your folks know all about me? How could you tell them?" My voice had dropped to a whisper, and I looked around to make sure we were still alone.

"I couldn't very well bring a date, and not tell them."

"What did you tell them?" I asked. My stomach was churning, threatening to bring up the coffee and toast I'd eaten earlier.

He leaned close, a seductive smile on his full lips. "That I was bringing the woman I'm going to marry." My jaw dropped open. His words left me speechless. My mind was reeling. Unable to resist the pressure he put on my back, we started moving down the steps again.

"How could you tell them that?" We were in his truck before I found my voice. "I haven't agreed to marry you."

"But you will." He leaned across the console. My mind turned to mush when his lips rested gently on mine. "Stop worrying. Everything is going to be fine." I couldn't seem to keep a coherent thought in my head when he kissed me.

I wasn't nearly as confident as he was concerning how the day would go. What if they recognized me? My entire life was fabricated out of whole cloth. I'm not certain what would happen to my job if the truth came out. I just knew I didn't want that to happen.

~~~

"That damn bitch," he grumbled to himself as he

watched her pull out of the apartment complex with Rafe. "She thinks she's safe just because she lives behind locked gates, and works for the cops. It's time to show her who the boss is." He chuckled. He'd always loved a challenge, but maybe she'd forgotten that or she wouldn't be working so hard to protect herself. He owed Rafe, too. "He's going to pay for taking what's mine."

Starting his rattletrap of a car, he made a U-turn in the street. He didn't follow them. "Off to a Thanksgiving feast with Rafe's family," he sneered, "while I sit in my ratty little apartment with a can of soup." The extended living hotel had kicked him out last week. Said he'd been there too long. He figured that snooty little desk clerk complained because he hung around the office when she was on duty. Thought she was better than him. "I'll show her. See how she likes me up close and personal." His evil laugh escaped through the cracked side window. "Just a little appetizer before the main course."

~~~

As expected Anita and her family were already at the Gonzales' home. They had moved out of the old neighborhood shortly after my parents were murdered. I was grateful I didn't have to see my old neighborhood. Rafe had told me few of the old neighbors had stayed after what happened.

Their home was just as warm and welcoming as the one I remembered from my childhood. Mrs. Gonzales greeted me with a friendly smile and a hug. "Rafe has talked about nothing but you since you met. You're the first girl to truly capture his heart. Welcome." She hugged me again.

Mr. Gonzales was a little more reserved but just as friendly. "Welcome to our family." He placed a peck on my cheek.

"Will you stop calling her a girl?" Anita spoke from behind her father before turning to smile at me. "They insist anyone younger than themselves is still a kid." She offered her hand in a friendly gesture. Memories of her no-nonsense manner floated through my mind. Being the oldest of three, she had always taken command whenever dealing with the neighborhood kids. "Don't let this one get away with anything." She poked Rafe in the ribs. "He's been spoiled all his life, so now he thinks he's entitled to whatever he wants."

"Nita, you're going to scare the poor girl off before she gets any further than the front door." Her mother scolded softly, moving us inside.

Before anything more was said, the front door opened, and five kids barreled into the room. "Gram, Gramps!" The two youngest threw themselves at their grandparents. They were followed closely by an older version of Rafe and a petite woman slightly older than me. This could only be Rafe's brother, Juan and his wife.

After introducing his parents, Rafe introduced the others like we'd never met before. "This bossy Bess is my sister Nita, my older sister," he qualified, earning him another poke in the ribs, "and her husband Jim. This is my big brother, Juan and his better half, Debbie. The two littlest rug rats are theirs, Juan Jr., JJ for short, and Juanita. In case you can't tell, they're twins."

Before he could introduce the other three, the oldest, probably all of six years old, spoke up. "Hi, I'm Rebecca, and these are my brothers, James and Christopher." No nicknames for her, I thought with a smile.

"And guess who her mom is," Rafe cut in. "Like mother like daughter." He laughed, tugging on her long pony tail. He picked up the twins who appeared about three years old, and everyone headed for the kitchen. A huge table holding enough food to feed an army took center stage. Debbie added the two large dishes she'd carried in, and Juan gave his mom another. The amazing aromas made my mouth water.

"You'd think this bunch of munchkins hadn't seen us in a month," Mrs. Gonzales laughed. She planted a kiss on each of them. "Five grandchildren under the age of six keep us busy, but there's always enough love for more." She smiled at me. Her meaning was clear, and I could feel my face turning red. I was going to throttle Rafe when we were alone.

"Enough, Mom," he warned.

She laughed at him, patting his cheek. "You can't blame a mother for trying. There are never too many grandchildren to love."

Both sets of grandparents added to the already big crowd a few minutes later, and I could almost fade into the background; almost. Rafe was always at my side, making sure I didn't disappear. Throughout the afternoon more people came and went, aunts, uncles and cousins. I couldn't believe the size of his family. Everyone was friendly and accepted me as part of their family. This only piled on the guilt. How could I keep lying to them? What would they think if they knew who I really am? It wasn't supposed to be like this. No one else was supposed to be involved but Eddie and me.

Watching Rafe play with his nieces and nephews, I knew he would make a wonderful father. Was it possible to have children, and not worry about one of them turning out like Eddie? What played a bigger role, nurture or nature, in how a person turns out? Science wasn't really clear on that.

Everyone gave me a hug as we were getting ready to leave, like I'd always been a part of their family. "Are you sure you don't want to get up at two-thirty in the morning, and go to all the after Thanksgiving sales with these two nuts and me?" Mrs. Gonzales asked, laughing at her daughter and daughter-in-law.

"I'm sure, but thanks for asking." I laughed with her.

"I don't blame you in the least, dear. Every year I say

it's the last, but come the next year they always talk me into going again." She gave me a hug. "Thank you for making my son so happy." Her whispered words caused me heart to lurch. Unable to find words, I nodded, following Rafe out to his truck. What would they think if they knew the truth?

My mind was reeling, and the silence stretched out as he drove to Tessa's parents' house. "What did Mom say that upset you so much?" He finally broke into my thoughts.

"Why would you think I'm upset?" I kept my voice light, forcing myself to smile at him.

He picked up my hand, bringing it to his lips. "Because your hands are like ice, and your whole body is shaking."

"Maybe I'm just cold."

"You're such a bad liar," he chuckled. "Now, tell me what Mom said as we left. And not about going shopping," he added before I could say anything.

I shrugged. "She just thanked me for making you happy. See, nothing to be upset about." I forced another smile.

"Uh huh." We pulled up to the Gordon house right then, preventing him from probing further.

I'd made deviled eggs, something I remember Mom making when I was a kid, and had given them to Tessa to bring with her so we didn't have to go back to my apartment. The evening with her family was less stressful with far fewer people than the earlier dinner had been.

Thinking about Mrs. Gonzales' words kept me awake all night. Most people would think little of it, but I knew I had to talk to her, tell her who I really am. Would she be upset Rafe wanted to marry me after I told her about what Eddie had done? I expected she would want little to do with me, and wouldn't want her son around me either.

I left a message for her to call when she finished

shopping and had a nap. It was just after noon when she called back, much earlier than I expected. "Thanks for returning my call. How was your shopping trip?" I couldn't get to the point without some idle chitchat first.

"About as productive as you'd expect," she laughed. "The lines were awful, but there were a few good bargains. It's always a good bonding time with my girls. Is everything all right?" She sounded worried.

"I was wondering if I could come over and talk to you or maybe we could meet somewhere. Is Mr. Gonzales home?"

"Now none of this Mr. and Mrs. stuff," she admonished. "We're Clara and Mario. I hope someday you'll feel comfortable enough to call us Mom and Dad." Without realizing it, she was heaping on the guilt. "We can have coffee or tea in the family room. Mario is entrenched in front of the TV with football games. I've never understood the attraction to that game, but men seem mesmerized by it." She laughed, "He's still in a food stupor from yesterday, and won't even know we're in the house."

I'd planned what to say, but seated in the comfortable family room with glasses of iced tea my mind was blank. How do I begin this conversation? Mr. Gonzales, Mario, I corrected myself, had given me a friendly wave as I walked through the living room, but his attention was really on the television. Men did have a fascination for the game of football.

"Is everything all right, dear?" Clara finally asked when I didn't say anything. "Has Rafe done something to upset you?"

"No, of course not." I fell silent again.

"Well, men can be insensitive sometimes when they don't mean to be." She waited for me to speak.

"Mrs...um, Clara, I need to tell you something about myself. You aren't going to be happy, but please let me finish before you say anything." She nodded, and waited again.

Clearing my throat, I decided the best way was just blurt it out. "I used to live down the street from you when I was a kid. Some bad things happened, and I left."

She picked up my hand. "I'll never forget what happened, or the sweet young girl they happened to."

"You...you know who I really am?"

"Of course."

"How? Did Rafe tell you?" He said he hadn't, but how else would she know who I am?

She shook her head. "He would never betray a confidence. He knew when you were ready you would say something to us. But if you never did, it would be all right with him, and with us."

"Then how did you know?"

She was still holding my hand. "When he told us he'd found the girl of his dreams, and he was going to marry her, I had no doubt who he was talking about. He's loved you since the first day he laid eyes on you all those years ago." She chuckled. "Rafael was about five or six when he came in after playing in the front yard. He was all aglow, and announced that he was going to marry Jennifer Miller someday. We laughed it off as something a young boy would say about a new friend. But that's never changed."

She gave another chuckle. "The day you gave him a black eye, he walked in like he'd just won the Pulitzer Prize. I was concerned he'd been in a fight at school, but before I could question him, he asked in that grown-up voice he sometimes used, even then, 'When a girl hits you for doing something wrong, that means she likes you. Right, Mom?' When I nodded, his grin grew even bigger. I wanted to know what he'd done wrong, and who gave him the black eye. He stated very matter-of-factly, 'Jennifer, of course. I cussed in front of the girls. She hit me, and told me not to do it again.' I don't think he's ever cussed in front of a girl or woman since. He loves you that much, dear."

I was too stunned to speak, but somehow I had to make her understand. "If you knew what Eddie's done, you'd feel differently. You wouldn't want Rafe to marry me."

"Whatever he did isn't your fault. Why are you blaming yourself?"

"He killed my parents," I whispered, unable to say the words out loud, unmindful of the tears running down my face. "He's a monster."

"And that isn't your fault either. Your parents should have had him committed years before they did, and they should have made sure he stayed there. Did they ever tell the police about all the things he did?"

I shrugged. "I don't know. They were ashamed, and didn't want people to know."

"It was their job to protect you," she said forcefully. "Child Protective Services wasn't as involved as they should have been back then, and they leave a lot to be desired even today, but your parents should have protected you instead of thinking about their own reputations." She was clearly indignant on my behalf. "You were a child!"

"He's still out there," I whispered. "And I suspect he's still killing people. I have to stop him."

"That's a job for the police."

"It's my job, too. I can't have a life until he's caught. I'm his prime target, but he'll keep hurting other people until he gets me." She had to understand. "Does Mario know?" What would he think of me? What about the rest of the family?

"Of course. There are no secrets between husband and wife, or at least very few," she chuckled. "But I didn't say anything to him. He knows his son. If Rafe had simply said he was getting married, that he was finally settling for second best, we would have known that it wasn't you. But you are the girl of his dreams, the one always preventing him from settling for someone else."

"What about the rest of the family?" I had to know who else knew my secret.

She shook her head. "It's up to you if you say anything to them. But even if they knew, they wouldn't care. Nothing that happened was your fault," she reemphasized.

Tears were running unchecked down my face. She pulled me to her, letting me cry like I hadn't cried since I left home, over fifteen years ago. Emotions I didn't even know I had, surfaced. She said nothing, just held me, patting my back comfortingly. I don't remember my own mother ever holding me like that, offering me comfort.

It took several minutes for me to gain control of myself. When I finally did, I sat back, wiping my face with the tissue she gave me. "I won't ever be that girl again. My name will always be Casey. That's who I am now." I had to make sure she understood.

"Of course. A name doesn't make you what you are. You're a wonderful person no matter what name you go by. You should be proud of what you've made of yourself."

She still didn't understand, and neither did Rafe. I hadn't pressed this point home, but I was going to have to before long. "Jennifer Miller is dead," I stated softly. "There's a death certificate to prove it."

Her look of surprise worried me again. But I had to go on with the story. "Once I figured out that I could use computers to do just about anything, I managed to hack into the public records department in the city where I lived then. It really wasn't hard to put a false death certificate online. As far as the government knows, she's dead. I never used that Social Security number for a job so there isn't any work record out there."

"When did you do this?"

Heaving a ragged sigh, I kept my eyes on my hands in my lap. "I was sixteen."

"My goodness, I always knew you were smart. I just didn't realize how smart. Is that how you got your degree in a different name?"

I nodded. "I have a birth certificate and Social Security number, everything a person needs to get around in this world. All done online. I look totally legal and real. I'm just not." I drew a deep breath. As long as I was confessing all that I've done, I might as well go all the way. "All the things I've done aren't exactly legal, and I could probably be arrested for computer hacking any number of times. Not probably," I corrected. "Definitely. Hacking is a crime, especially government files."

"Did you steal anything? Cause someone harm? Make yourself rich?" I kept shaking my head at each question. "And you did this to keep yourself safe, maybe find out information about Eddie?" This time I nodded in the affirmative. "The way I see it, you were forced to take these steps because the police didn't do their jobs at the time your parents were killed." She leaned close to me, and whispered. "I won't tell, if you don't." She gave me a conspiratorial smile, patting my hand.

I fell silent, I was all talked out. She didn't hold any of my past against me. In my mind, this was nothing short of a miracle.

By the time I left, she had filled me in on the years I'd missed with her family. She still saw a few of the old neighbors, but most had just moved on. "I'll let Rafe fill you in on his high school escapades." She winked at me. "He probably wouldn't appreciate me telling tales.

"Anytime you need someone to talk to, you're more than welcome to call me. You might also consider talking to your pastor. He could definitely help you with the guilt you're carrying around. I can't say it often enough; you did nothing that you need to be ashamed of." This time, I was the one to pull her in for a hug.

When I got home, Rafe was standing at my door; his

forehead resting on the jamb almost like he was praying. "Rafe? What are you doing here?"

He pulled me into a tight embrace. "Thank you, God." He breathed out a prayer. Just as quickly, he held me away from him, examining me from head to toe. "Are you hurt? Where the hell have you been? I've been calling you for the last two hours, but your phone went straight to voice mail. Did you see Eddie? Why would you do...?"

I put my hand over his mouth to stop any more words from spilling out. "Shut up. I'm fine."

"Why didn't you answer your phone?" He kissed my fingers before I could move them from his mouth. "I've been frantic thinking Eddie got ahold of you." He pulled me to him again; his heart pounding hard against mine.

"Why would you think that? I wouldn't let him get close enough to do something." That wasn't necessarily the truth. I never knew when or where he would show up. Sometime I might not have the opportunity to protect myself. Something Rafe was painfully aware of.

"Can we go inside? I don't think we need to play show and tell for your neighbors." He took the keys from me. His hands were shaking so much it took several tries before he got all the locks opened.

Once inside, he cupped my cheek in his hand, his kiss so gentle yet so fierce that my heart nearly stopped in my chest. By the time he released me, my thoughts were far from the current topic of conversation. "Why didn't you answer your phone? I've been imagining all sorts of things."

"I turned it off because I didn't want to be interrupted." Drawing a deep breath for courage, I finished. "I went over to talk to your mom."

"You went..." He smiled down at me, his arms still holding me tight. "I hope that's a good thing?" he asked, raising that eyebrow.

"Yes, it's good. Did you know they know who I am?"

"How could they? I didn't say anything to them. Honest. I wouldn't say anything unless you said it was okay." He led me over to the couch, but didn't let go of me, like he was afraid I'd get away if he did.

"Your parents know you better than you think they do." I repeated our conversation, leaving out my own meltdown. He isn't my husband, and we can have secrets from each other, at least for a while yet. I knew Clara wouldn't say anything about it either. She would leave that to me.

~~~

Too late I realized I should have gone shopping with Clara, Nita and Debbie after Thanksgiving. At least it would have given me some insight into what to get everyone for Christmas. I haven't had anyone to buy presents for in a long while; now there are a countless number. Even Tessa is a puzzle. She still needs things for her apartment, but I don't want to get something practical. I want something meaningful, something she will treasure for a long time. If I could find an armoire like mine, that would be perfect, but there wasn't enough time to search for it.

"Anyone up for some Christmas shopping?" Tessa asked as we left church. "The stores shouldn't be so crowded today, but the specials are still good."

Both guys groaned. "More shopping?" Joe spoke the words I knew Rafe was thinking.

"Of course, more shopping," I laughed at them. Spending every spare minute with Rafe, I sometimes felt a little smothered. This might give me the break I needed.

"It's Christmas," Tessa said. "Have you finished your shopping?" She raised her eyebrow.

Joe groaned again, but Rafe smiled. "I have the most important gift." He directed his words to me. Those pesky butterflies were back in my stomach, and my heart gave a little jump. I was afraid I knew what he was talking about, and I wasn't ready for that yet.

"I guess I could go and get something for everyone else," he said, putting his arm around my waist, and pulling me against his side. "We can pick out something for Mom and Dad, and I never know what to get those five little rug rats." I don't know why he thought I'd know what they'd like. I had absolutely no experience with children.

Lunch at Frederico's had become such a ritual we didn't need to discuss it. He had recovered from his mugging, but his attacker was still in the wind. In my heart of hearts, I knew it was Eddie, but we had no proof.

"I have some of my gifts already, but I always get stuck on what to get for my folks," Tessa picked up the conversation once we were seated. "When I ask for suggestions, they say they have everything they need, and can buy anything they want. That doesn't help me at all." She sighed dramatically.

"Your mom is still looking for accent pieces for her living room, isn't she? We can go to the antique stores in Glendale." I had an ulterior motive for this suggestion. Maybe I could find something for Tessa there.

I didn't get the break from Rafe I was hoping for, but the afternoon was more fun than I expected. He had suggestions for his family, and overrode my objections about buying gifts for everyone from both of us. "You might as well accept it," he said, leaning close, whispering in my ear. "We're a couple." He kissed my cheek before pulling away. Goosebumps moved up my arms, and it wasn't because I was cold. His little signs of affection always had this effect on me. If I was being honest with myself, I kind of liked them.

Tessa found a table that would be perfect for her mom, and I spotted one that would look very nice in her living room. It took some fancy footwork to pay for it, and arrange to have it picked up when she wasn't around, but we finally worked it out. Clara and Mario both liked antiques, and Rafe found the perfect gift for them. After that, we headed for the mall to find gifts for everyone else. The big question mark for me was Rafe. I had no idea what to get him. Maybe I could ask Joe for suggestions.

By the time we got back home it was already dark, and we were all beyond tired. Who knew a four-day weekend could be so exhausting? Joe went with Tessa to her place, and Rafe followed me inside carrying all our packages. I'd given up arguing about him searching the apartment, and just waited at the door until he was finished. It was easier that way.

When he came into the living room again, I stepped away from the door where I'd been leaning while he did his search. Before I could get more than a step, he backed me up to the door again. His lips played over mine, teasing lightly not really kissing me. My heart fluttered in my chest to the same beat as the butterflies in my stomach. "If you're going to kiss me, do it right." I wasn't even aware I'd said the words out loud until he chuckled.

That was all the invitation he needed. He gathered me in his arms, crushing me against his chest. He rained kissed over my cheeks, my eyes, that sensitive spot on my neck before finally settling his mouth on mine. My arms wound around his neck, pulling him even closer. We ended up on the couch, and I wasn't even aware we'd moved away from the door.

"You're driving me crazy, Casey." His words were nothing more than a soft breath against my lips. "If I asked you to marry me now, would you say yes?"

I wanted nothing more than to say the word he wanted, but now wasn't the time. Eddie was still out there. When I stayed quiet, he pulled slightly away. "I guess that's a no." He sighed.

"Not no, just not yes right now. There's no telling what Eddie would do if I got married. He killed Fred. I don't want that to happen to you." I took his face in my hands, holding him to me. "Please, don't be mad. It can't be much longer before he does something else, and we'll be able to stop him."

He turned his head to the side, placing a kiss in each of my palms. "I can't be mad at you for wanting to protect me when that's exactly what I want to do to you. I love you, Casey, with all my heart."

"I know. I l...love you." The words stuttered out before I could stop them.

"Do you mind saying that again? Please?" His dark eyes were alight as he smiled at me, the dimple in his cheek deepening as his smile grew.

Saying it a second time wasn't as hard. "I love you, Rafe, I love you very much!" The butterflies had finally stopped attacking my stomach; now I felt them flutter throughout my body. I'd only said those words to Fred once. In the space of a few seconds, I'd said them to Rafe three times. I knew in the deepest part of my soul I meant them.

"Will you marry me, Casey?" he asked again. "That isn't the romantic proposal you deserve, but if you will say "Yes" now, when I give you a ring, it will be down on one knee, the whole enchilada."

The pleading in his dark eyes was impossible to ignore or turn down. "As long as it is just between us for now, yes. YES!" The word erupted from my mouth. He laughed, smothering me in kisses. It was a long while later when he finally went home.

~~~

"That damn bitch broke my leg, and probably broke my balls as well." He shifted the bag of ice he had on his groin. "She was supposed to be dead, not nearly kill me," he continued to grumble. "I can't even go to the hospital to get my leg fixed because she's probably got the cops out looking for me." He didn't consider the fact that what he

did was against the law. It wasn't his fault. Nothing was ever his fault. She shouldn't have had him kicked out of that place.

He had to lay low until his leg healed, but that was going to take money. He had her car hidden for now. Eventually he would switch the plates so the cops couldn't trace it. At least, he had a better car to drive now. If he didn't hurt so much, he'd have chuckled at that fact.

It was still dark when he got back to this dump. He nearly passed out climbing the stairs, but he'd made it, picking up the ice on the way.

He needed to make plans, but first he had to do something about the pain. His stash of pills came in handy. Swallowing two, he began to float, the pain drifting away. He'd make plans when he woke up. He needed crutches, and a brace or something to stabilize his leg. Those were his last thoughts before the fog enveloped him, and his pain disappeared.

Several hours later the pain was back, but not as bad. His head was still foggy, making it difficult to think. Using the furniture in the small room as a crutch, he hobbled to the bathroom. After relieving himself, he splashed water on his face hoping to clear his mind. The ice had helped bring the swelling down between his legs. If he could stay off his leg for a few days, he'd get through this. He'd put up with worse. He just needed to figure out how to make money while he was laid up.

Panhandling with crutches and a leg brace might be a good gimmick, he thought, a crooked smile playing around his mouth. It couldn't be in Phoenix though. Chances of the cops spotting him would be too great even with a disguise. He thought over his prospects for several minutes. A small town wasn't a good idea either. Not enough people to give out money, and the cops in small towns were notorious for sticking their noses in where they didn't belong. Tucson was the next best thing, but how did he get there with a broken leg?

Driving from the parking lot after that bitch broke his leg, and stomped on his balls hadn't been easy. He was going to have to wait until the pain in both places went away. "Jennifer's living in the lap of luxury while I live in this dump," he grumbled. "Someday soon, Jennifer, you're going to pay for all this." It was a promise he made to himself often.

CHAPTER TWENTY-ONE

Going to work Monday morning, I felt like I was walking on air. I didn't know how I was going to hide my happiness, but I couldn't tell anyone when I'd sworn Rafe to secrecy, at least for now. It didn't take long to lose myself in work, putting everything else aside as I ran the evidence from several different crimes that happened over the holiday weekend.

When Jeremy came into the lab, he stopped next to me. "Are you looking at the evidence from the attack?" Excitement made his voice squeaky, alerting me that there was something unusual about the case.

"I haven't got there yet. Is there something special I should see?"

"Oh yeah." He shifted from one foot to the other so fast he was almost dancing. "We have more non-fingerprints. We might be able to catch this bas..creep with this one." He quickly changed his swear word for my sake.

My heart gave a leap. Was this the case I've been looking for? Then guilt took over. If Eddie attacked another woman, that meant she was dead. I didn't wish that on anyone. Even a prostitute didn't deserve that kind of end. "Tell me what happened to the poor girl. Was she mutilated like the other one?" I really didn't want to go there, but I had to know.

"He screwed up this time!" By now, he was so excited; he was just about hopping out of his skin. "He didn't kill her! She fought back, and managed to do a little damage of her own."

I leaped off the stool I'd been sitting on, gripping Jeremy's hands. "She's alive? Was there skin under her fingernails? Could she describe him?" I started looking around for the case file, and evidence taken at the scene.

"He picked on the wrong gal this time," he said. "He beat her up some before she turned the tables on him. He's one of the walking wounded now. From what she told the detective he might have a broken bone or two." He laughed at the prospect.

"Could she describe him? What about skin under her nails?" I still hadn't found the file. Too bad Rafe hadn't been the detective in charge of the case. At least Jeremy was on duty over the weekend. He didn't dismiss the non-fingerprints as though they weren't important.

Puzzlement replaced his excitement from moments ago. "It's kind of weird. He had on some kind of rubber suit or something; she couldn't get her nails into him. I guess that doesn't matter though. She knows who he is."

My heart started beating faster. This *is* what I've waited for. "Who is he? Did she give a name?"

Jeremy shrugged. "By that time, Detective Roberts noticed I was hanging around, listening in. He told me to get back to work." His sigh matched mine. Why did it have to be that guy? Does he think he can solve the cases all by himself, without the CSI team?

"Do you know if she was admitted to the hospital? Where did they take her?" I wanted to go talk to her, but I knew Mr. Watkins wouldn't let me leave work, no matter the reason.

Time dragged by all day. I didn't stay late, hurrying as I headed for my car. I hadn't heard from Rafe all day, and a few worries had crept into my mind by quitting time. I told myself he was wrapped up in any number of cases, but the worry was still there. Fred had left my apartment with the promise to be back first thing in the morning, and we would get married.

Rafe had left my apartment after I had said I would marry him. Had Eddie somehow known, and managed to get the drop on him? Fear that there was a psychic thread linking us surfaced again. I didn't want to have any connection to Eddie, psychic or otherwise. Brushing that thought aside, I concentrated on what I knew. It was very unlikely Eddie could get the jump on Rafe, especially after the beating he took at the hands of his latest victim. The evidence hadn't made it in to me yet, so I knew nothing more than what Jeremy told me. But I knew it had to be Eddie. I was going to see the victim now.

Headed to my Jeep, I pulled my phone from my purse. "Please let him be safe," I whispered a small prayer as I dialed Rafe's number. I wanted to let him know where I was going, but more than that I needed to know he was safe.

"Hi there, Beautiful. I'm heading to the station, and should be there in a few minutes. We can grab a bite to eat. I haven't eaten all day."

My heart skipped a beat at the sound of his voice. I tried to tell myself it was because he was safe, but I knew it was more than that. "I'm not going to be there, Rafe. I'm on my way to the hospital to see..."

"What? Are you all right? Did Eddie do something to you?" His questions spilled out with the panic I could hear in his voice.

"Whoa, take it easy. I'm going to see an attack victim."

His breath shuddered out on a sigh of relief. "Oh, thank God. You just about scared ten years off my life."

I laughed. "I hope not. I'd like to have those ten years at some point," It felt strange teasing with him.

"Sounds good to me. Now tell me what's going on. I've been out all day."

I filled him in on the attack, getting more excited as I talked. "This might be it. She knew her attacker."

"What makes you think it's Eddie? Did she give a name?"

It was my turn to sigh. "I haven't seen the file or the evidence yet. Detective Roberts hasn't brought it." I didn't know why he would keep the evidence since the attack happened early Sunday morning. He should have turned it in as soon as he got back to the station.

Rafe grumbled something unintelligible, which was a good thing. I might have had to give him another black eye. "What hospital is she in? I'll meet you there." He paused for a minute then spoke quietly, a smile lifting up his voice. "I love you."

I hope I never get tired of the thrill those three words give me. "I love you, too." It was still hard to speak them out loud, at the same time it was very freeing.

After checking with the volunteer at the front desk, and getting directions to the room of Beverly Johnston, I headed down the long maze of corridors. I don't know why they have to make hospitals so hard to navigate. Finally arriving at the right room, I was surprised there wasn't someone guarding her door.

She's a witness against her attacker who could come back to finish the job he started the other night.

I knocked softly on the door before pushing it open. If she was sleeping, I didn't want to wake her. A young woman, probably in her mid-twenties, was propped up in the bed, her eyes closed. When she heard the door give a slight swish as I pushed it open, she turned to look at me. My breath caught in my throat. One eye was swollen nearly shut, and turning a bright purple. Her lip was split, and she had a cast on her arm. Gauze was wrapped around her head.

"Hi, my name is Casey Gibson. I work for the Phoenix Police Department. Is it all right if I ask you a few questions?"

"Have you caught him yet? I told that detective who did this." She was angry, and I didn't blame her.

"Not that I know of," I shook my head. "Do you mind if I ask you a few questions?" I repeated.

With a weary sigh, she shook her head. "I guess it's all right. I don't know what more you need from me. I gave that detective his name."

"I know, but anything else you can tell us will help. How did you get away from him?" I didn't know what she had told Detective Roberts. I didn't want her to know he hadn't turned in the evidence yet. The man was another incompetent cop in a long list of them in my life.

She started to smile, but stopped when it pulled on the stitches in her lip. "I'm a martial arts instructor," she said. "If he hadn't hit me from behind, he wouldn't have been able to do all this to me." She raised her hand to a spot covered by the gauze bandage. "I was momentarily stunned, and couldn't fight back right away. That's when he did this." She gingerly touched her face. "Once I came to my senses, my training took over, and I fought back. He looks worse than I do, and he probably isn't walking very well either. Before he finally gave up, I got him in the groin. He might be peeing blood for a while. That's when he ran off; I should say limped off. He was dragging his left leg. It might be broken. He wasn't so bad off though that he couldn't drive." Her tone was bitter.

"Did you see his car?" This was getting better all the time.

"The damn perv took my car! I dropped my keys when he hit me. Somehow he managed to pick them up, and he took off in my car. Why haven't they found him yet? I gave them his name, and a description of my car, even the plate number." She was getting understandably agitated.

"There's an APB out for him and your car, Miss Johnston." I hadn't noticed when Rafe entered the room. "I'm Detective Rafael Gonzales with the PPD. I'm just following up on your attack. I know you've covered this with Detective Roberts, but if you could go over it again, it would help." His gentle tone helped to calm her, and his devastating smile didn't hurt either.

She nodded and he went on. "You called him a 'perv'. Why? Did he sexually assault you?"

"He is a perv, and I told that other detective!" She drew a shaky breath. "I work part-time at an extended stay hotel. This guy had been staying there for more than a month. Whenever I was on duty at the front desk, he'd sit in the lobby pretending to read a book or something. But I could feel him watching me. Sometimes when I looked at him, he'd lick his lips in a creepy way. He never did anything outright giving me a reason to call the police, but he gave me the creeps. I finally told my boss either this guy went or I did. I guess I'm more important than the weekly rent the guy was paying. Anyway, he was told he needed to move."

"What reason did your boss give him?" I asked. If Eddie thought she was the reason he had to move, that would be enough of a motive for him to attack her.

"Mr. Perez said he could only stay there for a month at a time, and he was already over that limit." She gave a slight shake of her head. "He didn't buy that excuse because while he was hitting me, before I started fighting back, he said he knew I was the reason he got kicked out." Tears had started running down her battered face. "I wasn't supposed to survive this, was I? He meant to kill me. What if he tries again?" I reached out, and took her hand. It was cold, and shaking from fear.

"We're doing our best to make sure that doesn't happen, Miss Johnston," Rafe assured her.

"What name was he using at the extended stay hotel?" She was so upset she didn't realize this was something he should already know from the report Detective Roberts had taken.

"Edward Miller," she replied as she struggled to get herself under control.

I didn't know if I was happy or sad. Eddie had

definitely attacked Beverly, and he wasn't even trying to cover his tracks by using an alias where he was staying. He was very confident in his ability to slip through law enforcement's fingers. Again.

"Do you have family you can stay with when you leave the hospital?" Rafe asked quietly. Since Eddie had her car, he had her address.

She nodded, "I'll stay with my parents. They'll be here when they get off work. He won't know where they live. He won't know where I live either," she added. "There isn't anything in my car that has my home address on it. I use a post office box on everything." She's a smart young woman; I just hope the police are smart enough, and fast enough to finally catch Eddie.

"Could you tell us what he was wearing that kept you from scratching him?" I asked.

She gave a humorless chuckle. "He had on a rubber wet suit and a swim cap. He looked like he was planning on going scuba diving in the middle of Phoenix. The only things that weren't covered were his hands and face. He didn't care that I could see him." She was crying again. "He was going to kill me, and it didn't matter that I knew who he was." A few minutes later, an older couple entered the room, rushing to her side when they saw her tears.

"What's going on here? Who are you people?" The man demanded. "Why are you bothering my daughter?" Rafe showed them his badge, and the man calmed down only slightly. "Why isn't there someone protecting my daughter? Shouldn't you have an officer at her door? What if this bastard comes back to finish what he started?" This brought more tears from Beverly, and now her mom was crying as well.

"Sir, I'll make sure there is an officer outside her door when I leave here. We will do our very best to make sure she's safe." Rafe ushered me out with his hand on the small of my back. I could feel his rage at Detective

Roberts vibrating through his shaking fingers.

He pulled his cell phone from his belt as soon as we were in the hallway, punching in a number. "Gonzales here, I want an officer outside the door of Beverly Johnston's hospital room ASAP! Her attacker is still on the loose, and he knows she can ID him." He gave the details needed to accomplish it, then snapped his phone back on his belt.

"What about Roberts?" I asked quietly. "Isn't this going to get you in trouble for interfering with his case?"

He released a disgusted breath. "It might, but I don't care. If there's any chance Eddie will come after that poor girl to shut her up, I intend to stop him. I want to know where that evidence has been since this happened. Roberts is just marking time until he can retire. I don't know why he doesn't do everyone a favor, especially the victims, and retire now." He sighed trying to calm down, but it didn't work. "He used to be a good cop, but he's gotten lazy. Now he's just incompetent." Neither of us spoke again until we left the hospital. "That useless baboon," he growled once we were outside. "It's guys like him that made me want to be a policeman, so idiots didn't rule the force."

He'd worked himself into an angry state, and I reached out to touch his arm, sliding my hand down, lacing my fingers with his. It was such an uncharacteristic move for me, I stunned Rafe and myself. His smile sent my heart racing, and blood flooding my face. I started to pull away, but he held on tight. Without saying anything more we headed for my car. Once there, he turned me to face him, my back leaning against the door panel. Bracing his hands on each side of me; he leaned down until his lips were just inches from mine. "You're good for me, Casey, you ground me. Thank you." He closed the distance between us, his lips resting gently on mine. "I love you."

Before either of us could say anything more, someone hollered across the parking lot. "Gonzales, what the hell do you think you're doing?"

Tension shot through him again, but he kept his tone mild when he turned to the voice. "I'm kissing my girl, Roberts. What does it look like?"

"Don't play dumb with me," Detective Roberts snapped as he stormed up to us, getting in Rafe's face. "You know damn good and well what I'm talking about. Why did you order a guard put on that girl's room?"

"Because you didn't," Rafe answered. His calm tone angered Roberts further.

"Why does she need a guard? If she really broke the guy's leg, he isn't going to be coming after her any time soon. Of course, if she's lying, that could be a problem." He had a smirk on his face now.

"Why would you even think that, Detective?" I inserted myself into the conversation. "If she hadn't defended herself, she'd be dead right now. Would you have preferred that?"

He dismissed me with a roll of his muddy brown eyes, turning back to Rafe. "Stay out of my case, Gonzales, or I'll have you cut back to beat cop."

I gritted my teeth, clenching my fists to keep from smacking the man. In his view, I wasn't even worth answering.

"Where's the evidence from the crime scene?" Rafe ignored the threat, stopping the other man from walking off. "Why didn't you turn it in? Are you trying to undermine the case before we even get a chance to investigate?"

"I turned it in before I left the station tonight. That's when I heard you were trying to take over my case. Back off!" The last was a mean growl, and he stomped off.

By this time, Rafe was so mad he was shaking. Taking his hand again and turning his face to mine, I spoke softly. "Let's get something to eat. I still have plenty of food at my place. I'll cook." Going to a restaurant didn't seem like a good idea given the mood he was in. Besides, I wanted to show him I really did know how to cook.

Once again we moved around the small kitchen like we'd been doing it for years, each doing our own part of the meal. "It's only a matter of time now before we pick Eddie up," he picked up the conversation like we never stopped to drive here in separate vehicles. "There's an APB out for Miss Johnston's car and Eddie. If he's staying in another extended stay hotel, or in some flea bag motel, we'll find him. This is almost over."

"It won't be over until he's permanently behind bars, or in the ground, not some mental facility." I stated as matter-of-factly as I could. "I know that sounds harsh, but he's really good at conning people. If they put him in another hospital, he'll be out in a few years, and this will start all over again." I was afraid to look at him, afraid of seeing disappointment in his deep brown eyes. "I don't have your faith yet, Rafe. I can't just accept that everything will turn up roses. And I can't forgive what he's done."

He pulled me into his arms, resting his forehead against mine so he could look into my eyes. "Nowhere are believers told that life will be a bunch of roses. Just the opposite, in fact. We're always going to have troubles. We're promised that we won't go through those troubles alone. Jesus said to forgive, not to forget. So eventually you'll be able to move past what happened, but you won't forget, so it doesn't happen again. Hate hurts only you, not the person you hate, so letting it go will be very freeing."

I wasn't sure I agreed with that, but I didn't argue. When his stomach rumbled and mine rumbled in response, we both laughed, breaking the tension that had built up. For tonight, we let the subject drop.

The next day I went over the evidence Detective Roberts had finally brought in. The report was bare bones to say the least. He didn't even bother to mention that the suspect was wearing a scuba divers wet suit, and swim cap. This explained why there was never any hair or fiber left behind when Eddie attacked someone. The smudges Jeremy had lifted matched the ones from the previous murder, but they weren't included in the evidence from the detective. As far as he was concerned, Jeremy had messed up the prints. He wasn't even aware that Jeremy had brought them to me. I wasn't sure what good they'd do in a trial since they weren't part of the original file.

~~~

"Why can't they find him?" Bitterness tinted Beverly Johnston's voice two days later when she was released from the hospital. I went to see her while she waited for her mother to pick her up. "I gave them everything but his current address. Wasn't that enough?" I didn't blame her for being bitter or angry. I'd felt the same for years. If Detective Roberts was the only one working the case, I would agree that the police weren't doing a very good job. But Rafe was also looking for Eddie, just not officially. I knew first-hand that he wouldn't be easy to find. He was a chameleon when he wanted to hide, somehow managing to hide in plain sight. Until he showed himself to me again, we wouldn't know where to look.

CHAPTER TWENTY-TWO

Two days before Christmas, I found what I'd been afraid I would find on the internet. Fifty miles from Kansas City the unidentified remains of a male had been found three years after Fred disappeared. Since the police hadn't taken my report seriously, and failed to file a missing persons report there was nothing to indicate who it was. In my heart of hearts though, I knew it was Fred. My heart ached for the sweet, tender man he'd been.

I looked through subsequent issues of the Kansas City paper that had reported finding the remains. After three days, nothing more had been reported. I even looked through the small town paper closer to where he had been found. Nothing had been done to learn who he was.

Printing out the sparse articles, I'd show them to Rafe later, but there wasn't anything either of us could do. I had nothing of Fred's that would have DNA to match to the remains, and I didn't know if a dentist would still have records. Bodies that are found and unclaimed are often buried in an unmarked pauper's grave. I would have to do some research to find out how I could at least put a marker on his grave.

"Merry Christmas, Fred," I whispered. My thoughts were in the dumps, but I didn't want to bring everyone else down with me.

Christmas in Phoenix is nothing like other places I'd lived. The temperatures were in the forties first thing in the morning, but it would warm up into the high sixties or seventies later in the day. It was a given that I would spend the day with Rafe and his family. Tessa's family had us over for Christmas Eve dinner, then we all went to the candlelight service at church. It was a beautiful and meaningful service that brought tears to my eyes.

Eddie had disappeared again. Since the attack on Beverly Johnston, he hadn't been seen. He never showed up at any hospital to have his leg set. My hope was that he had been hurt worse than anyone knew, and had crawled into a hole somewhere to die. Not exactly the attitude Rafe or Tessa would approve of, but mine all the same.

Christmas day at the Gonzales home was more chaotic than Thanksgiving had been, if that's even possible. There was food on every flat surface, and more people coming and going all day. Aunts, uncles, cousins, more people than I could imagine. Clara still made her wonderful tamales, and the aroma was mouthwatering. Turkey and tamales is quite a combination, but I couldn't wait to start eating. Long before that happened, though, I was ready to leave. I was definitely feeling overwhelmed. Compared to all the Christmases I'd spent alone, or even those before my family imploded, this was more than a little daunting.

The kids were dancing around, anxious to open their presents. "That's what the junk food is for," Rafe explained. "It keeps the hunger pangs away from the adults while we open gifts. Then we can start on the real food. Come on." He laced his fingers with mine, tugging me towards the table, piling every kind of junk food imaginable on a plate before heading to the great room where everyone was gathered around the tree.

My heart did a funny little stutter when he handed me a small gift wrapped box. Everyone had their eyes on us. He'd said he'd wait before giving me a ring. It had only been a month. That wasn't long enough. Eddie was still out there somewhere.

I held my breath when I opened the box, releasing it on a sigh that was almost a laugh. A beautiful cross pendant on a gold chain was nestled in the satin lining. No one would understand if I laughed, including Rafe. Until he opened his gift from me, that is. Clara and Mario seemed slightly disappointed that Rafe hadn't given me an engagement ring, but I was relieved.

A few minutes later he opened the small box I gave him, and he started laughing. Showing the cross and chain to the others, they joined in the laughter. "Great minds run on the same track," he joked before placing a soft kiss on my lips. "Thank you." When I had called Clara to ask for suggestions, her response wasn't helpful. "He'll love anything you pick out," she'd told me. I wasn't sure if he'd wear a chain, but I thought the cross was appropriate for him.

It was dark by the time we pulled through the gate at the apartment complex. I was exhausted, but I had to admit I'd had a good time. Rafe's family was loving and accepting, if a little noisy. "Want to go see Joe and Tessa?" Rafe asked nodding his head at Joe's truck parked not far away.

"I'll call her when we get all this stuff inside." I couldn't believe the number of gifts his family had showered on me, a virtual stranger to most of them. Instead of taking the stairs like I usually do, we rode the elevator to the third floor. It was always safe, but I still have trust issues, I guess. Today, it didn't matter. There was just too much to try carrying it up three flights of stairs.

A note was taped to my door, the complex logo at the top of the paper. My stomach churned uncomfortably. The office had never left a note on my door before, and this just didn't feel right. I pulled it off as I unlocked the door. If this was something bad, I wanted to be inside before reading it.

My unease transferred to Rafe, and he made a fast search of the apartment. When he came back to the living room, I was frowning at the sheet of paper. "What's it say? Is everything okay?"

I couldn't decide if everything was okay or not. A

messenger had delivered a package addressed to me, and they were holding it in the office. "Who's sending you presents? Is this someone I should be jealous of?" He tried to make a joke of it after reading over my shoulder.

"Only if you're jealous of Eddie." My voice was sharper than I intended, but I couldn't help myself. This could only be from Eddie.

"Hey, I was joking. You don't know this has anything to do with him. We haven't been able to locate him since Thanksgiving. He could be anywhere by now."

"I'm sorry I snapped at you." Until the words were out of my mouth, I didn't realize I'd broken one of my/Gibbs' rules. I guess I'm getting away from my fictional family after all. "He's still here," I continued. "This is just like something he'd do. He wants to keep me off balance."

"Well, it's not going to happen this time," he stated firmly. "If he did send the package, he made a mistake. Now we know he's still here, and we can trace the messenger service. They'll have a record of who sent the package." Maybe he was right. This could be a good thing.

The label on the box was from FedEx, not a messenger service. It could have been sent by anyone from any number of outlets. I doubted it could be traced back to Eddie. Maybe there would be fingerprints though. That thought was uplifting. Maybe now I could match those smudges we'd found at the other crime scenes to Eddie. The return name and address meant nothing to me, but he wouldn't be foolish enough to use a name and address that could lead us right to his door. Rafe would check it out anyway.

Getting latex gloves and a fingerprint kit from his truck, Rafe sliced the outside wrapping. With a lot of people handling the package, it would be useless for prints. The inside was where we were hoping to find something useful. As he sliced through the tape I grabbed his hand. "What if there's a bomb in there? Maybe we should call someone."

"I'll be careful. If it even looks suspicious, I'll call the bomb squad. I doubt he'd send a bomb through FedEx though. Too much chance it would go off before it got to you." He continued removing the wrapping. Everything was generic, nothing to give away where he was.

Leave it to Eddie to ruin my first Christmas with any kind of family in more than fifteen years. I'm going to hurt him as bad as he's hurt me, I promised myself.

There wasn't much in the plain brown box, just a white sheet of copy paper sitting on top of something. "Merry Christmas" was typed on the paper, nothing else. I got tweezers so Rafe could pick up the paper without disturbing any possible fingerprints that might be there. As he put the paper in a clear evidence bag, I stared at the remaining object in the box.

"What's wrong? What is that?" He was looking from me to the box, and back to me.

"That was my doll when I was little. After the first time Eddie molested me, it disappeared. Mom said I had left it somewhere, but I knew I hadn't. She said she'd get me a new one, but that never happened." My voice sounded more than a little sad and forlorn. I cleared my throat, reaching out for the doll, but Rafe stopped me before my fingers touched it.

"Fingerprints," he cautioned.

My face burned at my probie mistake. "Sorry, I slipped back a few years."

"You can play dolls with our little girl someday." He leaned over, placing a kiss on my lips, sending my head spinning and my heart rate off the charts.

The idea of having children with Rafe both excited me and scared me to death. Would they turn out like Eddie? Science had never been able to prove whether you are born with a conscience or it developed as you grew. Still, the idea of loving Rafe, making a life with him was a heady one indeed.

I could feel my face getting warm, and I looked back at the package to distract my wayward thoughts. "How are we going to get this processed? Mr. Watkins won't let us run the prints if there isn't a case, and it isn't a crime to send someone a package. Besides, I don't want to have to explain why someone would send me an old doll."

"One thing at a time," Rafe said. "First, we have to find out if there are even any prints on this." A few minutes later I wanted to scream when there was not a single fingerprint anywhere on the box, note or doll. Everything had been carefully wiped clean; even the fingerprints of the small child I'd been when the doll disappeared were wiped off.

Rafe released a frustrated sigh. "I'm not holding out much hope, but I'll still check out this return address, and check with the FedEx office where it was mailed. Maybe someone will remember him." Eddie wasn't that careless, but I didn't say anything.

CHAPTER TWENTY-THREE

He limped around the small shabby room. He was getting cabin fever from being forced to stay inside most of the time. His leg was finally healing, but he was probably going to have a limp for the rest of his life thanks to that damn bitch. How was he supposed to know she knew karate? It was time to end this game, he was tired of playing, and he was tired of this scratchy beard. He scratched his cheeks then raked his hands over his bald head. He was tired of that, too. Shaving his head everyday was worse than shaving his face. It was the best disguise he had right now though.

After the attack on that bitch, a drawing of him had aired on all the television stations. It was a close likeness, but not exact. There weren't any pictures of him, not even from a driver's license. He laughed now. The license he gave at the hotel had his real name and picture, but it wasn't in any state data base. Same with all the other licenses he had stashed. Each one had a picture of him in a different disguise. He should have used one of them when he checked into that stupid hotel. They'd be looking for some guy who didn't exist instead of looking for him. Of course that bitch wasn't supposed to live to identify him. He'd pay her back for that someday. First, Jennifer. It was time for him to claim what was his.

His car had been towed a few days after his leg was broken because he couldn't go get it. The tab just kept rolling up against her, and someday he was going to collect. There wasn't anything in the car that would lead the cops back to him, not even his prints. Hell, it wasn't even his car. He laughed out loud at that. He took it from some homeless guy sleeping in the back seat. Probably *wasn't his either; he probably took it from some other homeless guy.*

His plan to go to Tucson and panhandle there until his leg was better had fallen through. For the first two weeks he could barely walk across the room, let alone drive two hours to Tucson. The manager of this dump fell for his story of being beaten by some homeless guy who stole his car, and she took pity on him. The story was true, just the roles were reversed. In his version, he was the victim. She was a little old for him, but in his present persona he was older, so it didn't matter. She brought him food when he couldn't go get it for himself, and she'd proven useful in other ways as well. A nasty chuckle erupted from his throat.

His mind was wandering again. That's what happens when you're cooped up for too long, he thought. There wasn't even a decent TV in the crummy room, and reception was spotty at best. He needed to get out, get some air. He did go out on Christmas, hoping to see what Jennifer thought of his little present. Of course, Rafe was with her. Lately they'd been joined at the hip. Well, he'd fix that soon enough. Once he had Jennifer back, he'd make sure she and the rest of the world never saw Rafe again. The thought cheered him up. Too bad they couldn't have had a New Year's celebration together. That would have been fun. At least for him. Oh well, soon enough. His evil laugh filled the small room.

~~~

"What if they don't like me? What am I going to do?" Tessa paced around my living room. Joe's parents were coming to visit for a week, and her past experience with a boyfriend's parents was haunting her now.

"What's not to like?" I asked, trying to lighten the mood. "You're a sweetheart, and Joe is nuts about you. Why wouldn't they like you?"

She frowned at me. "Because I'm not good enough for their son?" She turned it into a question.

I started to laugh, but coughed instead when she glared at me. "Joe isn't that shallow, and like I said, he's nuts about you."

"That's reason enough for them to hate me. Oh, I wish you and Rafe were going with us tonight. I need moral support."

This time I did laugh. "Tessa, your parents are going to be there. They aren't going to let anyone be mean to you."

She waved that off. "Mom and Dad always see the best in everyone. They won't even notice if Joe's folks don't like me." Tears sparkled in her eyes.

Without giving it any thought, I wrapped my arms around her, trying to comfort her. "Try to relax and calm down. You'll see. Everything is going to be fine."

She clung to me for several seconds then stiffened her spine. "You're right. Everything is going to be fine. I hope." She whispered the last.

A few minutes later she got ready to leave, only slightly calmer than when she came in. "Call me when you get home tonight," I said, giving her one last hug. "It doesn't matter what time, just call me."

It was after midnight when someone knocked on my door. I'd fallen asleep on the couch waiting for Tessa to let me know how dinner with Joe's parents went. The knock came again, a little louder this time, causing my heart to thud against my ribs. Had Eddie somehow gotten through the gate and the front door of the building? Anything was possible where he was concerned.

I sat undecided whether to answer the door or ignore whoever was there when I heard Tessa's soft voice. "Casey, are you awake?"

Rushing to the door, I pulled it open, and she hurried inside. I couldn't tell if she was upset or excited. "I'm sorry it's so late, but everyone just left, and I had to show you." She held out her left hand, wiggling her fingers where a

254

beautiful diamond sparkled on her ring finger.

"Oh, Tessa!" I wrapped her in a hug, and we jumped around too excited to stand still. "I'm so happy for you. I take it his parents approved of you."

She nodded her head, her straight shoulder-length hair bobbing around her beaming face. "Joe was so sneaky. On Christmas day he talked to Dad and asked for permission to marry me. Then he called his folks and told them. I guess that's why they suddenly decided to visit." She drew in a deep breath. "They wanted to check out their future daughter-in-law. Anyway, at dinner Joe asked me to marry him. He even got down on one knee, right there in the restaurant. It was so romantic, everyone cheered for us, and like a fool, I cried." She grabbed me in another hug. "When is Rafe going to finally ask you? I know you're in love with him. We could have a double wedding. That would be great!"

I felt like scum not telling her. "We're not ready yet," I hedged. "Maybe someday. Right now, this is all about you and Joe. Did you set a date yet? You need to find a dress, and I need to plan a shower."

It was after two when we both fell asleep on my couch our feet propped up on the coffee table. Not very comfortable, I decided a few short hours later when I woke up with a stiff neck and my legs cramping from resting on the hard table. I gently shifted Tessa around so she was lying down on the couch, covered her with an afghan and went to bed. My alarm would be going off all too soon, and I needed to get some sleep to make it through the day.

~~~

I'm not sure Tessa's feet touched the floor the entire day. She was still beaming when she woke up on my couch, and I'm sure she didn't stop until she fell asleep again in her own bed that night. "You'll be my maid of honor, won't you, Casey? Oh, there are so many plans we need to make. I want a spring wedding instead of being a June bride like every other bride in town. How fast do you think we can organize a wedding? Mom and Dad were so excited! When my brothers got married it was different; they weren't in on all the planning." Her words and sentences tumbled on top of each other without giving me a chance to say anything.

She finally stopped when she ran out of breath, gulping in more air. She was ready to start again, but I managed to forestall her. "I'm sure your mom will be glad to have Joe's mom help out. I've never planned a wedding, but I'm sure you can get this organized by next spring."

Tessa looked horrified. "Not next spring, this spring. I'm not waiting more than a year to marry Joe. Before I came over here last night, Joe and I talked it over. We decided on this April."

It was my turn to be horrified. "That's just four months! I've never planned a wedding," I repeated, "but I think it takes longer than four months."

"Then we'll just have to work harder. I'm getting married in April; this April not next year!" There was a stubborn set to her jaw that I hadn't seen before. She relented just as quickly, taking my hands. "I'm sorry, I didn't mean to sound so nasty. I just don't want to wait. I love him, and I want to be his wife. Everyone will think we're rushing it for the wrong reason, and they will be counting to see if I'm pregnant. But I'm not. You understand, don't you? I know you love Rafe."

I wanted to deny that, but couldn't. Instead I went in another direction. "I'll help any way I can." We spent the rest of the day with the two mothers, making as many plans as we could. Joe and Rafe were glad we left them out of the fray, and watched football with the two fathers. By the time Rafe walked me to my apartment that evening, I felt like I'd worked harder than I ever did at my job. Planning a wedding certainly wasn't for weaklings.

"When are you going to let me put a ring on your finger?" Rafe whispered against my lips just before he closed the distance between us, his kiss tender and passionate all at once.

My heart was thudding against my ribs. Like Tessa, I didn't want to wait forever, but I was afraid of what Eddie would do to Rafe if we got married before he was locked up. It had been more than a month since he attacked Beverly Johnston, but we knew he was still close by. The package with my childhood doll in it proved that.

"There's no telling what Eddie would do to both of us if we got married while he's still on the loose. I can't take risks like that with your life." I tried to move away from him, but he pulled me onto his lap as he sat down on the couch. "I know he's out there watching me," I said. His skeptical look caused me to bristle angrily. "You think I'm imagining things, but I know it." I crossed my arms around my waist, sitting rigid on his lap. "Just because I'm paranoid doesn't mean Eddie isn't really out to get me."

"Sweetheart, I'm not saying he isn't dangerous. I know better. What I'm saying is I can protect myself and you. Why won't you trust me on that?" He nibbled on my neck, sending goose bumps all over me. I wanted to stay angry, but he wasn't making it easy.

"Because I know him better than you do," I said weakly. "I've seen his handiwork. He doesn't care who he hurts to get what he wants." This was a conversation we'd had numerous times in the past. I just wasn't getting through to him.

His lips were now playing around my ear, tugging on my earlobe. A shiver passed through me that had absolutely nothing to do with being cold. In fact, I was feeling very hot right about now. I was also having a hard time concentrating on what he was saying instead of what he was doing. When his lips captured mine, I gave up the argument, at least temporarily.

Finally lifting his head, his breathing was as ragged as mine. This was what I wanted, and so much more. Was it a possibility? Did I dare take the chance?

"You've said you'll marry me. Right?" His voice was raspy against my neck. "You haven't changed your mind?"

I laughed. "You can ask that when you make my resolve disappear with just a kiss?"

"Well then, maybe I should kiss you some more." He put his words into action. Several minutes later he moved me off his lap. "I'm not sure whose resolve just disappeared, but if I want to keep my intentions honorable, I need to put a little distance between us for a few minutes." His hands were shaking with his effort.

I leaned close, placing a soft kiss on his cheek. "You're a good man, Rafael Gonzales, and I don't ever want anything bad to happen to you." I headed to the kitchen. "Would you like something to drink? A bottle of cold water?" I looked over my shoulder, a teasing smile tugging at my lips.

"Has anyone ever told you you're a tease?" He gave a fake growl, coming after me. The rest of the evening we kept things playful and light.

~~~

It was a lot of work in a short time, but Tessa was determined to have her wedding this April. She'd found the man she wanted to spend the rest of her life with, and she wasn't going to wait any longer than she had to. Finding a wedding dress for her had been easy. She wanted to wear her mom's. They were almost the same size, so there were only a few alterations necessary. Tessa added some personal touches by beading flowers on the bodice. She also decided to make her own veil and head piece. That meant we only had to find dresses for me and the two bridesmaids. Everyone has heard horror stories about the awful dresses brides pick out for their attendants, but Tessa let each of us choose our own dress as long as the colors were compatible.

Gina Gordon was as gracious with Joe's mom as she'd always been with me, and was grateful for any help she could offer. Since they lived in Colorado, Gina and Wanda spent a lot of time on the phone and email coordinating their efforts. Both women enjoyed cooking, and were setting up a buffet menu that would feed a small army. With everyone pitching in, it looked like Tessa was going to get her wish for an April wedding.

CHAPTER TWENTY-FOUR

He felt no remorse for what he'd done. It was simply necessary. She was getting too possessive, wanting him to move in with her. Her usefulness had come to an end. Fortunately, she made it extremely easy to make it look like an accident. She enjoyed taking long soaking baths with candles ringing the tub and a bottle of wine. All he had to do was keep pouring the wine until she passed out, slipping below the water. When the water started to bring her around, he just held her under. She was too drunk to put up much of a struggle.

Of course, he now had to pay for his room, but that was okay. He had the crutches and leg brace she gave him. That would add to the sympathy factor when he went out panhandling. He didn't like the feeling of owing anyone anything. Of course, that feeling never lasted long at any one time. Now he didn't have to worry about it.

Six weeks and his leg still hadn't completely healed. As he'd suspected, he was going to be limping forever. She'd done more damage than he thought; his knee didn't work quite right, and ached something fierce when the weather turned bad. "Damn bitch," he grumbled. He could play it up when he was panhandling, but he needed both legs to work right if he had to make a fast get-away sometime. Was he getting too old to play this game?

~~~

"Why do you keep poking around in my cases?" I was pouring over the evidence of an accidental drowning when Detective Roberts stormed into the lab. "It's bad enough when Gonzales sticks his nose in my cases, but a lab rat has no business doing it."

"I'm not a lab rat; I'm a forensic scientist, and your

cases would go nowhere without those of us in this lab."

"You're making more work for me. This is an accidental death, so why are you wasting your time and mine snooping around?"

"Every death is suspicious until proven otherwise." That was another 'Gibbs-ism.' I had adopted. "And this one looks suspicious to me," I finished.

"She drowned in her bathtub because she was drunk!" he all but shouted. "What's suspicious about that?"

"Well, let's see. She was extremely drunk, but there was only one bottle in the bathroom. This is the third case with these funny smudges instead of fingerprints, some of which were on top of her prints. Doesn't that seem a little suspicious to you?"

He ignored my question. "I can't help it if the lab rat who took the prints is incompetent."

"Jeremy isn't incompetent, and neither is anyone else in this lab. These smudges are proof that someone else was with her when she drowned, or at least while she was drinking. I want to know who that was."

"How do you figure that?" He sent me a fierce frown, hoping to intimidate me. "A smudge is just a smudge."

"No, they're consistent with the size and shape of a finger. Until I can match them to a person, I intend to keep a file on them."

He shook his head in disgust. "You're wasting city resources. If you keep messing with my cases, I'll get you fired."

I laughed at his threat. "I seriously doubt you have that kind of pull."

He didn't like being laughed at, and his face mottled with anger. Unable to intimidate me, he stormed out of the lab.

He could probably cause some problems for me if he went to Mr. Watkins, but neither of them could argue with my record of assisting in closing cases. I'd also assisted with several cold cases. I knew what I was doing, and could back it up with facts. I put him out of my mind, and went back to work.

Every time I looked at a case with those smudges, my stomach churned. Only one thing would cause that kind of reaction. Eddie was involved. My problem was proving it. Until I could get his prints from his fingers, I couldn't prove in a court room these smudges belonged to him. Everyone would be as skeptical as Detective Roberts.

I looked over the report for the third time hoping I'd missed something, but I knew I hadn't. I had it memorized. Suddenly I realized I actually was missing something. The victim was the manager of a shabby motel in downtown Phoenix that allowed homeless people to stay there full-time. This was just the type of place Eddie would gravitate to after being kicked out of the extended stay hotel he'd been living in.

"I wonder if he's still living there," I muttered to myself. He's just cocky enough to believe he got away with murder again, and would see no reason to move as long as the police wrote it up as an accident. Maybe Detective Roberts had done me a favor after all. After work I'd drive by the place, trying to scope out the area. Tessa and Joe were going to several florists after work, and Rafe was tied up on a case. This was the ideal opportunity. No one needed to know what I was doing.

In late January, it was already dark by six o'clock when I left work. I wouldn't be able to observe much at the motel, but it would give me an idea what I was up against in my surveillance. I had no idea what name Eddie was using now, or what he even looked like. He's a master of disguises, but I was relying on my own gut reactions to tell me if I saw him. Hopefully, he didn't have the same reaction when I was nearby.

Right after Beverly Johnston was attacked, detectives

had canvased all the area hospitals, showing the drawing of Eddie. No one had gone to any of the hospitals with a broken leg. That meant he was staying inside, and off his leg. I had no idea what kind of car he drove. Beverly's car was still missing. If Eddie had been mobile enough, he probably sold it. It was either in Mexico or cut up and sold for parts.

Sitting on a dark side street, I watched the parking lot of the motel. 'Run down' barely described the place. Weeds grew through the cracks in the lot, even in January. Paint was peeling off the exterior. There were several light poles in the parking lot, but only one had a lit bulb. The few cars and trucks that were parked there were all run down, maybe barely running. Any one of them could belong to Eddie. No one walked around the building. In this neighborhood, I'd be afraid to walk around after dark, too.

I had just made it back to my apartment when Rafe knocked on my door. Hanging up my coat before opening the door, I ran my hands through my hair and tried to look like I'd been home all along. "Hi, Sweetheart." He pulled me close; lifting me until just my toes touched the floor. His kiss was as devastating as always, my head was spinning by the time he released me.

"Where've you been?" he asked when he set me back on my feet. "Your cheeks are still cold from being outside."

"Oh." I rubbed my face, stalling for time, hoping to come up with a plausible lie. Unfortunately my mind was blank. I sighed, and turned my back on him as we went into the living room. "I wanted to look at a crime scene." I flopped down on the couch, hoping he wouldn't question me further, but of course I was wrong.

"What crime scene? Did something happen today that I don't know about?" He sat down, cradling me against his side, kissing the top of my head.

I was going to have to tell him my suspicions, and he wasn't going to like what I did. "You did what!?" I hadn't even finished explaining about the smudges, and why I went to the motel before he exploded. Turning sideways on the couch he stared at me with a fierce frown. "What would you have done if you saw Eddie? Would you have confronted him?"

"Of course not!"

"And if he'd seen you, and come after you? What would you have done then?" By now he was pacing around the room.

"Like you, I carry a gun, and can defend myself. Besides, I was in my Jeep, parked on a side street. He wouldn't have known I was there." I was trying to remain calm, hoping it would help calm him down some.

"Oh, that makes me feel soooo much better. In that part of town, after dark, nothing bad could ever happen to you."

His sarcasm was beginning to tick me off. "Do you think I'm stupid?" I got right in his face.

"No!"

"Then why are you treating me like I am?" My fists were braced on my hips, and I was glaring up at him.

"I'm not treating you like you're stupid, just reckless." With each word, his voice got a little louder.

"Let me tell you something, Detective Gonzales. I've been on my own since I was fourteen years old, and I haven't let anyone hurt me or boss me around. I'm not going to change just because you think I should. You need to go home. I don't want to talk to you anymore tonight." I turned away from him to open the door so he could leave.

I only took two steps before he pulled me back. "Don't you get it, Casey?" he whispered against my hair. "I don't want to change you; I want to protect you. You aren't alone anymore. You have people who love you; I love you." He turned me in his arms; his dark eyes boring into mine. "I lost you once when you left town, I couldn't stand to lose you again." He closed the distance between our lips, placing a gentle kiss on mine.

It was all the persuasion I needed. I melted into him, my arms wrapping around his neck to pull him closer. Our hearts were pounding in tandem when he lifted his head.

"If I promise not to get mad, will you finish telling me what made you go there tonight by yourself?" We sat down again; this time I was on his lap. "I promise I won't say anything until you're finished," he added.

I raised a skeptical eyebrow, but didn't comment. Starting at the beginning, I told him what was in the case file, Detective Roberts' conclusions and mine. When I finished, I added, "Someone was with her, and I think it was Eddie. I just wanted to see what the place looked like."

My mind was in the lab, going over the evidence again. I waited for him to say something, but he was silent for so long, I wondered if he'd fallen asleep. Sitting up, I looked at him. A frown drew his dark eyebrows together. "You said Roberts didn't want you looking over the evidence? Why not?" He paused, but answered his own question before I could say anything. "He wants this to be an accidental drowning instead of murder, so he can close the case. That man needs to retire." He set me on the couch, and stood up to pace around the room again. This time he wasn't mad at me.

"Okay, I'll talk to the captain," he finally said. "Do you think Eddie would still be there? Is he that stupid?"

"Not stupid," I corrected, "confident. He thinks he's smarter than we are. He's managed to remove his fingerprints somehow, and doesn't think there is anything that can tie him to this crime or any of the others. That's why he had on a wet suit and swim cap when he attacked Beverly Johnston. He doesn't want to leave behind any hair or fibers that can be traced to him, and his victims can't scratch him through the wet suit. He's probably been doing that for years." I started pacing alongside him. "You have to admit it's a pretty ingenious idea. He has probably also shaved all his body hair since we didn't find hair on the prostitute he raped and murdered."

We were still going over the case when Tessa and Joe knocked on my door. "We have our flowers picked out!" Tessa bounced into the room. "They're so pretty. I just love this. We're going to have everything arranged in plenty of time. I knew we could do it." As with anything to do with the wedding, Tessa was so excited.

"Now can we eat?" Joe pleaded. "I haven't eaten all day." As if on cue, my stomach rumbled with an answering one from Rafe and maybe even one from Tessa. I offered to fix something quick, but the idea was vetoed, and we headed to Frederico's.

~~~

The next night I was sitting on the same side street watching the dingy motel, only I wasn't alone now. Rafe was with me. We'd stopped for fast food on the way. The comforting scent of French fries and fried fish patties filled the cab of his truck. Until now I'd forgotten all about this one luxury my parents had indulged in while Eddie was locked up: a local fish and chips joint with the best fish and homemade sauce I've ever had.

Finishing off his jumbo order, Rafe wiped his hands on a napkin, putting his trash in the paper bag. "Do you really think he's still here? How will you know it's him if he's wearing a disguise?" He still didn't understand the connection or the hold Eddie had over me.

"I believe his ego is big enough to convince him he can get away with just about anything. Maybe I won't recognize him in disguise, but I'll still know it's him."

"How?" He frowned, not questioning me, just wanting to understand.

"When I was little, really little, maybe four or five years old, and I would be playing in our backyard, it didn't matter if I was alone or with a friend, whenever Eddie

266

came outside it was like a cloud came over me. The other kids never felt it, just me. I didn't have to see him, but I knew he was there. That feeling has never left me when he's close. I always knew when he'd been in my apartment no matter where I lived. It's like he leaves a cosmic footprint that I can feel." I gave a nervous laugh. "That sounds kind of crazy and 'other worldly,' but that's the only way I can explain it."

He nodded. "Okay, I can buy that. I don't call it a cosmic footprint; I call it my gut, but I know when I've got the right suspect even when I don't have all the evidence yet."

I almost laughed; he sounded so much like Gibbs on *NCIS*. Maybe someday I'd tell him how I'd adopted those characters as my family for so many years. Instead, I leaned over, placing my hand on his face, turning him to look at me. "Thank you for believing me, and for being here with me." I moved a little closer to him, placing my lips on his. It was the first time I had initiated a kiss.

When I sat back, he drew a shaky breath. "Damn these bucket seats. I don't know why they did away with bench seats. You sure can't get close with a console between you and someone else." This time I did laugh, even while silently agreeing with him.

After sitting in the truck for more than two hours and drinking a large iced tea, not only was I getting cold, but I had to go to the bathroom. There'd been no activity in or around the motel and parking lot. "I guess we can call it a night. It doesn't look like anyone is going out tonight." I could hear the disappointment in my voice. "Stake outs aren't much fun, are they?"

Rafe laughed. "Bored?"

"Kind of, I really expected Eddie to put in an appearance by now." I cleared my throat, squirming a little before asking, "What do you do when you have to, ah, go the bathroom while you're on a stake out?" I could feel my face getting hot, and was glad it was dark.

Rafe laughed again, handing me his empty soda cup. "Thanks a lot." I slapped at his arm. "That isn't going to do me much good. Can we call it a night?" I was beginning to get desperate, and squirmed again.

By now he was laughing so hard if he had to go to bathroom as bad as I did, he'd pee his pants.

As we pulled away from the curb, a shiver passed through me. Turning around in the seat to look behind us, all I could see was darkness. It seemed like even the few street lights in and around the motel had dimmed. "What's wrong?" Rafe looked over at me. The greenish light from the dash board gave his face a weird glow.

I gave myself a shake, still looking out the window. "Nothing, I guess. Do the lights look dimmer to you than they did before?"

He looked in the rear view mirror, shaking his head. "No, why?" He slowed down, pulling over to the side of the road.

I looked back again, and everything was normal. There was only one explanation. Eddie had been there in the dark. Whether he knew I was there, watching me as I watched for him, I didn't know. I just knew he had been there, somewhere. I shook my head. "No, I guess not. Let's just leave. Nature is calling my name." I wasn't certain Rafe believed me, but at the moment, nature took precedence over Eddie.

"Was Eddie there? You think he knew we were watching him?" His voice was very matter of fact.

I frowned at him, trying to see his face in the dark truck. Was he making fun of me? Finally deciding he wasn't, I shrugged then realized he couldn't see me in the dark while he was driving. "I don't know. I wouldn't be surprised though. If luck is on my side, he was just walking around in the dark. He always manages to stay in the shadows."

"We're going to catch him, Casey." He reached for my hand. "Once we find him, we have him for assault, attempted rape, and attempted murder on Beverly Johnston. She's willing to testify against him."

I sighed in frustration. "I guess I should be happy with that, but I really want him put away for good. My life will remain unsettled, and up in the air as long as there is a chance he'll ever walk free again."

"When we get him in custody for one thing everything else will fall into place." He gave my fingers a squeeze.

"You're right." I released another sigh. "With all the evidence from other cases, we'll be able to tie him to them once I can match his non-fingerprints to what we have in evidence. I have to remember that science won't fail me."

Rafe laughed. "I think I've heard that line on some TV show, but you need to remember it is God who won't fail you. Science is a collection of facts that can be manipulated one way or another." I wanted to argue, but couldn't. I'm beginning to understand what he and Tessa have been telling me.

Another few days parked on different side streets with the same results, even the dimming of lights as we pulled away, and I was ready to give up. "This has been an enormous waste of time," I grumbled. "I think we can forget it. He's not going to show himself. Let's go." I slumped down in the soft leather seat, feeling dejected. But not so much that I didn't keep an eye on the side mirror as Rafe pulled away from the curb.

"Lights dimmed again?" He lifted one eyebrow in that questioning way that I found particularly sexy. "You think he knows we've been out here all this time?"

I dragged my wayward thoughts back in line. "Most likely. If I know when he's around, he's probably just as aware of me. I wish I knew which room he's in. I'm willing to bet it's one that doesn't have a working light outside the door."

"If he knows we're out here, why hasn't he confronted us? Or even tried something?"

"That's not his style. He doesn't do anything out in the open or up front. Besides, his leg might not be healed enough to get around fast. He knows we both carry a gun. If he's still having trouble getting around, he's not going to do anything that will give us the advantage."

I was silent for several minutes trying to tamp down my frustration. I was getting very tired of this game. "What do you do when you have evidence or even an eyewitness, but don't have the suspect in custody so you can tie him to the evidence?"

Rafe sighed out his own frustration. "You just have to keep digging, keep looking. Eventually you'll get the one piece that will tie it all together."

"The one piece we need is Eddie. I have enough evidence to hang him several times over, and we have a witness who will testify against him. I wish we could go through all the rooms back there, forcing him out."

"We'd be playing his game then by breaking the law. I've shown the desk clerk the composite of the guy who attacked Beverly Johnston. He said there isn't anyone registered there that matches the description or the name. Until he does something else, we just wait." His voice was tight with anger and frustration.

~~~

He chuckled as he watched the big pickup pull away from the curb. She thought she was being so clever, hiding in the dark, hoping to catch him doing something. Did she think he was stupid? That he'd do something right in front of her and that idiot cop? His stomach rolled slightly when he wondered how many nights they'd been parked on one of the side streets before he paid attention to the alarm bells going off in his head. Had they been there the night

270

he'd paid his last visit to the stupid manager's apartment? He shook his head in denial. They couldn't have known where he was staying until after the old sow died. Then it had been only a guess. If they'd known where he was all this time, and saw him leaving her apartment, he'd be behind bars by now. Not even that bumbling cop who investigated her drowning could ignore the fact that he'd been in her room right before she drowned.

The fact that he was still free was proof that they still didn't have anything on him. The thought let him relax, and he stood up from the chair he'd been sitting in for the last hour. The immobility and the chill that had settled into his bones made his leg ache and creak when he first put weight on it. Someday that little karate bitch is going to pay the ultimate price for what she did to me, he promised himself. "No one gets away with doing that to me," he muttered under his breath as he limped towards his room. The fact that she could identify him was added incentive to put an end to her existence. He'd bet his last meal she'd be willing to testify against him. "But I need to take care of Jennifer and that damn Gonzales first. He's going to pay for taking Jennifer away from me." He kept repeating that mantra to himself. Planning exactly what he was going to do to them cheered him up, and he embraced his pain. It gave him a motive to keep going.

CHAPTER TWENTY-FIVE

It had been three months since Eddie attacked Beverly Johnston, and six weeks since the manager of the rundown motel drowned, but Eddie was still in the wind. His leg was probably completely healed by now. Who was he planning to kill next? Or was he planning my abduction and murder? Although I have always known it could come down to just that, I now had a lot to live for, and didn't want that to happen. For the first time I could envision a life for myself, a normal life with a husband and family. I want that, but I have to stop Eddie, or he will destroy all I hold as precious.

After watching the motel that one week, we'd given up the surveillance as a lost cause. Eddie wasn't going to show himself. I wanted to start knocking on doors to see if he'd answer, but Rafe was against that on more than one level. I wouldn't even need to knock on his door to know which room he was in; I would be able to feel his presence, but we didn't have cause to break into his room. Getting a search warrant on my feelings or vibes, or whatever you called it, wasn't likely to happen. A judge wouldn't go along with that.

Plans for Tessa and Joe's wedding were coming together. I knew Rafe wished we were planning ours. He didn't push me; in fact, he hadn't said anything more about giving me a ring. Still, I knew he was getting impatient. Truth to tell, I was feeling just as impatient. I was more than ready for this game with Eddie to end.

I was lost in these thoughts as I left work, paying little attention to my surroundings. Not a smart move, considering Eddie was still somewhere close by. Feeling a presence beside me, I whirled away, reaching into my purse for my gun. "Whoa, Sweetheart, it's just me." Rafe held up his hands.

I sagged against him, thumping my fist against his chest. "Don't sneak up on me like that! I could have shot you." This was the third time I'd been so preoccupied, that I let someone get the drop on me. It could have been Eddie instead of Rafe. The thought made my stomach hurt.

"You were concentrating so hard you weren't even aware I was right behind you when you left the building. What were you thinking about?" He frowned. "Is everything okay?"

This was my chance to tell him I was ready to move forward, but I didn't know how to say it. What would he think? Finally I hedged, hoping he would take it as a hint, "Just thinking about Tessa and Joe's wedding. She's going to be a beautiful bride."

"That she is." He draped his arm around my shoulder, pulling me in to his side as we walked to my Jeep. "Not as beautiful as you'll be someday though." I felt slightly let down that he didn't understand what I wasn't able to put into words.

"Joe and Tessa are meeting us at Frederico's at six-thirty." He changed the subject. "I'll follow you back to your place, and we can take my truck."

"That isn't necessary. Call and tell them to come over and I'll cook." Since Rafe became a constant in my life, I'd taken to keeping a well-stocked kitchen even though he often liked to eat out.

He dipped his head, placing his lips lightly on mine. "I'm hungry for some green corn tamales; you can cook tomorrow night. Okay?"

Still feeling slightly disappointed or unsettled inside, I listened as Rafe and Joe discussed the latest case they were working on. Since I was involved with the forensic side of most cases, I was only half listening. When Rafe reached across the table for my hand, I jumped in surprise like I had earlier in the parking lot.

"Wool gathering again, Sweetheart?" He raised that one eyebrow I found so fascinating. "What's got you so preoccupied?"

"Just thinking about things." I lifted one shoulder in a shrug. Maybe later, when we were alone, I'd explain.

He lifted my hand to his lips, placing a kiss in my palm and folding my fingers over it like he's done so many times. Still holding my hand, he stood up, coming to my side of the table. To my utter astonishment, he dropped to one knee, looking up at me. "Casey Gibson, will you do me the honor of marrying me?" He held a small velvet box and opened it.

Where did that come from? The thought was totally irrelevant, and was gone as fast as it appeared in my mind. "How did you know?" I whispered. "I wanted you to ask me." I didn't realize tears were running down my face until he brushed them away with his thumb.

"Is that a "Yes"?" He was still kneeling in front of me, waiting for my answer.

"Yes, yes!" I threw my arms around his neck, nearly knocking him over, raining kisses all over his face. It wasn't until the other people in the restaurant began clapping and cheering that I remembered we weren't alone. My face heated up, but I really didn't care. Rafe had just asked me to marry him, and I'd said yes! Taking my hand, he slipped the most beautiful ring on my finger, a single white diamond with a blue diamond on either side.

Frederico and Marisol came to congratulate us along with just about everyone else in the restaurant. I was glad it was a slow night for them. There were less people watching us.

I was still admiring the beautiful ring Rafe had placed on my finger as I stepped outside when a chill swept over me. Eddie was here! Before I could take the two steps back inside, he grabbed my arm, the sharp point of a knife pressed into my side. I could feel the point slice through my clothes, piercing my skin. I tried to draw away from the slight pain but he pressed harder, and I felt the knife go in farther.

"Go back inside, Gonzales," Eddie snarled at Rafe, "and tell your little buddy not to come out."

"Not gonna happen, Miller," Rafe said. He'd already pulled his gun, pointing it at Eddie. "Put your knife down, and step away from Casey."

"Not gonna happen, Gonzales," Eddie sneered, throwing Rafe's words back at him, mocking him. "And you know her name is Jennifer, so stop calling her that stupid name," he shrieked the last part. He was losing all control. He pulled me in front of him using me as a shield. If Rafe tried to shoot him, he would risk hitting me as well.

I could see Tessa at the window; her blue eyes as large as saucers in her pasty white face as she watched the drama unfold. I hoped Joe had gone out the back to sneak up on Eddie. I sent up a silent prayer that no one else would get hurt. This should be just between Eddie and me.

"You had no right to take her away from me, Gonzales," Eddie snarled. "She's been mine since she was four years old."

"No, Eddie, you had no right to Jennifer then, and you have no right to Casey now. Let her go." His voice was calm, trying to talk Eddie down.

"Drop the knife, and step away from her," Joe ordered from behind us.

Startled, Eddie jerked around, loosening his grip on my arm enough that I could pull away. Spinning around, I kicked his injured leg, still in a brace. With an animal-like howl, he went down, dropping the knife to grab his knee.

It was over in a flash. Rafe pulled me against him. "Are you all right?" he whispered against my ear. "Did he stab you?" His hands ran over me.

"I'll be fine." I didn't feel anything in my side, but that wouldn't last long. I looked over to Joe. "He'll live," Joe stated matter-of-factly, flipping Eddie on to his stomach, putting handcuffs in place. I didn't know if I was relieved Eddie was still alive or disappointed.

Tessa rushed outside pulling me out of Rafe's embrace. "Are you all right? That's the guy who was stalking you, right?"

Three police cars, sirens blaring, pulled into the parking lot before I could answer. I kept my hand clamped against my side to staunch the blood seeping between my fingers. Eventually I would need stitches where Eddie's knife had sliced through my sweater into my side. First there were a multitude of questions to be answered. Could I prevent them from discovering my true past?

Eddie screamed, whether from pain or anger I didn't know or care. A young officer jumped out of the first car, running up to Rafe. "What happened? Who's hurt?"

"I'm hurt," Eddie yelled at the officer when he heard the question. "I need an ambulance. These two goons attacked me. She wrecked my knee. I'm going to sue you for police brutality." No one was paying any attention to him which made him shriek even louder. "I want to talk to my sister. I didn't do anything wrong!" It was his usual dog and pony show; put the blame on someone else.

An older officer with sergeant strips on his sleeve joined us after talking briefly to Eddie. He nodded at Rafe and Joe, then introduced himself to me as Sergeant Dunn. "What happened? Do you know this guy?" He nodded in Eddie's direction.

"He's been stalking me for several months," I said, giving an account of all that Eddie had done. I spoke softly so Eddie couldn't hear. Anything I said would make him protest louder.

"His ID says his name is Robert Stark. Does that ring

276

any bells?" When I shook my head; he continued questioning me. "He says he's your brother." He left the sentence hang there; I suppose to trip me up or something.

"I don't have a brother, sir. I'm an only child."

"Why would he say you're his sister?" His suspicions were beginning to unnerve me, but that was probably his purpose. I needed to remember who I am now.

"I think I can answer that better than Miss Gibson," Rafe said. We were sitting on a bench in front of the restaurant. I could feel the warm blood running down my side; the numbness had begun to wear off, pain taking its place. "Unless I'm mistaken, I know this guy, and his name isn't Robert Stark; it's Edward Miller. He's wanted for assault, attempted rape, and attempted murder." This momentarily threw the sergeant off his game. For the next few minutes Rafe explained about the attack on Beverley Johnston, and everything in my life. Only he made it sound like it had happened to someone other than me. His story was so convincing I almost believed him, but I couldn't let him do this. He was lying in an official investigation.

I touched his hand still wrapped around my waist. "Um, ah, Rafe."

"It's okay, Honey." He kissed my temple. "I told you we'd catch him. He's not going to bother you again." He looked at the sergeant, a small smile tilting his lips. "We just got engaged tonight."

"Um, congratulations." Dunn was silent for a long moment, then he turned to the young officer and said, "Load him in the squad car, and get him downtown for booking."

"No, you can't do this," Eddie screamed. "Gonzales, you can't have her, she's mine." The car door slammed shut; cutting off anything else he was saying.

Sergeant Dunn walked away to question Joe, and I turned to Rafe. "What are you doing?" I whispered. "You could lose your job or worse; you could be charged for lying in an official investigation. I can't let you do this."

"It's okay. There's no reason for them to doubt what I said."

"What if Eddie convinces them that I really am his sister? What if they compare my prints to the ones from my parents' house? What if they want to do a DNA test to compare it to Eddie's? They'll know you lied."

"None of that is going to happen. Eddie can't wiggle out of the attack on Beverly Johnston, or what he did to you tonight. Did you get cut?"

"What if they do a background check on me?" I ignored his question. "Maybe I didn't do a good enough job when I set up this identity. What if they find there really isn't a Casey Gibson?"

He gave a small laugh. "Where's that smart girl I fell in love with back in grade school? The police department runs a background check on all prospective employees. Everything is just as you say. You are Casey Gibson."

"But what if..."

"No what ifs," Rafe whispered against my lips. "We have him in custody. Now you can run his fingerprints. This is what you were hoping for. Remember?"

He was right. This is what I'd been hoping for. I was finally going to be able to put him away for good. If nothing else, he will go to prison for the attack on Beverly Johnston.

"Did you get cut?" He repeated his question. Moving my hand away from my side, color drained from his face. My hand was caked with sticky blood. At his sharp bellow, everyone turned as one, and people moved in fast forward to get me to the hospital.

The knife hadn't gone in far enough to cause serious damage, but I needed stitches. The bruises where he gripped me hurt almost as much as the stitches, and would probably take longer to heal.

~~~

It was the next day before a public defender was assigned to Eddie's case, and during that time he didn't say a word to anyone. Jessie Smith, the detective in charge of the case let Rafe watch the questioning, but wouldn't let him in the room. "His lawyer's good," Rafe said, "but he's also honest. I don't think he'll try to pull any fast ones." I hoped he was right, but I also knew Eddie. If he thought he could work the system to his advantage, he would do just that, putting the blame on anyone but himself.

Beverly Johnston picked Eddie out of a lineup; but he denied any knowledge of her or the attack. He said he broke his leg when he fell down a flight of stairs at some motel. He couldn't remember the name or where it was located though. According to Eddie, Rafe's story that they knew each other as kids was just that, a story; he didn't know him. Asked why he kept screaming at Rafe before the police took him away and claiming I was his sister, he denied ever saying such a thing. He still claims his name is Robert Stark.

"He's preparing his defense," I told Rafe. We were sitting in my living room two days later. He was keeping me up to date on everything since I couldn't work up any of the evidence. "He's going to claim insanity or some dis-associative disorder. He'll end up in a mental hospital, and be out in a few years." Frustration laced through my voice as I began pacing around the small room.

"Yeah, that's what I figure. The lawyer tells him not to answer a question; he nods agreement then keeps right on talking, sometimes babbling about nothing, sometimes answering a question the lawyer just told him not to answer."

"What does he say about his fingerprints? How did he manage to remove them?"

Rafe just shook his head. "He doesn't know what

they're talking about. Of course he has fingerprints, everybody does. Even when they took his prints and showed him there was nothing there, he denied doing anything to his hands; he says the tech screwed it up to make him look bad. He also claims he was in a mental hospital a long time ago; maybe they did something to him there. No one can find a record of any Robert Stark in the system anywhere, and of course he doesn't recall where the hospital was, even what state he was in. He claims they hooked him to some kind of 'electric shock thingy,'" Rafe made air quotes around Eddie's words. "He doesn't remember much from his past.

"He keeps saying he hasn't done anything wrong, and doesn't know why he's under arrest. Says you attacked him. When Jessie asked how you got a knife wound in your side and the bruise where he gripped your arm, he just shrugged, said maybe I did it." He shook his head again.

"Once they found out where he's been staying, they got a warrant and went in. I told the CSI team to go over his room with a fine-toothed comb. He wouldn't leave anything out in the open for a maid to find. He'd pulled up the carpet in one corner of the room and another in the closet. They found several drivers' licenses with different names, but his picture. Unfortunately, there wasn't one with his real name. There were also pictures of your family. Or they would have been of your family if he hadn't cut out your parents. It was just you and Eddie together."

My stomach dropped to my toes. "Have they connected me to the pictures?" I whispered. What would happen if they discovered I'd lied about my identity?

Rafe shook his head, "They were so faded it was difficult to see details. When Jessie said they'd searched his room, Eddie came out of the chair like he'd been shot from a cannon, saying they had no right to do that, he's innocent. His lawyer tried to get him to calm down and not say anything. That lasted for about a minute. Jessie showed him the pictures, asked who they were. He played dumb, said they weren't his; they probably belonged to someone who rented the room before him. He even tried to deny the ID's belonged to him. In each picture, the subject looks slightly different; hair color, beard and mustache, bald. There's even one with a visible scar on his face. He's a master at disguising himself. After that he got smart and clammed up; wouldn't say another word. The lawyer said that was enough for now. He needed to confer with his client. So far, he's still not talking."

"He's setting up an insanity defense," I said again. "What happens now?" I sank down on the couch. Was I going to spend the rest of my life looking over my shoulder, waiting for Eddie to jump out at me? I wanted more than that now. I wanted to get married. I twisted the beautiful ring Rafe had given me just two nights ago.

Bringing my hand to his lips, he kissed my finger over the ring. "We get married; that's what happens now. Even if he tries for insanity, it will be months before he goes to trial. Bail has been set so high he won't be able to come up with it on his own, and he doesn't have anyone who will post it for him. He's going to sit in jail until his trial date."

My stomach fluttered. Marrying Rafe was what I wanted most of all, but did I have the right to put him in jeopardy? "Did they find anything to link him to the death of the motel manager?" I asked, dragging my thoughts back.

Rafe shrugged. "The prosecutor might try to tie those smudges you found to him. It will be a stretch though. They're checking into my version of the story, and checking out one Edward Miller and family. They've reopened his parents' murders and the disappearance of his sister." He said it like he wasn't talking about me or my parents. I didn't want them to check so closely that they would discover my real identity.

"You said there is a death certificate on Jennifer Miller?" Rafe's words brought my thoughts back to the room. "If they find that, will there be questions about how she died? There couldn't be a police investigation since no body was found, and you didn't really die."

It was sort of creepy, and a little confusing to talk about myself in the third person, and at the same time talk about my own death. "The death certificate says death by natural causes. She froze to death the winter after I left here. I doubt anyone will question it. I was classified as a runaway."

"Where did this supposedly happen?"

"New York City. I figured that was where runaways congregated, and was big enough that no one would remember a case from that long ago." I gave him a weak smile. "There is a file just in case someone goes poking around."

"How did you manage that?" His voice held a touch of awe.

I lifted one shoulder in a shrug. "I'm a computer expert?" I made it a question. He laughed, pulling me against him.

CHAPTER TWENTY-SIX

"Have you and Rafe set a date yet?" Although Tessa's question was innocent enough, the sparkle of excitement in her eyes should have given me a clue that she was up to something. But my mind was still wrapped up with Eddie, hoping he would eventually be convicted of all his crimes.

"So much is going on I haven't had time to think about setting a wedding date," I shrugged. "When they figure out what they're going to do with that guy, maybe we'll decide then." My mind was still somewhere else.

"I have a suggestion; see what you think of this." She paused before pushing on. "We could have a double wedding! That would be so great."

The noise from the happy hour crowd, and my preoccupation made me think I hadn't heard correctly. "What are you talking about?" I leaned closer so I would be sure to hear correctly this time. "Say that again."

"I said we could have a double wedding!"

"No, that's your special day, you and Joe." I shook my head. "You shouldn't have to share it with someone."

"We wouldn't be sharing it with just someone; we'd be sharing it with our best friends," she argued back. "Joe and I have already talked about it, and he agrees it's a wonderful idea. He's going to talk to Rafe about it."

"Tessa, your wedding is two months away; all your plans have been made. You can't go changing them now. There isn't enough time to add another whole wedding party." Even I didn't think I sounded very convincing. To marry Rafe as soon as possible would be wonderful; to share that with Tessa, my best friend ever, my 'sister by heart', would make it even more meaningful.

"Nothing is set in stone. I know Rafe has a large family, but the reception hall is large enough to hold twice as many people as Joe and I invited. Everyone would fit, and it still wouldn't be crowded." The excitement in her voice was contagious, and I could feel myself wanting it to happen just as she said. "Ask Rafe," she continued, "I'll bet his mother would be willing to help you in any way possible."

Before I could argue further or cave in to her suggestion, Rafe and Joe came up behind us, wrapping each of us in a hug. Rafe kissed my neck and nibbled on my earlobe sending goose bumps all over my body.

"What are you two discussing so seriously?" Joe asked. "This is Happy Hour, not Serious Hour." He was kissing Tessa's neck. "Now this is happy hour." He continued kissing her neck and face.

Tessa's happy giggle floated across the bar prompting one of the other officers to holler at them. "Hey, you two, get a room."

"Two more months and we will," Joe returned with a laugh, sitting down beside Tessa.

The bar was getting crowded with police officers and other city employees preventing her from broaching the subject of a double wedding again. I was grateful for the reprieve until I could consider all the problems of getting married before Eddie was locked up for good. Would he start talking, spilling the truth of everything he's done? That would be a good thing, but it could also be bad for me. My thoughts ran in circles until I was almost dizzy.

"Did something happen at work today?" Rafe asked as he walked me to my car later. "You've been awfully quiet tonight."

"Just thinking about things." As much as I wanted to marry Rafe, I wasn't sure it was safe while there was still the chance Eddie could be set free.

"Things like getting married in two months?" He cocked his head, looking down at me in the dark, his teasing smile tilting his mouth. So Joe had mentioned it to him. "Shall we save this conversation until we're at your place?" He kissed me softly as he opened the car door.

Cuddled against his side a short time later, Rafe picked up the conversation where he left off. "I take it Tessa suggested we make it a double wedding?" When I nodded without saying anything, he tipped his head down to look me in the face. "Does your silence mean you don't want that?" His tone was flat.

"No, I'm mean yes, I mean..." I was making a mess of this. Sitting up, I turned to face him. "Their wedding is only two months away. That wouldn't give your family much notice." This wasn't my only concern, but definitely right near the top.

"So?" He was confused.

"You're the youngest in your family, your parents have been looking forward to a big wedding like Anita and Juan had. We couldn't..." He placed his fingers over my lips to stop me from saying more.

"This isn't about my folks or my family; this is about us. I want you to have the type of wedding every little girl dreams of having some day. I don't want you cheated out of anything."

"Until I met Fred, I never dreamed of a wedding of any kind; then it was a very short lived dream. When he disappeared, I gave up all thoughts of getting married. I never expected to live long enough for that to happen." This last was more of a thought than words for anyone to hear.

He gave me a little shake. "Listen to me. I'm not going to let Eddie, or anyone else hurt you again. He's in jail, and he's going to prison. If not for what he did to you and your parents, then for what he did to Beverly Johnston."

"What about your parents?" I asked. "What would they think? Don't you want your family there? Two months isn't very long to prepare."

"As long as you're there, I don't care who else is. Until you came home, I never thought I'd get married, period. Now I plan on having a very long and happy marriage." He kissed me before asking, "Do you miss him very much?"

"Miss him?" I was confused now. "Who?"

"Fred." For the first time I heard something in Rafe's voice I never expected to hear from him: insecurity.

"I would have been the best wife possible if he had lived, but what I felt for him isn't..." Embarrassed, I stumbled over the words. "There was no passion, no heat," I whispered.

"So, you're saying there's passion and heat between us?" He waggled his eyebrows suggestively.

I poked him in the ribs. "The heat isn't always the good kind. You can be exasperating sometimes."

"But you love me anyway?" That dark eyebrow rose, forming a question mark above his eye.

I gave in to the desire to kiss him. "With all my heart and soul," I whispered, cuddling closer.

I finally pulled away from him; his heart was beating rapidly in time with my own. "Do you think your parents would be disappointed if we got married with such short notice?"

He laughed. "Mom will just be happy I'm finally getting married. I think she gave up on the idea about the same time I did. They both know I've been in love with you most of my life. I've waited a long time for this. It can't happen soon enough for me."

~~~

Even though I'd agreed to a double wedding with Tessa and Joe, I couldn't help but worry about Eddie somehow messing things up. His actions at the jail were growing more and more erratic. "He's going for an insanity plea," I told Rafe again when he told me what Eddie was pulling.

286

"He's smart, probably as smart as me. But he has a screw loose. That's the technical term the doctors used when Eddie was locked up before." I gave a bitter laugh.

"He never wanted to put his intelligence to good use though. And he's always been able to work the system to his benefit. The doctors back then thought they could 'reprogram' him and turn him into a productive citizen." I shook my head at their stupidity, or maybe it was a sign of their own egos, thinking they could change someone who didn't really want to change. "Instead he just convinced the doctors that he'd changed so they'd let him loose. He'll do it again if they put him in a mental hospital instead of prison."

~~~

Three days later Rafe came into the lab. His expression clearly said something was wrong. My first thought as always was Eddie had done something. Had he started a fight at the jail and been killed? God forgive me, but I didn't think that was a bad thing. "What's wrong? What happened?"

"Let's go into the office where we can talk." He took my arm, leading me into the small office where we wouldn't be overheard.

I didn't give him a chance to explain. "What did Eddie do? Who's dead?"

"No one's dead." A silent 'yet' hung in the air, and I held my breath, waiting for him to continue. "Sometime early this morning, two inmates escaped. One of them was Eddie." Rafe was holding my hands, expecting me to fall apart. That didn't happen. I'd been half expecting something like this all along.

"What do you mean, sometime early this morning? When exactly did he escape? Who did he hurt to get away?" I knew in my heart, if Eddie had a chance to hurt someone, he'd do it, just for the fun of it.

"It happened sometime between five and seven this

287

morning. Eddie and another inmate claimed they were sick. The guard took them to sick bay around five. That's the last anyone saw them. The medic was stabbed. He wasn't found until a guard went looking for the two sick inmates, and found the medic on the floor. He's in pretty bad shape, but hopefully he'll live. You're going to have round-the-clock protection."

"I don't need protection! I'm not the one in jeopardy! Beverly Johnston is more of a threat to him than I am. She's the one who can put him in prison right now. You need to protect her." Urgency had my voice rising. I just hoped Rafe believed me.

"I've already sent someone to her house. We're going to put her in protective custody until Eddie's caught."

"It's after noon. When did you learn about the escape?"

Rafe didn't say anything for several long seconds. With a sigh, he finally answered. "Not until about an hour ago. I wanted to come tell you right away, but other things needed to be done immediately."

My heart sank. If Eddie had been on the loose for over five hours, he could have caused a lot of destruction. "You're sure Beverly is safe? He didn't get her before you knew he was gone?"

"She's safe," Rafe assured me, and I sagged in relief. "I still want a protective detail on you."

I shook my head. "You and Joe are in more danger than I am. You're the ones he'll blame for me getting away again, and putting him in jail." He started to argue, and I cut him off. "Don't tell me you're a cop and you carry a gun," I said angrily. "That won't help you at all if he puts a bomb in your car, or something equally as destructive." He didn't look convinced, but didn't argue.

"Every law enforcement officer in the state is going to be looking for them," Rafe said. "We don't take kindly to having one of our own hurt. They won't get away." He was a lot more confident than I was. Eddie had been getting away with all his crimes for years. What made Rafe think this would be any different?

I wanted to call off the wedding, but no one, including Tessa, would listen to reason. The inmate who escaped with Eddie had been captured that same day. In fact, he turned himself in, ranting about 'Robert Stark' being crazy. He'd rather be in jail than on the loose with the guy.

After a week, there was nothing new on Eddie. He'd gone to ground again. The protection detail on Beverly Johnston wouldn't last long if they didn't find him soon. No law enforcement agency could afford to give her protection forever. As soon as it stopped, she'd be vulnerable, and Eddie would remove the threat against him. He wouldn't care if he was the only suspect. As long as he didn't leave any evidence behind he'd figure they couldn't convict him.

As another of Eddie's victims, I went to see Beverly. I had to make sure she was safe. "I'm staying with my parents for now," she told me. "I don't go anywhere alone, and I'm still a kick-ass martial arts instructor. Unless he tries to shoot me from a distance, I guess I'm about as safe as anyone can be in these circumstances." She put on a brave face, but I could see the fear below the surface.

I wanted to tell her he definitely wouldn't try to shoot her; he'd want to see her fear up close. Telling her that would bring on questions I couldn't answer, so I remained silent.

~~~

Eddie had been on the loose for over a month. The medic at the jail had recovered, and the powers that be decided he had left the state. He was no longer a threat to anyone, including Beverly.

It broke my heart to tell her and her parents she was on her own. "Don't worry about it," she said with a whole lot of bravado. "I'm not going to let him take over my life. I'll have a few surprises waiting for him when he comes after me." I noticed she said when, not if. She knew he would come after her.

"She reminds me of you," Rafe said as we headed back to his truck. "I wonder what she's planning."

We didn't have to wait long to find out. Two days later, Eddie went after her. "It's over," Rafe said when he woke me up in the middle of the night. "Eddie's dead."

Relief flood through me, but it wasn't just for me. "What did he do to Beverly? Is she all right?"

By the time we reached her parents' house, the alarm company and police were there. There was a body on the ground covered with a sheet. A paramedic was working on someone in the back of the van. My heart jumped into my throat. What had he done to her?

"What happened?" I wanted to know how she had accomplished what I hadn't been able to do for most of my life. Before she could answer, I turned to the paramedic. "Is she okay?"

He finished wrapping gauze around her arm, taping it in place before stepping back. "She needs stitches and her wrist set, but she's alive. More than I can say for that guy." He nodded at the covered form on the ground. Giving one last pat to Beverly's arm, he stood up. "Get this taken care of tonight." Eddie had used a knife on her, but she still got the best of him. Her parents hurried over to her as the paramedic put his equipment away.

"Do you feel up to telling us what happened?" Rafe asked. His cop face was firmly in place.

"Is that necessary right now?" Her father scowled at Rafe. "She needs to go to the hospital."

"I'm fine, Dad." She turned to Rafe. "I strung bells below every window in the house, even upstairs. If he managed to get past the alarm system, I wanted a warning that he was there."

Rafe snorted a laugh. All the high tech equipment in the world hadn't been able to stop Eddie, but simple bells had been his undoing.

"He tripped over the bells and fell on his knife," she continued. "He was bleeding, but wouldn't stop coming after me." An involuntary shudder shook her, and her mother wrapped the blanket tighter around her shoulders. Holding up her arm, she stated simply, "That's when I got this. He hit me with something and broke my wrist."

"How did you…" Rafe's look brought my question to an end before I finished it.

"Just because I couldn't use my arm, didn't mean I couldn't kick the shit out of him" Beverly continued. "He probably has more broken bones than what he got when he fell out the window."

"How did that happen?" Rafe continued questioning her.

"Besides martial arts, I practice kick boxing," she explained. "One good kick to the solar plexus, and he crashed through the window."

It was several hours later when Rafe brought me home. After all the scenarios I'd run through my mind over the years, this felt rather anticlimactic. I wasn't even involved in bringing him down, but Eddie will never hurt Beverly, me or anyone else again. The ME said he died of a broken neck from his fall from the second story window.

For a few days, I felt at loose ends, like something important was gone from my life. But the feeling didn't last long. My wedding was only weeks away.

~~~

The wedding went off without a hitch. Eddie is gone for good. My past is just that, my past. For the first time ever, none of that crossed my mind for an entire day. The people I care about most, love me unconditionally. As I lay in Rafe's arms as Mrs. Rafael Gonzales, his soft, warm breath feathered across my cheek. I said a grateful prayer, thanking God for all He has given me and for leading me home.

I thank God for giving me the words and talent to write this book. Without Him I can do nothing. My thanks and gratitude also goes to Diane Scott, Gerry Beamon, and Cathy Slack for their suggestions, editing and encouragement.

OTHER BOOKS BY SUZANNE FLOYD

Revenge Served Cold
Rosie's Revenge

Coming Soon

Man on the Run

Dear Reader:

Thank you for reading my book. I hope you enjoyed reading it as much as I enjoyed writing it. If you enjoyed A Game of Cat and Mouse, I would appreciate it if you would tell your friends and relatives and/or write a review on Amazon.

Thank you,
Suzanne Floyd

P.S. If you find any errors, please let me know at: Suzanne.sfloyd@gmail.com. Before publishing, many people have read the book, but minds can play tricks by supplying words that are missing and correcting typos.

Thanks again for reading my book.